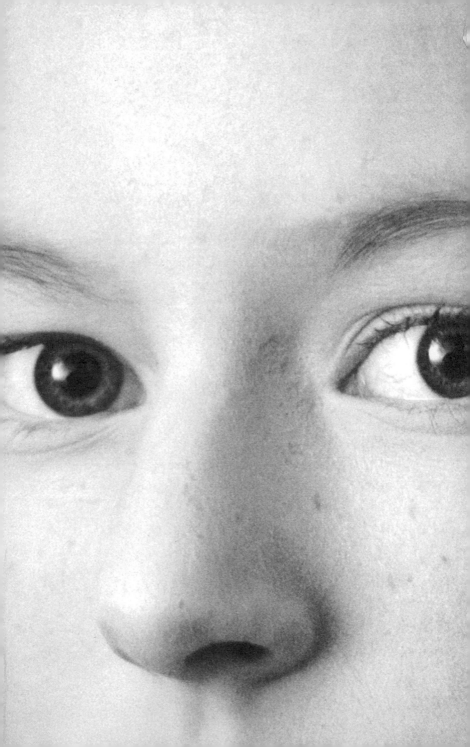

Anna North is a journalist working for the *New York Times,* whose writing has previously appeared in *San Francisco Chronicle, The Paris Review,* Jezebel, and BuzzFeed. She lives in Brooklyn.

The Life
and Death
of
Sophie Stark

Anna North

WEIDENFELD & NICOLSON

First published as an ebook in Great Britain in 2015
by Weidenfeld & Nicolson.

This paperback edition first published in Great Britain in 2016
by Weidenfeld & Nicolson,
an imprint of the Orion Publishing Group Ltd
Carmelite House, 50 Victoria Embankment
London EC4Y 0DZ
An Hachette UK Company

1 3 5 7 9 10 8 6 4 2

A CIP catalogue record for this book
is available from the British Library.

ISBN 978 1 474 60125 2 (mass market paperback)

Printed in Great Britain by Clays Ltd, St Ives plc

The Orion Publishing Group's policy is to use papers that
are natural, renewable and recyclable products and made
from wood grown in sustainable forests. The logging and
manufacturing processes are expected to conform to the
environmental regulations of the country of origin.

www.orionbooks.co.uk

For my family

Allison

WHEN SOPHIE FIRST SAW ME, I WAS ONSTAGE. THIS GIRL IRINA who I lived with at the time had organized a storytelling series at a bar in Bushwick, and after a couple weeks of watching I decided I wanted to tell a story too. I wasn't like the other kids in the house; I'd never assumed I'd be an actor or a writer or anything creative. When I was growing up, everybody figured I'd stay in Burnsville, West Virginia, and have some kids. But there I was in New York and for ten minutes I could make people listen to me and treat me like I was important. The theme that week was "scary camping stories." I was wearing my only pretty dress, a blue halter with a full skirt that I'd bought for seven dollars at a vintage store, and I got up onstage after some girl talked for twenty minutes about seeing a possum. Here's the story I told, the one that started everything for Sophie and me.

My school had some good kids, Christian kids, kids who got married at eighteen before they started popping out babies. But my family was one hundred percent trash for five generations back, and I didn't fit in real well with the church crowd. Instead I used to hang out with this guy named Bean.

Bean was a couple years older than me, and he'd dropped out of high school to sell weed, and he made enough money to rent half a run-down old farmhouse outside of town. He was nice—he always shared his weed, especially with girls, and he'd give me a place to stay when things got bad at home. But he had an edge to him—his dad was a Marine and he had taught Bean this trick where you snap someone's neck in a single motion. And Bean always made you feel like you were so cool, part of this secret club with just him, and you wanted to do exactly what he said so you could be in the club forever.

I never saw a girl turn Bean down until he decided he was into Stacey Ashton. Stacey was my only friend who was a good girl. She was in the French club and she didn't smoke weed and she wanted to go to Emory someday—she had a sweatshirt from there and everything.

Maybe that's why Bean liked her, because she was so different. But she wasn't interested. He'd go up to her at a party and she'd just be polite and then turn away, talk to some other guy. It made Bean really angry. I'd never seen him mad before—things usually went so well for him. But now every time Stacey turned her back on him, he got that look on his face like pressure building up.

Bean convinced me to talk to Stacey for him—he said maybe she'd go out with him if we double-dated. I didn't like the weird, angry Bean, and I wanted to bring the happy one back. Plus, he promised me an eighth of weed. Stacey wasn't easy to sway—she kept saying he creeped her out, there was something off about him. I said she was crazy, everybody loved him—anyway, me and Tommy, this guy I was sort of dating, would be there the whole time. Finally I told her that if she didn't have fun, I'd buy her these butterfly earrings she liked at the mall. Stacey loved all that girly shit.

So Bean showed up that Friday and him and Stacey and me and Tommy drove to the campground where we usually went to drink and make out without anybody bothering us. There had been a lot of stories about this serial killer that summer, not in our area but in Virginia and North Carolina. He used a bowie knife to kill his victims, mostly girls in their teens or twenties. The paper called him "The Charlottesville Stabber," but we called him "Stabby," and whenever we went out in the woods, we'd tease each other that Stabby was going to get us. On the car ride I kept poking Stacey in the ribs to make her shriek, and then I'd yell "Stabby!" When we got there, we roasted hot dogs and drank beer and had a good time, and I could tell Stacey was kind of loosening up. Bean moved closer to her, and she didn't move away, and then he put his arm around her, and she didn't stop him. The night got colder, and she actually snuggled up against him a little bit. Then Bean winked at me, and I turned and started kissing Tommy, and I heard Bean say, "Let's go for a walk and give them a little privacy." Then I heard them both walk off toward the creek.

I didn't love Tommy but I liked fucking him, and since we both lived in houses full of kids and stepdads we were pretty used to doing it on the ground at the campsite or in the backs of pick-up trucks or on football fields or wherever we could get a minute to ourselves. So we were all sweaty and happy and pulling on our clothes when Bean came walking out of the bushes by himself with a look on his face I'd never seen before.

"We need to leave," he said.

"Why?" I asked. "What's the matter? Where's Stacey?"

"She went off to pee," he said, "and then I couldn't find her. I called and called. I looked all over."

"We can't just leave," I said.

I started calling Stacey's name.

Bean took my arm. He looked at me, and I saw fear in his eyes for the first time.

"I think we need to get the police," he said. "I mean, I'm sure she just got lost or something, but in case . . ."

He trailed off, but I knew what he meant. None of us wanted to bring up the Stabber's silly nickname. I told Bean to give me another minute, and I walked just a few steps outside the campsite, but I started to get scared, and we all drove to the police station where we told our stories to Officer Gray, who spent most of his time breaking up our parties or arresting my stepdad when he tried to drive home drunk from Red's on a Tuesday night.

The police searched with dogs for miles around the campsite, but they didn't find her body. Sometimes a thing like that brings people together, but this just blew the three of us apart. Tommy and I didn't hook up anymore after that night. Bean didn't come to high school parties anymore, and then he moved away without telling anybody or saying good-bye. The Stabber killed another victim, this one in South Carolina. I felt the joy drain out of me. I dropped out of high school, left my sisters and my brother to fend for themselves, and took a job waiting tables at a pasta restaurant in Charlottesville.

I'd been working there about six months when I saw in the news that they'd found Stacey's body. She'd washed up on the shore of Moncove Lake, about a half mile from the campsite. The police said it was probably the work of the Stabber, since Stacey fit the profile of his other victims. But they noticed a change in his MO—Stacey's neck had been snapped.

Another year passed. I turned twenty. I was just marking time in my life. And then—I remember it was a Friday, the restaurant was crowded with students ordering carafes of our gross wine—he showed up. He had a woman with him, a pretty, thin girl with strawberry-blond hair. She was well dressed, well cared for, nice skin and expensive shoes. She looked the way people look at that time in their relationship when they're absolutely sure the other person loves them and they haven't started to love that person any less yet. The hostess seated them at one of my tables, and I went to take their drink orders. I didn't even think about running away. I wanted to see what Bean ordered, what his girlfriend's voice sounded like. It was more than curiosity—as I walked over, I had the feeling of finishing something.

And then he saw me, and we looked right at each other for just a moment, and he didn't look frightened all. His face had no expression on it. For a second I thought he might pretend not to know me, but instead he smiled wide and said, "Allison! It's been forever."

"It has," I said. I didn't know what to say next. I hadn't thought beyond walking up to the table, looking at Bean, and seeing what he did.

"Allison was my best friend back in Burnsville. Allison, this is my fiancée, Sarah Beth."

Sarah Beth extended her hand and I saw the ring sparkling on the other one. Bean had come up in the world. He was wearing a sweater and a collared shirt. He looked like he had stopped dealing drugs.

"What are you doing here?" I asked him.

"Sarah Beth and I just bought a house in Sunflower Court," he said. "I'm working at Alton Kenney."

Alton Kenney was the biggest real-estate agency in Charlottesville. I looked at Sarah Beth and then back at Bean and thought: rich father-in-law, job, house, wife, life. I wasn't disgusted—I just felt like I'd slipped into some other universe, one that had even less justice than the one I'd grown up in. I felt like I was moving through water. I took their drink orders and told them about our specials and even remembered to smile. Bean smiled back. I went back and got the drinks—white wine for her, red for him— and I took their meal orders and brought them their pasta, and then I went in the kitchen and stood for a minute staring at the wall.

That's when Bean found me. He touched my elbow—not hard, not a grab, just a tap—and he asked me if I'd come outside with him for a minute. I thought about whether he would kill me too, just snap my neck the way he'd snapped hers, but I didn't think he'd do that with his fiancée so close, sipping her wine and thinking he was normal. And I wanted to hear what he had to say. I let him lead me out to the parking lot.

"You know why I wasn't surprised to see you?" he asked.

"Why?"

I kept my back against the kitchen door so I could let myself in quickly if I needed to.

"Because I've been keeping track of you. I knew when you moved here, and I knew where you worked, and I came here to see you."

"Why?" I asked again.

"Because I wanted you to know that I can always find you."

And then he reached behind me and opened the door and went back inside.

That was three years ago. I quit that job, I changed my name, I moved here. But I still check behind me every time I let myself in my apartment. I still have a panic attack every time I see someone his height, his build. I've never told anyone this story before. I guess I keep hoping I'll forget it, but I never do.

After I finished, everyone applauded. A blond girl with perfect teeth came up to tell me how great I was. A guy who said he had a magazine gave me a homemade business card and told me to send my story to him. I was sleeping with this guy Barber at the time, who was in a band and who everyone thought was going places, and he put his arm around me and kissed me on the head and said, "That was so powerful, dude."

Sophie waited until I was alone—Barber and Irina had gone off to get drinks when she came over. She was tiny, wearing a boy's button-down shirt and jeans rolled up above scrawny ankles. Her hair was slicked back and her face was pale, pointy, wide-eyed. She looked about sixteen years old.

"That's not a true story," was the first thing she said to me. "Is it?"

7

"Excuse me?" I said. But she was right.

Bean was actually my best friend in high school. Everybody called him that because in third grade he'd gotten a bean stuck up his nose and had to go to the emergency room and his dad beat him so hard that he had to stand in the back of the classroom for a week instead of sitting down. He was six-foot-four and skinny as a bug, with this desperation about life that made him talk so fast his words turned into nonsense, or show up at my house in the middle of the night so jazzed and agitated about zombies or racism or the terrifying infinity of the universe that I would have to shout to get him to settle.

It was true that sometimes when Bean and I drove around at night in his gold Buick with the windshield wiper that stuck straight up like a clock striking midnight, I did feel like we were the only people in the world—especially after he calmed down a little and started to talk more slowly, and I could listen to his voice and watch the dark going by around us like it was a blanket that would wrap us up and keep us safe. But of course eventually he'd have to take me home, and my stepdad would be screaming in his nightmares or trying to drink them away at the kitchen table with his face like a deflated balloon, or my fourteen-year-old sister would be having sex with her twenty-two-year-old boyfriend, who my mom liked because sometimes he brought over hot dogs or oranges from his job at the Kroger, or my eleven-year-old sister would be sleeping in my bed because she was afraid of something she couldn't name that lived in the hills behind our house and came in at night to lie on top of her, invisible and terribly heavy, trying to crush the breath out of her lungs.

I'd seen the real Bean angry plenty of times. I saw him rage about his dad, who tried to toughen him up by putting him in headlocks and calling him a pussy when he couldn't get out of them, about our stupid high school he couldn't wait to escape, about the hard guys who played football and shot deer with their dads' guns and wrote "FAG" on his locker. About how all the girls wanted to go out with those guys instead of him. Bean's rages weren't scary—if anything, they made me sad. He was like a dog running in circles until it tires itself out; he was like a kid all out of breath from crying who's just discovered the world is unfair.

There was no Tommy, there was no Stacey. There was no Stabby. It was just me and Bean in the woods that night. We used to go there when he was really worked up, because the trees and the silence and the smells of the long-dead campfires would slow him and calm him down. But that night he was really going off—he and his dad had gotten into a fight about the garbage, and his dad had shoved him and then laughed when he fell down. Bean went pacing and pacing in circles, and finally I got him to sit down and I was rubbing his back a little, the way you rub a kid with a bad chest cold. I'd done this for my sisters in the fall and spring, when the phlegm would catch in their throats and stick in their lungs and they would beg for lemon tea and Vicks cough drops and someone to sit up with them at night and sing. But my sisters had never wheeled around and kissed me hard on the mouth. My sisters had never held me tight when I tried to pull away and stopped my mouth with their tongues when I tried to yell. My sisters had never pushed me to the ground and unbuttoned my pants.

The whole time Bean was raping me, I kept my eyes shut and tried to pretend he was someone else. Not someone I wanted, someone I'd agreed to have sex with, but someone evil and mean who I could completely hate. It didn't work. When he came, I opened my eyes and saw Bean, panting, an awful guilt dawning in his eyes, and I wrapped my arms around him and held him for a long time, because it seemed so important to let him know that he hadn't lost me, that I would still be his friend.

Bean and I didn't avoid each other after he raped me. Instead there was a weird energy between us, a brightness. We laughed too hard at each other's jokes and argued loudly over nothing and ambushed each other from behind with big bear hugs. Some of my other friends asked me if we'd started sleeping together. And then we did.

At first I thought it was a way to erase what had happened. I thought that making it okay to have sex with him now would reach back in time and make it okay then. It didn't, and once I knew it wouldn't, the sex got violent. I banged my body against him, I bit his chest, I dug my nails into his back until he bled. He was rough with me too—he'd hold me down, grab big handfuls of my hair and yank my head straight back. It reminded me of the first time and I got scared, but I never told him to stop. I thought everything we did was fair somehow—in some way through this a score would be settled. Afterward we didn't hold each other. We lay side by side sweating and panting, like boxers.

By the time graduation rolled around I started to worry I'd do something to really hurt Bean—gouge his eyes with my thumbnails while he fucked me, tear his lips off with my teeth. Something scary was awake in me and I wanted to put it back to sleep. I bought a bus ticket to New York with money I stole from my stepdad's wallet over the course of a month, and I told my fourteen-year-old sister where I was going and that she was in charge now. Then I saw Bean one last time.

I don't know why I told him where I was going. I know I wanted to get away from him—that night in bed my body was itching to leave. But also our fucking was less angry than usual, almost tender, and I came, and afterward he held me and I felt not peace but some kind of stillness. The next day I left town for good.

My first days in New York were like a bad dream. I moved into a basement apartment with no floor, just dirt under our feet, which my three roommates thought was funny. They were an NYU student whose parents had supposedly cut him off but still called every day demanding to talk to him; a part-time art restorer named Lady; and a forty-year-old guy named Charles who did odd jobs and might've been a drug dealer, but not a very good one, because he never had any money. Charles had adopted a cat with a broken jaw but he couldn't afford to take her to the vet, so he mashed her food up in water into a runny paste, some of which always leaked out of her mouth as she ate and for a while afterward, so when she sat on your lap you ended up with little drops of spit and mashed cat food on your pants. No one I knew back home lived like that, not even the Mastersons, whose mom was schizophrenic and made them wear surgical masks to school every day to keep the chemicals out. I worked at a diner until my manager started stealing my tips, and then as a bar waitress until a customer tried to follow me home, and then at a bodega where I had to stay because I had no ideas left, even though the owner always pressed his crotch against my ass when he walked behind me and yelled at me for not selling expired food. I felt like I'd come to a place for people who didn't know how to be people, and if I was there I must not really know how to be a person either.

After a couple of weeks I started expecting Bean to call. I hadn't given him my phone number but my sister had it—he could easily ask her. At first I just wanted him to call me up and talk to me like nothing had happened, like he was just an old friend reminding me where I came from, that I'd once had a real floor and a dog instead of a fucked-up cat and a life that, even if it wasn't that good or that happy, still made a little bit of sense. When it had been a month and still he hadn't called, I started wanting him to say he missed me. I wanted him to tell me that he'd been stupid to let me go, that he wanted to see me again and he thought we could work things out. I felt terrible for the whole two months or so that I thought this way, and at the same time I imagined myself saying I missed him too, and yes, and yes, and yes.

And then I started wanting him to apologize. By this time I'd managed to get a job waiting tables at a decent place in Williamsburg, and I was making enough money to move to the house with Irina, which was also dirty and crowded and full of cats, but at least it had real floors. I started to feel a little bit more in charge of my life, and I found myself standing on the subway platform or walking down Atlantic Avenue or carrying a slice of birthday cake to a customer, shielding the candle's little flame with my hand, and suddenly wishing, as hard as I'd ever wished for anything in my life, that Bean would say he was sorry. I didn't want him to explain, I didn't want him to tell me he loved me or he missed me or he wished things were different—I just wanted him to say those two words and never talk to me again.

The night I told the story it had been almost two years since I'd left Burnsville, and I still hadn't heard from him. It had gotten weaker, but I still had the feeling that he had something of mine that he needed to give back, and that I couldn't rest until I had it.

Maybe that's why I told the story about Bean that night, instead of one of the others I could've told—he still had a hold on me, and my mom and dad and my sisters and my stepdad didn't, or at least I thought they didn't at the time. But I wasn't about to tell the real story and have everybody know my business, and I guess I thought I could fool people—usually Brooklyn kids would believe anything you told them about West Virginia. I hadn't expected this little stranger standing in front of me, acting like she knew something about my life.

"When people lie about their past," she said, "they push their chests out and stand up straight, like someone's going to challenge them."

"And I was doing that?"

She nodded. "But some of it was true," she went on, "because sometimes your whole body relaxed, like you knew the story in your sleep."

I was annoyed with her for pegging me so well. I told all kinds of little lies about my life to Barber and Irina, to people I met, making my family and my town sound better or worse than they really were depending on the situation. I'd always gotten away with it, and I was happy to be able to make my own past and have people accept it. But I sometimes hoped somebody would catch me out, so I could feel like they really knew me. And the first person to do it was a girl who didn't know me at all.

"What are you," I asked, "some kind of psychologist?"

"I make movies about people," she said, "and I'd like you to be in one."

I thought she was fucking with me then. The arty kids I knew put on shows in crappy bars or made websites with a few cartoons on them—no one made movies. Either it was a joke, I figured, or she was one of those people who always had a crazy plan and never followed through. Plus Barber came back just then with a beer for me and wound his arm all the way around my back so he could touch the side of my left breast.

"Sure," I said. "I'll be in your movie, whatever."

"Good," she said. "I'll come by next week."

I DIDN'T KNOW HER NAME, and I hadn't told her where I lived, and I figured I'd never see her again. But there she was the following Monday, at my door.

"I'm Sophie," she said, and sat down on my bed without asking.

She kicked off her sneakers—her feet underneath were sockless, long and thin and graceful. She smelled good, like the dark valleys back home, cool even in the summer and full of ferns.

"We start shooting in three weeks," she said. "I need to raise a little more money, but I already know where I'm going to get it."

"Okay," I said. I started to take her a little more seriously. My friends with their shows and websites rarely talked about raising money.

"You're going to star, so you need to be there pretty much every day."

"Hold on," I said. Over the weekend Barber had told me that we needed to have an open relationship, because he and the bass player of his band, a tall blond girl named Victoria, needed to have sex.

"It's not even about the physical," he said. "She's just such an amazing artist."

I didn't care that much about the open relationship—I hadn't really been aware we were in a relationship at all. But I was jealous that he was so impressed with her; after my story I'd quickly gone back to being unimpressive.

"I'm not an actress," I told Sophie. "I can't star in a movie."

She waved her hand in the air like she was swatting away a fly.

"That doesn't matter," she said. "You're the one I want."

She was staring at me. She reminded me of the boys I liked in high school, the pretty, intense boys with their fake swagger, their soft mouths. They wrote bad songs and sang them well, and their girlfriends talked lovingly about how fucked up they were, how they should've been born in another place, another time. They always had girlfriends; those had never been the boys who liked me.

"What's the movie about?" I asked.

"It's about your story," she said.

I was flattered, but I was worried again—I figured no real director makes a movie after hearing a ten-minute lie from someone she's never met. And practically speaking, that meant she probably didn't even have a script yet. Maybe this was all a joke, a way to fuck with me by making me think I was important.

"That doesn't make any sense," I said. "That's not how people make movies."

She shrugged. "It's how I do," she said. "Movies are how I get to know people."

I laughed; she sounded so cocky. "How's that working?" I asked.

"Pretty well so far."

"For you or the people in the movies?" I asked.

"Both," she said.

After that she came over every day so we could work on the script. Always my place, never hers—I don't even know where she lived that year. She always sat close to me on my bed, but I wanted her closer. I wasn't even sure if it was sexual at first—I just wanted to feel her sleek hair, her narrow bones. Her body gave off so much heat, like a field mouse, an animal that has to survive in the wild. I wanted to know what she looked like under her boys' clothes—I imagined something neither boy nor girl, something I'd never seen before.

On the third night we worked together she asked for the real story of what happened to me back home. The room seemed too small all of a sudden, and I made us go for a walk. It was summer, after midnight, warm as a bath. Williamsburg was still ugly then—as I talked, stray cats skulked in the gutters, all bullet heads and scrawny shoulders. I felt so far away from home.

After I finished, we didn't talk for a while. My chest felt hollow. We looped back, and when we got near the house I felt Sophie staring at me. I didn't meet her eyes. I thought maybe I'd call Barber—telling the story made me lonely, and I wanted someone in my bed. But Sophie stopped outside the door, her hand on my arm. She made a face I'd never seen before—very serious, but with tenderness fighting through, like it almost hurt to show it. Like a knight from an old movie, I thought later, a hero.

"I want you to know something," she said.

"What?" I wasn't sure there was anything she could say to make me feel less lost.

"I would never do that to you," she said. "I would never do anything you didn't want me to do."

I wanted to laugh at first. Who was she to assume she'd get that opportunity? She didn't even know if I liked girls—I didn't even know. And even if I did, what was this little mouse going to do to me, when I had four inches and forty pounds on her? Then she took hold of my right wrist. Her hands were strong and she had me fixed with her giant eyes, and I thought maybe she could hurt me after all. I took a step toward her.

It didn't matter much that I'd never been with a woman before. Her body was so different from mine—her sharp hip bones, her boy's ass, her breasts you could cover with tablespoons. She fucked me like a man too—not like the boys I'd been with, but like the men I'd meet later on, who'd learned to read a woman's body and knew without asking that I wanted them to hold me down. She always knew how far to go and when to kiss me on the forehead or loosen her grip on my wrists so I didn't get too scared. Every now and then something would surprise me—how delicate she looked when she was sleeping, how when she showered and put on deodorant, she smelled just like me. And I knew my mom would cry if she found out and say it was my dad's fault for leaving us alone. But once I started spending all my time with Sophie, I didn't think about anything but us. That summer she was a hot wind I blew through the city on.

For a while after we got together, the movie seemed both real and not real. We talked about it all the time, and I helped Sophie with the screenplay. She submitted it for grants and fellowships—she was businesslike and organized and already knew what to do. I learned she was twenty-three, older than I was, that she'd already made a short film called *Daniel* and spent a year in a big-deal filmmaking program, that she knew dozens of people who worked on real movies and shows. I was always asking her to let me see *Daniel*, and she said she would, but somehow it never happened. All I knew about it was that it was about a boy she went to college with—which made me curious and jealous—and that she thought it had a lot of technical problems.

"This one will be better," she said. "I know how to make a movie now."

I liked this side of her, that talked about a complicated thing like it was easy and asked people for thousands of dollars like she knew they would say yes. And at the same time, I never thought we'd really make the movie. I thought we'd be working on it forever, the two of us, a project to keep us close, and all the other things that I now know make up a film seemed so strange and far away that I figured they'd never actually arrive.

And then it was November and Sophie got a grant. It wasn't quite enough to make the movie, but it was enough to start, and suddenly she was scouting out locations, calling grips she knew, and teaching me what the word "grip" meant. I started to get scared then. I'd made the whole story of the movie from something terrible, and I was worried I'd be punished somehow. Everybody in my family believed in ghosts, and my grandma said it wasn't just bad people who turned into them, it was bad deeds too. I was worried I'd made Bean's bad deed grow.

Sophie said the world didn't work that way. And she said even if it did, we should be punished if we *didn't* make the movie, because we'd be depriving something great of the chance to exist. She never doubted herself in those days. She was more sure about everything she said than I'd ever been about anything. Eventually I got her to change my character's name at least—I picked Marianne because I'd always thought it was perfect, plain but a little bit classy too. I told myself that made the movie just based on me, not really about me, and that made me feel better, for a while.

I was still working at the bar then, and Sophie did all the casting without me. So I didn't meet the guy she picked for Bean until our first day of shooting. He hadn't come to the read-through—Sophie's assistant director, a stuck-up girl named Susan who I already didn't like, read his part in a schoolteachery voice. But there he was the first day, at the community center that was supposed to be my high school, wearing a white T-shirt that looked like it had been dipped in pee.

"This is Peter," Sophie said.

I stuck out my hand, but he just nodded at it. He didn't look like Bean, but he looked like the scary, cocky Bean I'd made up for the story. He wasn't tall, but his arms were ropy and his hands were big, a fighter's hands. His face was ugly in that way a lot of girls like, hard angles and slitty eyes. He held his body like he didn't trust people.

In the first scene that day, he was supposed to ask me about Stacey. The community center had a hallway with olive drab lockers that looked a lot like a high school; we took down the signs for senior-citizen groups, and Sophie had Peter lean up against one of the lockers like he was waiting for me. I didn't like how she reached out to move his left shoulder down. He didn't like it either; he rolled it away from her and gave her a junkyard-dog look. She didn't back down, though. Instead she said, "You're not mad in this scene. You're relaxed."

"This is what I look like when I'm relaxed," he said.

"Well that's not what Bean looks like when he's relaxed. I need you to lower your shoulder."

He looked at her for a hard minute, and when she didn't break her gaze he did drop his shoulder, but slowly, like it was a favor. Then the camera was ready; Sophie sent a couple teenagers we'd paid ten dollars to be extras down the hallway first, and I followed, carrying a backpack. People always talk about what a "natural" actor I am, like

I don't actually have any skills and I just grew out of the ground like this, some prized tomato. But really I have to think carefully all the time, because I don't have any formal training. You learn a lot of things in drama class that I had to teach myself. Especially back then I was thinking constantly, because I wanted so hard to show Sophie she wasn't an idiot for picking me, and also because I wanted everyone to see how great we both were, how well we worked together. That day in the hallway I was thinking about how I was in high school, ornery and impatient but starved for the feeling of being liked, for the feeling of somebody seeking you out to spend time with, not because you were making them dinner or fixing their broken doll or telling them no, they didn't mess their life up. I thought of how it was to walk down the hall and see the real Bean, before he hurt me, the pleasure of running into somebody I didn't have to make any effort with, and how it might have been to see fake Bean, who was supposed to be cool and scary and who I would have wanted to impress, and I tried to mix those things in my face and my body and the way I walked. It felt like a long walk down that short hallway with cameras on me for the first time ever, and when I reached Peter, I was relieved.

But his face looked funny, like he was lost or something, and instead of saying his line he growled, "What are you looking at?"

"That's good," Sophie called out. "But your line is actually, 'Come here a minute, Marianne.'"

What about that was good? I wanted to ask.

But Peter just rocked back on his heels and slipped his thumbs into his pockets and said, "I know. I was just messing with Allie."

I hated when people called me that, but I thought Peter was trying to get a rise out of me, and I didn't want to let him. I knew something else was going on too. Peter looked nervous. He took his hand out of his pocket to scratch his nose. I wondered if he was on drugs. I walked up again, and this time he said the line right, and I said, "What's up?"—which was my line—and then he just said, "Not much," and I looked up at Sophie because that wasn't his line either—he was supposed to say, "How well do you know Stacey Ashton?"

"Okay," Sophie said. "Take a minute and look over the script again."

The skinny kid who was our production assistant handed Peter a copy of the script, and then Peter did something weird. He flipped through the whole thing for a minute, not even stopping on our scene at all.

"Okay," he said, "I'm ready."

We went through it again, and this time instead of bringing up Stacey he said, "I have to talk to you about something."

Sophie was getting frustrated.

"Just stick to the script," she said. "You don't need to ad-lib."

But I knew Peter wasn't ad-libbing. I'd seen that lost, defensive face before, on Arnie Phelps, who finally got passed to seventh grade because he was too big for the grade-school chairs. Peter couldn't read.

He must've known I knew, because he dropped the script on the floor and mumbled, "Whatever, this is bullshit," and walked down the hall and out the door.

Sophie stood empty-handed in the hallway. She looked as lost as he was.

"What just happened?" she asked me.

"He can't read," I said.

"That doesn't make any sense," Sophie said. "He was reading the script."

"He wasn't," I said. "He was pretending. Where did you find him anyway?"

"He was working at this bakery I go to," she said. "I liked the way he looked. Why would somebody pretend to know how to read?"

"He's embarrassed," I told her. "He doesn't want anyone to find out."

"Why?" Sophie said. "Who cares if he can't read?"

I was quickly learning that even though Sophie seemed to understand me so well at times, there were things she didn't understand at all. That day I didn't feel like explaining how normal people cared what everyone else thought of them or how if you weren't good at school you always felt nervous around people who were, like any minute you might have to prove you really were as smart as them.

"He thinks you'll think he's stupid," was all I said.

Sophie had a habit when she was frustrated—she would rake her fingers through her hair and pull it back hard from her face. It made her look like a hawk, diving.

"It's okay," she said, more to herself than to the rest of us, who were gathered around looking confused.

"It's fine. We'll just explain the story to him and let him ad-lib it."

She waved at the production assistant. "Chris, come here, we'll make some notes. Allison, you want to go out there and get Peter?"

I didn't. I didn't like Peter, and I didn't like that Sophie did. I didn't like that she liked the look of him, all skinny and hard everywhere that I was soft. We hadn't talked much about men but I knew she'd been with them, and I thought maybe what she liked in them was the opposite of everything about me. I was worried that one day she'd be with a man and tell him I was disgusting—my big ass, the way I submitted to her without question. I loved her in that headlong way that makes people jealous and anxious and greedy.

But loving her also meant I loved it when she was strong and in charge, when she knew what she wanted and she took it, even from me. And she wanted Peter to be in our movie.

"Fine," I said.

Peter was outside, leaning against the dirty wall of the community center, smoking a cigarette. Across the street was a park where the grass was dead for the winter, and some starlings were pecking at it. He was watching them.

"Hey," I said.

He jumped a little bit, and I felt good that I could startle him.

"What?" he asked.

"I came to tell you that you don't have to read off the script," I said. "You can just ad-lib from now on. Sophie says it'll be fine."

He dropped his cigarette on the sidewalk and ground it out with his shoe. "No," he said. "I'm done with this shit. I told her I wasn't an actor."

There was a wooden bench pushed up against the wall near where he was standing, and I sat down on it. I wanted to show that I wasn't afraid of him.

"Look," I said, "I don't know you. I don't know if you can act or what. But Sophie wants you to be in the movie, and she knows what she's doing."

He didn't say anything.

"She's going to be a big deal someday," I added.

I hadn't thought about this before I said it, but I realized it was true. Right then I imagined the day I would be talking about Sophie in the past tense, when people would ask me about her. I hoped I'd say, *That was the beginning of our life together.* But Peter didn't ask anything. He ran a hand through his oily hair. That's when I saw the tattoo, black-green on his white inner arm. It was an amateur job—a tiger with a head way bigger than its body, and one leg all long and wiggly like a hairy snake. The edges were blurring—ten years and it'd just look like a bruise.

"Where'd you get that?" I asked him.

He looked at me then, and his mean mouth had gone a little bit soft, and I realized he wasn't much older than I was, probably twenty-five. He didn't answer, but he seemed like he wanted to, kind of.

"Prison?" I asked.

He shrugged. "Juvie."

"What did you do?"

He shrugged again.

"My dad was in prison," I told him.

Peter lit another cigarette.

"What'd he do?" he asked.

I used to make up stories about my dad, like he was a bank robber or a gunrunner or a hit man. But I didn't think Peter would like those stories, so I told him the dumbest, saddest one of all, which was the truth.

"He stole a car outside of Richmond and he was going to take it home to my mom and me to surprise us. But then he got lost and he pulled in to a gas station for directions, and the gas station was across from a police station, and the cops recognized the car and arrested him."

Peter shook his head. "Your dad was a dumb-ass."

My mom used to say this about him while he was away, from when I was three to when I was seven. When he came back, though, she cried and wrapped her legs around him, and they tried to make it work for a while and even had one of my sisters. But he was just

24

missing the thing that lets people get by in the world, and he was always getting in trouble for no reason, getting thrown out of McDonald's for trying to smoke or fired from jobs for skipping three days just because he felt like it. He wasn't evil or even all that stupid; he was just really, really bad at following rules, and eventually he left us and moved out to the desert, where he said there were no rules at all. I didn't tell Peter this, though. I just said, "Yeah." I didn't want him to think he'd riled me.

"I didn't do anything," he said. "Some older kids were selling weed and I was the lookout, that's all."

"How long were you away?" I asked him.

"Well once I was in there I kept getting in trouble for other stuff. Fighting. So six months and then another six, and then I got transferred and then two years. So three years."

"That's a long time," I said, and then I took a little risk. "I bet you missed a lot of school."

"Yeah," he said. "So?"

"Listen," I said. "Where I grew up the schools were shit, and a lot of kids didn't go anyway. I knew a lot of people who couldn't read."

"Don't fucking condescend to me," he said in a low hot rage-whisper. "I know she thinks I'm a fucking retard and I don't need you to explain it to me."

His face went all tense the way boys' faces get when they're trying not to cry. I realized then that even if he didn't care much about acting, he cared about impressing Sophie. I wondered if all the cast and crew were people like us, people who loved Sophie a little or a lot and were willing to do whatever she said. It made me jealous—I wanted to be the only one. But it also made me feel warm toward him; we were in the same boat.

"Sophie didn't even know you couldn't read. She thought you were just being a jerk, and she didn't care. If she wanted trained Shakespearean actors, she could've gotten them. She wanted us. And that should make you feel good."

"Why do you care about this so much?" Peter asked. "It's not like you like me."

"I love her," I said, "and I want to make her happy."

This was true, but there was something else I didn't say—I could tell people were going to start coming between me and Sophie, and if I could take charge of Peter, maybe I could take charge of the next one too. And if I was in charge, maybe they wouldn't make it as far in and it wouldn't hurt as much.

Peter give me a little smirk then, held up two fingers in front of his face, flicked his tongue.

"So you guys are, like, lezzies?" he asked.

I almost liked him then; he looked like a twelve-year-old kid.

"Yeah," I said, bugging my eyes out, making fun of him, "we do this." And I flicked my tongue between my two fingers too.

He laughed. Then he shook two cigarettes out of his pack and handed me one without asking. I've never been a big smoker, but I had a cigarette with him and watched the starlings, and then we both went inside.

THE NEXT FEW DAYS were exciting ones. We were constantly behind schedule, and the production assistant quit, and the nineteen-year-old grip dropped one of the lights and sprayed broken glass all over the floor, and the little trust-fund girl who was playing Stacey cut her foot and cried and talked about a lawsuit, but Sophie just powered through all that with this kind of scary joy. She was barely eating and her collarbones stuck way out and her eyes were huge. One night she yanked my hair and snarled and bit me on the thigh, and I wore a short skirt the next day so everyone could see the bruise.

Because Peter was ad-libbing we all ended up doing it a little, and we kind of got into a rhythm with each other, especially Peter and me. Hating each other was a joke we kept pushing further and further. Once during a take of the scene where Bean tells Marianne he knows how to snap someone's neck, we just busted up laughing for no reason, and Sophie came charging over yelling at us, asking what was so funny. We couldn't explain. I could tell she was a little jealous, and I didn't mind. Peter started to flirt with me—he asked me did I ever date guys, and did girls have special tricks, and could they ever teach them to a man or were there things only a woman could ever do—and I didn't mind that either. I still didn't think Peter was good-looking, but there was something raunchy and sneaky about him that I liked. He always smelled like sweat, and I liked that too.

The day we were supposed to shoot the big scene at the restaurant was the first day of February. Our version didn't end the way my story had; instead of letting him leave, I was going to shove a knife into Bean's belly. We were in the parking lot behind a Turkish restaurant in Bay Ridge whose owner loved movies. Inside we made it bright and cheesy-looking with checkered tablecloths and menus we printed out at the DP's mom's house, but the parking lot was still dirty and lonely, a sad place to end up. I took my mark, my back against the faded red door. Peter stood in front of me. The makeup artist, who was the nineteen-year-old grip's big sister, had given him a close shave, and in his polo shirt and khakis and leather shoes he looked like a stranger. The wedding ring we borrowed from the other grip fit like it was his.

"You ready?" I asked him, smiling, trying to get comfortable.

He nodded, but he was looking past my shoulder at the beat-up door. Sophie counted down.

"You know why it didn't bother me, running into you today?" he asked.

His voice was different—he sounded slick, polite almost. For the first time, I realized he was good at this, at being someone else.

"Why?" I asked.

"Because I came here on purpose," he said. "Just to see you."

Then he moved close to me, the way he'd been in the run-through, so close I could smell him and feel the heat coming off his chest. And then he came closer. He was fully against me, pressing on me with all his weight. I looked at him to get him to ease up, but his eyes were flat. I looked at Sophie but she was staring over the DP's shoulder at the picture of us in the viewfinder. Peter pressed harder, and I could feel his cock against my belly, through those stupid khaki pants, and I wanted to scream so he would stop, but the take would be ruined and everyone would know how weak I was, how someone could scare me just by pretending.

"Why would you come to see me?" I asked him, and people who love the movie have told me this is their favorite part, the fear and anger in my voice feel so real, so authentic. I hate it when people say that.

"Because I want you to know that I know how to find you. Wherever you go, I'll always be there."

And then he grabbed my chin and put his mouth on my mouth.

People who have been raped talk about flashbacks, and I believe them. But that's not what I felt while Peter was holding me against the door and mashing his lips against mine. What I felt was pure shame. I'd gone to such trouble to tell a good story about my life, a story that was exciting and didn't make me look bad, and now the cast and crew and anyone who saw the movie would see the other story anyway. They would see me letting Peter do something I didn't want; they would see me fearful and helpless and struggling. And even though it was just a movie, even though I was supposed to be Marianne and he was supposed to be Bean, Peter was taking my dignity away, and everybody knew it.

It went on for a long time before I remembered I could stop it, and I felt even worse that I'd forgotten. I took the retractable knife from my apron pocket and jabbed him in the ribs, hard enough to bruise. He fell back, crushing the blood packets in his shirt; the red paint bloomed from his body, and I wished it was real. After the cameras stopped rolling, he asked me if I was okay, but I ignored him. I left the set and walked down the street in the cold to a coffee shop. I ordered a mocha, which I've always hated, and I sat at the table staring at it. After a while Sophie came in. She sat down across from me and put her hand over mine on the table, but I pulled away.

"What's wrong?" she asked.

"Nothing," I said. "I'm fine."

I hated girls who pretended nothing was wrong when they were obviously mad, but if Sophie actually didn't understand why I was upset, I didn't think she deserved an explanation.

"That's not true," she said.

I shrugged. The whipped cream on top of the mocha was melting.

"Are you upset about how Peter played the scene?"

She said it slowly, in that way she had of puzzling out things that would've been obvious to any normal human, and this time it made me furious.

"You think?" I asked. "You think I might not like how he held me down and kissed me without any warning, in front of everyone? You think I might be a little upset about that?"

I realized then that I'd never really yelled at her before. I didn't know what was going to happen. Maybe she'd break up with me. Maybe she'd cry. I was scared, but I was excited too, like I'd climbed up to a high place and I was looking down. But she didn't cry, and she didn't yell back. She just looked at me for a minute, and then she said, "I'm sorry. I didn't know he was going to do that. I should've stopped him."

This was also the first time she'd ever apologized to me. The words sounded weird coming out of her mouth, like a foreign language, but hearing them made my heart crack open a little bit. I felt like I was seeing a part of her I'd never seen before, a part that wasn't totally sure she was right all the time, a part that could admit she'd fucked up. And seeing that made me love her more than I had the whole time we'd been working on the movie, when she'd seemed so perfect and competent and impenetrable.

"It's okay," I said. "It wasn't your fault."

"I'm sorry anyway," she said. "I wish I could've protected you."

This time I reached out and took her hand. "It's okay," I said. "You didn't know."

We still had a few scenes to shoot, and they went easily. Sophie promised to edit the kiss out of the final cut, and I felt closer to her than ever. She'd moved into my room at the house with Irina by then, and we started talking about what we'd do when the movie was finished, how we'd enter it in festivals where everyone would see how great it was. We talked about winning at Cannes, how we'd go up together to accept the award. We talked about how I'd look in my red-carpet dress.

I didn't see Peter again until after the shoot was over. The last day had been odds and ends in what was supposed to be Burnsville, footage of me sitting on bleachers, waiting for the bus. It made me laugh, how little it was like home—the cameras in my face, the bright light, the city poking out through the smog on the horizon. Later I'd see the movie and shake for days at how real it looked, and forever after the fake memory would lie on top of the real one in my head, covering it over. But that day the air was sweet with the beginning of spring, and I was happy, and Peter came to the house to see me.

I was in our room, drinking wine from a jar and trying to hang the pretty Indian cloth I'd just bought for curtains. Sophie was in the editing room, and I'd just started to wonder when she'd be home. These days I wanted her to spend all her time with me, lazy in our bed, like I imagined she'd do if I were pregnant. But it was more like she was having the baby, and she had to work hard every day to make sure it got born right.

One of our housemates must have let Peter in. I heard someone on the stairs and I ran to the door with my face all shining, ready for Sophie, and when I saw Peter I turned away. I was embarrassed to let him see me so happy, like I was waiting for him.

"Hi Allison," he said.

"What do you want?" I asked.

My mother always said good manners were for people who deserved them. This attitude used to get her in a lot of trouble, but it was one of the few things I ever learned from her that I liked.

"I want to talk to you," he said.

"Well I've got nothing to say to you."

It wasn't true. Really I wanted to ask him why, why he thought he could act that way to me, just shove himself against me without warning when we'd already gone over the scene. I was worried there was something about me, something that said, *Do what you want with this one*, some kind of smell on my skin. That's why when Peter said again that he wanted to talk to me and asked if he could come in, I moved aside and let him sit at the edge of the bed. I stayed standing, holding my wine, looking down at him like that would give me the advantage somehow.

"First," he said, "I want to say I'm sorry."

"A little late," I said.

He went on. "I'm sorry because I knew you'd be scared when I kissed you, and I did it anyway."

He was talking fast and flat, like he'd written the speech out beforehand, and he wasn't meeting my eyes. I didn't want to give him any more power than he already had; I didn't want him to know how much he'd rattled me.

"I wasn't scared," I said. "It was just a shitty thing to do, that's all."

He looked up at me then. "I knew it would scare you," he said, "because Sophie told me it would."

Sometimes when something bad is about to happen, I get this rushing feeling, almost like joy. Right then I wanted to jump in the air or throw my jar of wine across the room. Instead I sat down on the bed next to Peter.

"What did she tell you?" I asked.

He stared at the floor. I was embarrassed about the T-shirts and panties and wine corks that lay there, all the evidence of the months we'd been fucking and drinking and sleeping and loving in that room, but it was too late to clean anything up.

"She said she didn't like the way things were going. She wanted the last scene to be different."

"What do you mean?" I asked. "What didn't she like?"

He paused. I could tell he was choosing his words and that he wasn't very good at it.

"It wasn't that she didn't like your performance. She liked it. It's just, she wanted something more intense for the end."

I could feel acid rising up my throat. Ever since the beginning, Sophie'd had only good things to say about my acting. She was always talking about how we were going to make so many more movies together. I wanted to kick Peter out, tell him he had no idea what he was talking about, but I also wanted to hear the rest of the story.

"And?" I asked.

"She said I should get in your face a little bit, to make the scene better."

"Get in my face?"

He stuck his hands in his hair, looked at his shoes. "I don't remember how she put it—she just said I should get close to you, even kiss you maybe. She told me to do that. I wouldn't have come up with it on my own."

I thought I had him figured out. He acted all hard, but really he was one of those guys who couldn't stand to have anybody hate him. Now that he'd had his fun freaking me out, he was going to pin everything on Sophie and look like the good guy.

"Bullshit," I said. "Get out of here."

He stood up. I stood too. I'd expected him to try to argue, but he looked defeated, almost relieved.

"Okay," he said.

But at our door, he turned back to me, and now he looked scared.

"She told me this other thing," he said. "She told me that because of something that happened to you, you might get really mad if I tried to kiss you. That you might even leave the set. But that I shouldn't worry because that was part of it. Whatever happened to you—she didn't say what—was going to make the movie better."

I had to sit back down.

"I didn't ask what it was," he went on. "I should have. I knew we were doing something fucked up to you, and I did it anyway, and I'm sorry."

And then he did leave, and I was alone, and I didn't know if I believed him, but I noticed that I was picking all my clothes up off the floor, like I didn't want them touching hers anymore.

SOPHIE CAME HOME HOURS LATER. I'd finished the bottle of wine and started in on somebody's cheap vodka from the kitchen freezer, and I was in what my mom used to call a bloodred mood. I wanted Sophie to ask me what was wrong, but she came in all important, talking about her day, wearing a new suit jacket she'd bought, and finally when she lay back on the bed and started talking at the ceiling without even looking at me, I gave up and interrupted.

"Peter came to see me today," I told her.

She didn't look worried. She didn't look at me at all. She was still staring at the ceiling like something was written up there.

"I thought you weren't speaking to him," she said.

"I wasn't," I said.

Sophie looked at me then. She sat up on her elbows and fixed me with those giant eyes, but still she didn't look angry or upset. She just looked focused, like she was in the editing room, cutting a tough scene.

"Did you tell him to kiss me?" I asked.

"Did he say that?" Sophie asked.

"Is it true?"

I wanted so badly for her to say something that made sense, something simple and obvious that would make Peter the liar and not her. Instead she stood up, took her jacket off, ran her fingers through her hair. She still just looked like she was thinking.

I started yelling. "Tell me if it's fucking true!"

"Can we talk about this in the morning?" she asked.

She held her hand out to me the way she did when she wanted me to come to bed. I took it and dug my nails into it the way I did when she was making me feel so good it hurt.

"Did you tell Peter to kiss me?" I asked again.

She looked away. "I did," she said.

I threw my jar of vodka against the wall. When it shattered into a million pieces, I picked up the bottle and threw that too. I was looking around for something else to throw when Sophie started talking in a new voice, loud and with a panicky edge on it.

"Allison, you know when you want something to be perfect?"

"No!" I shouted.

"Well, you know when *I* want something to be perfect?"

I turned to face her. My blood was pounding in my ears.

"Sometimes I just want that so badly that I don't think about what will happen or how other people feel. I can't think about it, even though I know I should."

"Why can't you?" I asked.

Her eyes were wet. I realized she was scared now, as scared as I'd ever seen her. She raised her arms in a silent shrug, and I remembered how small she was, how fragile.

"Well, you need to learn," I said. I wasn't yelling anymore. I was hoarse. "You can't be like this forever."

"I know," she said. She held out her hand again, and this time I took it and lay down on the bed with her. But all that night I dreamed a dog was chasing me, barking and biting at my heels.

MY GRANDMA AND MY GRANDPA loved each other, and when he died she cried for one whole day, my mom said, and then she went out and got a second job baking bread at the women's prison. She was smart and fast, and soon she was promoted to line cook, then kitchen manager, and she was able to quit her first job at a factory that made wooden dishware, and she worked at the prison until she died. My mom and I visited her when I was four or five years old, before my sisters were born, and she made bread with a soft cheese baked inside it and I kept wondering what magic she used to get it in there. Another woman was staying with my grandma then, a lady named Elma who had been a prisoner. She had a big square body and a face that had seen a lot of sun, and I remember she taught me how to peel an orange in a spiral so you're left with a bouncy, sweet-smelling snake. She also told me a story about her grandfather that I didn't believe but that I loved. She said he was a sailor who was captured by pirates, and they were about to make him walk the plank when he made a special Masonic hand signal, and since they were Masons too, they not only let him go but taught him all their pirate secrets and codes and ways of avoiding the law. Elma had round cheeks and deep wrinkles at the corners of her eyes, and when she smiled, I thought she looked like Mrs. Claus, and I told her that, and she laughed.

That night when my grandma was putting me to bed, I asked her what Elma had done to go to prison. My grandma didn't believe in lying to children, so she told me that Elma's husband used to beat her and her daughter, so one night Elma killed him. I was scared then—not because I thought Elma would kill us but because I was worried that the nice lady who I'd started to love the quick way little kids do was actually evil and I'd have to hate her.

"Is Elma a bad person?" I asked my grandma.

"What she did was bad," she said. "But not as bad as letting somebody hurt you over and over and not doing anything about it."

I knew she was talking about my dad, which wasn't fair, because he was just a screwup who never hit anyone in his life. But I remembered this forever, how bad she thought Mom was for taking shit from him. And I thought of it the day I packed up my stuff while Sophie was editing and moved to a new apartment across town.

Despite Flaws, *Marianne* Makes an Impression

R. Benjamin Martin, Class of 2005

This weekend's independent film festival at Bolcher Auditorium featured a number of worthy and wholesome efforts. *Bogdan* in particular, the story of one young boy's triumph over astigmatism, will no doubt be a contender this Oscar season. But it is not of *Bogdan*, nor of *Woolly Bear*, the majestic tale of an annual caterpillar migration, that I have come here to speak. I want to talk about *Marianne*.

Marianne is not a perfect movie. It is not beautifully lit, nor, it must be said, even competently edited. The sound has roughly the clarity of an expiring person shouting for help from the bottom of a very deep well. The supporting actors are occasionally embarrassing.

And yet *Marianne* is by far the most interesting film this critic had the pleasure of seeing at the festival, and perhaps the most interesting one his editors have ever assigned him to review (though *Death Slash 8* did, to be fair, have its moments). Many films try to convey the experience of being trapped in one's hometown. I'm still waiting for the movie that shows everyone what it feels like when your mom comes home every night with another part of her body ruined from her job—first her back, then her eyes, then the hands that spanked and comforted you as a child—and your dad, already ruined long before, lectures you from the couch every night on the importance of the education that he never got and that he has no idea how to pay for, and all your friends cut class to smoke pot and talk about dreams heart-wrenchingly out of step with anything the world will ever allow them. *Marianne* doesn't hit all these notes (eager viewers will have to wait for this critic's screenplay to be picked up, an event surely in the offing), but the way the camera crowds Marianne in her family's tiny house captures the hemmed-in, desperate feeling underlying them better than any film I've seen.

My editors at the august *Daily Mongoose* have recently requested that my writing be less "personal." I do not think this is an objection to personal writing per se, as a colleague's account of her (admittedly tragic and ultimately lost) battle with acne was met with great praise. I think it is an objection to the substance of my personal anecdotes, and thus to my life. Given this I will refrain from discussing at length how *Marianne* captures another aspect of small-town misery: the impossibility of escape. Being followed by a murderer from your past isn't quite the same as having the undeniable luck to win an academic scholarship, then arriving at college to find that everyone there has had the same set of four experiences, none of which are yours, and that when you try to talk about any of your experiences you are met with either suspicion or horror and exhorted to "lighten up." These topics are perhaps beyond the scope of *Marianne*, but later readers of my collected works (no doubt forthcoming within the next ten or twenty years, depending on the velocity of my rise) may find them revealing as an illustration of my perspective. In any case, leaving aside those matters apparently out of place in a paper of the *Mongoose*'s stature, I will say merely that *Marianne* accomplishes the difficult feat of conveying deep emotion by means not generally considered emotional: the framing of a shot, for instance, or the blocking of actors in a scene. The film's themes arise organically from the visual, rather than being forced upon the viewer through melodramatic dialogue or sentimental acting, as in many films that I could name but will not, since I already know I differ with many of my readers (and, indeed, my editors) in my opinion of them.

In an effort to make my film reviews more conventional, I have been asked to award films "stars." I have been told that the number of stars I assign will be printed in the paper, no questions asked. I award *Marianne* 3,468,994.2 stars. Note to copy desk: Please print this exact number of stars or I will be forced to conclude that the *Mongoose* editorial staff not only has no regard for accuracy but may not be able to count above ten.

Editor's note: ★★★

Robbie

SOPHIE RAISED ME, KIND OF. WE RAISED EACH OTHER. OUR DAD was dead, and our mom was just young and sad and indecisive, and one day she was into Amway and the next day she was into Jesus, and she was never that into us. Sophie taught me how to read and how to draw and how to crouch quietly in the grass behind the drugstore and spy on people, like teenagers making out and our third-grade teacher crying and once our mom looking at photos of a man we didn't know with an expression we'd never seen before. I taught her how to boil a hot dog and clean a cut and talk to grown-ups to get out of being in trouble—she never got good at the last one, so a lot of times I had to do it for her.

That makes it sound like we were best friends, and we were, but also she did all kinds of things I didn't understand. She was terrible at school—she didn't care about pleasing the teachers, and she didn't care about fitting in, and when she was in eighth grade, she started wearing the same men's black button-down shirt as a dress every single day, with a leather belt around the middle and boxer shorts underneath. The other kids called her "Crazy Emily"—she was still plain old Emily Buckley then, after our grandma—but she didn't seem to care. I was in sixth grade then, and I'm embarrassed to admit I tried to pretend I didn't know her; I even made fun of her when my friends did, though not as harshly and not when she was around to hear. It didn't work—the school was small, and everybody already knew we were brother and sister. Even if they hadn't, it was obvious: She and I had the same black hair and sharp faces, the same every-thing, except her eyes were even bigger than mine. So I tried to con-vince her to act more like a normal kid. It didn't work, until the eighth grade when boys started throwing chocolate milk and mushy straw-berries at her, and even then her only concession was buying some girls' jeans.

In high school she started trying a lot of different things—one week she went running every morning wearing her crappy black sneakers and twisted her ankle so hard she limped for a month. After that she started smoking weed—I'd find her in her room red-eyed, petting the wall. Then she tried other drugs, ones I didn't know. She started coming home covered in sweat, her pupils pinpricked, and once she drew tiny figures all over her bedspread in permanent ink, men and women with their faces all turned up like they were staring at the sun. She still didn't have any friends at school, but there were rumors about her—about girls, about boys, about older men I was sure she'd never have anything to do with, as much as I could ever be sure about her. Twice she stayed out all night and wouldn't tell me where she'd been. Once I caught her outside the drugstore begging for spare change.

When she was seventeen, she said she wasn't going to college.

She said she was going to move to Chicago and draw portraits of people on the street for money. Maybe I should've let her do it. I don't know if she was happy then, but she had this kind of drive in her, and maybe if I'd just let her go, it would've pushed her in the right direction. But a family has to have one practical person, and I wanted my sister to have a nice life. Also, even though she still embarrassed me at school, part of me was proud of her. I thought she was a genius, and I thought no one had seen it yet, and I wanted them to see.

So I convinced her to take the SAT, and then I found some colleges that didn't seem to care that much how you scored on it. I filled out the application for her. I said I (Emily) was an avid artist and also president of the French club (which we didn't have) and a volunteer at the senior center (it was true that she'd been a big hit on our high school's trip there, because she'd been willing to sit silently and listen to the old people for hours). I said my goal in life was to help people through art. My sister's only contribution was in the "nicknames" field, where she wrote "Sophie Stark."

"I'm changing my name," she said.

I asked her why.

She shrugged. "Do I look like an Emily to you?"

I had to admit that she didn't. I sent her applications off, and in the spring she got into Drucker, a liberal-arts college in eastern Iowa, about a hundred miles from our town. Mom had a party with scented candles and hard cookies shaped like fish, and it was just the three of us plus a lady from her church, and then one day late in August my sister was gone, and there we were in the house by ourselves.

I still had two years of high school to get through. I tried on some different things, too: I started listening to a lot of punk music and wearing band T-shirts, and then I tried out for and managed to get on the baseball team. Both of these worked out sort of okay—no one thought I was a loser, and I made a couple of new friends. But I didn't get a girlfriend or become extremely cool, and I felt kind of cut loose, like as soon as I left school in the afternoon, I didn't know what to do or how to be. I missed my sister. I kept starting a sentence in our silent house and realizing she wasn't there to hear.

When I got into Drucker, it was obvious I'd go. I'd gotten into a couple of other schools, and I made a show on the phone with my sister of weighing my options, but all she said was, "You should probably come here," so I did. I remembered how she'd been in high school, but I'd heard that college was supposed to change people— my friend Tyler's brother had come back a Jehovah's Witness—and I thought there was a chance Sophie had become cool. When I sent in my acceptance letter, I imagined her talking about me to a bunch of girls in black clothes, who played it cool because they were artists but who were all secretly excited to meet me.

But Sophie was even weirder in college than she had been in high school. She'd started wearing old-lady floral dresses that didn't fit any better than the men's shirt had, and it seemed like she wasn't washing her hair. As far as I could tell, she had never taken more than one class in any given subject. She still had no friends. Every night she came to my room and sat on my bed for hours, not talking to me, just drawing stick figures in a notebook she had. Nothing I said about my classes seemed to interest her much—I was planning to declare premed, so I was taking mostly science—but she perked up when I mentioned Intro to Cinematography. This was an elective I'd picked because it wasn't full, but soon it was my favorite—I'd always assumed that people who made movies just tried to make them look as much like real life as possible, but I was learning that movies could make life look different, could make time go faster or slower, make the world seem flat or deep, put a woman in red far in the background and let her draw everyone's eyes. Whenever I talked about that class, Sophie would listen really closely, and sometimes she'd write something down. It made me feel proud of myself, that I could teach her something for a change. Then, after a couple of weeks, she said, "I need a video camera."

"For what?" I asked.

"I'm going to make a movie about Daniel," she said.

Daniel Vollker was the guy my sister was in love with. He was on the basketball team and lived in an off-campus house full of jocky guys, and he looked like the star of a sci-fi movie about genetic engineering. He had a beautiful (though supposedly slightly crazy) girlfriend who was the vice president of the campus Christian fellowship, and he routinely hooked up with equally beautiful but less wholesome girls who then cried about him in campus bars and made him famous. He didn't go for unconventional-looking women, and he didn't move in the same circles as my sister, who as far as I could tell moved in no circles at all. The only reason he knew she existed, it turned out, was because she'd been following him around for weeks, even skipping her own classes so that she could go to his. And now she wanted to film him.

"Why?" I asked.

"I took a lot of pictures of him," she explained. "But I want to show him moving."

Sophie had gotten a little point-and-shoot camera for her fifteenth birthday, and she'd taken photos off and on since then. She'd taken one of me when we were both in high school that I still love— I'm sitting on our front steps eating an ice cream sandwich, and I look more like myself than I've ever looked in any mirror, a little bit angry but a little bit hopeful, too, like I'm looking forward to not being mad. Now she was cutting most of the few classes she was actually enrolled in to take pictures. They were different from the ones I'd seen when we were kids—sometimes she'd take ten or twenty shots of a crowded quad or a person sitting in the corner of the student union, and she'd always just shrug when I asked about them, like she was trying an experiment she couldn't or wouldn't explain. But photography was a thing normal people did, unlike drawing people for spare change on the street, so I was happy to encourage it if I could. I was starting to worry that my sister and I were falling down a misfit hole we'd never climb out of.

"Just make sure you don't break it," I said. "We got a big lecture on how fragile they are."

"Oh," she said, "you're coming. I don't know how to work the camera by myself."

Right away we ran into trouble. We spent a Saturday standing outside the big, dilapidated row house where Daniel lived, waiting for him to come out. It was October, not cold yet but getting there, with that gold pretty light that falls across the Midwest right before winter, and for a while I felt good, standing out there with my sister, showing her the few things I'd learned. But Daniel never came out, and the next day in English the guys who sat in the back made fun of me.

"I hear your sister's a stalker," said one.

That was not what either of us needed.

"Can't you make a different movie?" I asked her.

"Why?" she asked.

"Daniel's friends are starting to talk shit," I said.

We were at her place for once, an apartment above a bar that she shared with a med student. Her kitchen was clean and organized, with a bowl of fruit on the table next to a loaf of her roommate's homemade bread. Sophie's food tastes had stalled out around age ten, and she kept all her own food—oatmeal packets and canned fruit and white bread and sugar—in her bedroom, which looked like a homeless person's shopping cart, like if she didn't keep everything she owned in a giant pile right next to her body, someone would steal it or throw it away. She cleared a space for herself amid all the papers and socks and candy wrappers on her bed and sat down.

"Are you worried about this because you want to hang out with those guys?" she asked me.

Sometimes I assumed that because Sophie didn't care what was going on around her, she didn't understand it either. I was always wrong.

"No," I said. "I just— Why don't you make a movie about someone who wants to have a movie made about them?"

Sophie cleared a space for me to sit, too. Her messy room looked and smelled like home, and I missed the years when I couldn't sleep and she'd make a space for me on the floor next to her bed. Sometimes she was the one who couldn't get to sleep; she had night terrors that made her howl in fear with her eyes wide open, and I was the only one who could comfort her. I'd put my two hands around her head and squeeze gently, like I was holding her brains together, and slowly she'd calm down and sleep.

"If you want to try and be friends with them," she said, "you should go ahead. They have a lot of parties. They get a lot of girls."

From someone else this could've been manipulative, but Sophie always meant what she said. And she was right—I did want parties and girls. The closest I'd come to sex was a party senior year of high school when Tracy Schneider stuck her hand down my pants and stroked me until I was hard, then mysteriously lost interest and walked away. What I didn't understand was why Sophie didn't want the same things. She might not care about making friends, but she did care about Daniel. Sophie was weird, but I was old enough to know she wouldn't be the first person to fake being normal in order to get laid.

"Maybe you should go to parties," I said. "Talk to people. Talk to Daniel. That's a better way of getting his attention than stalking him with a camera."

Sophie got a crumpled look on her face then that I'd only seen a handful of times before.

"You think I don't try," she said, "but I try."

She pulled her knees up to her chest and rested her head on them.

"When I first came here," she went on, "I decided I was going to fit in. I got a haircut. I got a short skirt."

I tried to imagine my sister dressing like the other girls. I tried to imagine her looking like them, her face all happy and nervous as she laughed with them on the way to class.

"And what happened?" I asked.

"It worked. I had girlfriends. I had these girls, and we went out for pizza together, and we went to the bars and tried to get older guys to buy us drinks, and afterward we talked about which guys were cute and which ones liked us. I even went home with a guy once, who I didn't even like, just so I could tell the girls about it at breakfast the next morning."

It almost made me jealous, my sister having a social life I knew nothing about.

"Where are they?" I asked. "How come you're not still friends?"

Guys were yelling in the street outside the window. There was a football game that night, and the tailgates were starting.

"Two of the girls had a fight. Jenny and Carla. Carla wasn't speaking to Jenny, and I met Jenny for coffee—that was something we used to do, meet each other for coffee, even though none of us liked it—and Jenny was crying because Carla wouldn't talk to her. She said she kept thinking of things she wanted to tell Carla, just little things that only Carla would understand. She said the feeling of having no one to tell those things to was so terrible, and she said it like she knew I'd understand, but I'd never had a thing I'd wanted to tell any of them that badly. To me, hanging out together was like acting— putting on the right face, laughing at the right time. It was interesting, and I liked it in a way, but I didn't need it like Jenny did. That's when I knew that I could spend time with people but I was never really going to be friends with them the way they were with each other. And so I just stopped trying."

Sophie pushed some T-shirts off her pillow and lay back with her hands behind her head. Now she looked relaxed, or resigned. I was mad at her for giving up, and also I was worried—if those girls had been so easy to give up, would she be able to drop me like that, too? When she went off to college and I was back in high school, she never called home. At the time that had made it easier for me to imagine she was cool, but now I wondered if she'd forgotten I existed.

"You're acting like you can never feel close to people," I said. "Does that mean you don't feel close to me?"

She looked upset then, like I'd insulted her. "That's different," she said. "You're my brother."

"How is it different?" I asked her.

49

Now she was annoyed. She got up, went to the kitchen, came back with a glass of chocolate milk.

"It's different because I love you," she said.

It didn't explain anything, but still I was relieved. I didn't have to say it back; I knew she wouldn't even want me to.

"Can I have some?" I said instead, and she handed me the glass.

NEXT WE FOLLOWED DANIEL to a basketball game. It was a pre-season game against a college somewhere in Missouri that was even smaller than ours, whose players looked kind of dazed on the court, like they'd just come up from underground. I didn't know anything about basketball, but it was easy to see that Daniel was dominating the game. Over and over he drove down the center of the court and put the ball in the basket with total ease, leaving the Missourians just standing there blinking. Daniel didn't yell or pump his fist after a basket, but you could tell he was enjoying himself. He was light on his feet, like my high school friend Tyler the day after he slept with his girlfriend for the first time. Daniel looked as if the ball and the basket and his team and the crowd were all pouring energy into him and he was radiating it back out.

By the half we were up twenty points. I thought Sophie would want to take a break from shooting, but she started pointing the camera into the crowd, shooting kids high-fiving and eating M&M's and talking about the game. People were looking at us, and I tried to get her to stop so we wouldn't draw attention to ourselves, but she ignored me. Then I saw two girls stepping over the bleachers to get to us. They had long, shiny hair, one blond and the other dark, and they were wearing tight jeans and T-shirts with our college's name and looking pretty and confident and carefree. I'm not proud of it, but I moved a little farther away from my sister as they got close, so I could plausibly pretend I wasn't with her, but the blond one sounded interested when she pointed to the camera and asked, "Are you making a movie?"

Sophie didn't answer, but she swung the camera around to shoot them. The dark-haired one giggled and waved, but the blond girl stared straight at the camera like she thought there was something hidden inside it.

"Yeah," I said. "You want to be in it?"

"What's it about?" the blond girl asked.

My sister didn't say anything, so I answered for her. "It's a documentary about Daniel Vollker. Do you have any . . . uh, thoughts about him?"

The dark-haired girl didn't hesitate. "He made me care about basketball," she said. "I didn't know anything about sports when I came here, but he's just so good, and you can tell he's also a really good guy."

The blond girl rolled her eyes. "He's overrated," she said. "I mean, he's good and all, but good for our school doesn't mean that much. He doesn't really have a shot at the NBA."

We were drawing a crowd. More and more people came swarming toward us, crowding in front of the camera and yelling. Sophie peeled her face away from the viewfinder and looked at me with knitted brows.

I wasn't sure what I was supposed to do. Any minute someone was going to have the idea to beat us up.

"Okay!" I shouted. "Everybody who wants to be in the movie, get in a line behind me!"

For a second, everyone just yelled more. I started to plan a path to the exit. Then a girl hopped over a row of bleachers to stand behind me. And another. And a third. And then a pack of guys, still yelling. Pretty soon there were twenty people all lined up behind me, just because I'd told them to. Sophie swung the camera around to capture them—shoving and joking and eating Skittles but waiting their turn.

I didn't have a chance to interview any of them, though, because two security guards in windbreakers came up the bleacher steps to ask us if we were authorized.

"Yes," said Sophie, still filming.

"Okay," said one of the guards, big and balding, with those brown bits of hair clinging to the sides of his head that made me scared of getting old. "Show us your form."

Sophie lowered the camera and looked at the guard blankly.

"You can't record a game without the permission of the athletic department," the balding guard said. "You're going to have to leave."

All the way back to my dorm, I felt pleased with myself, like I'd gotten away with something. In a way we had—they'd kicked us out, but they hadn't taken the tape.

AFTER THAT, things were different for me. The kids in film class heard about the movie and were either curious or dismissive in a way that let me know they were actually curious. They'd all been doing just the class projects, things like "record something that is moving." Some of the more advanced kids started talking to me in the lab room where we signed out the camera—one of them volunteered to help us edit. The girls in my English class still ignored me, but the blond girl from the basketball game started saying hi to me around campus. She told me her name was Andrea and she was a sophomore, a history major. She had a sad edge to her voice that made me like her hair even more.

We couldn't shoot at games anymore, and we couldn't shoot at Daniel's house, but we could shoot at the outdoor courts on the edge of campus where Daniel usually showed up early in the morning to practice on his own. And we could shoot at the bars that the team liked to hit on weeknights, Jacky's and Bar 9 and the Sports Page. Daniel always ignored us, and his girlfriend stared at Sophie like she wanted to skin her, but other people came up to ask questions and try to get on camera. Everything I'd hoped for at the end of high school was coming together. I felt famous and important; I felt like Sophie's ambassador.

I was in my dorm room, not out filming, when Daniel's girlfriend came to see me. CeCe was tiny and honey-blond, and everybody said she was the hottest girl in school, but to me her face looked prematurely old, like she was a mom with a lot of worries already. I offered her a seat and a Coke—I was learning to be polite and generous in my fame—but she said no to both. My roommate was out; I sat in my desk chair, and CeCe leaned against the desk. She looked down at me like she was kind of annoyed that circumstances had forced us to interact.

"You need to keep your sister away from my boyfriend," she said.

"Why don't you talk to her?" I asked.

"I did," said CeCe. "She doesn't listen. She just looks at me like she's retarded or something."

"Sophie's not retarded," I said.

Actually, Sophie had been IQ-tested in fourth grade, because she

53

couldn't or wouldn't answer questions in class. She'd done so badly that she was briefly placed in special ed and put back in the mainstream class only after the first math test, on which she'd not only scored perfectly but also drawn a series of geometric diagrams she wasn't supposed to learn about for another four years. Later, when I asked her about the IQ test, she said, "They tell you stories that don't make sense and ask you questions where the answer could be anything. It scared me. I just decided not to say anything."

"Whatever she is," CeCe said, "she doesn't have the right to keep following us around like this."

"Daniel hasn't said anything," I said.

I actually had no idea how Daniel felt about the movie. For all I knew, he liked being the center of attention—I'd like it, I thought, if my sister decided to make a movie about me.

"Of course he wouldn't," she said. "He'd never admit how much it bothers them."

She was digging her fingernails into the flesh of her arms. It looked like she did it a lot; the skin there was covered with little scabs. I wasn't sure why she was so upset. I didn't know why Daniel's friends were mad either, now that I thought about it. I didn't really care. Sophie and I didn't need to suck up to people. The life I'd dreamed about for us was starting, I could feel it.

"Look," I told CeCe, "you're not his mom. If he has a problem with it, he can talk to Sophie. You don't have to do it for him."

She leaned closer to me. She smelled like vanilla perfume and something I couldn't place, something metallic.

"You don't get it," she said. "Everyone just wants to take and take and take from Daniel. They see how great he is, and they just want to take advantage."

"And you're so different?" I asked. "You're not enjoying being with the most popular guy in school, having everyone jealous of you?"

I thought she'd yell, but instead she got really quiet.

"You think I don't know what goes on?" she asked. "I know he fucks other girls. I know that when I go home to see my brothers and sisters, he's got freshman chicks with big tits coming in and out of his room all weekend. And I put up with all that because I know he needs me to. He needs me to support him and let him be who he is and not try to control him, so that's what I do. Who else would be there for him every day like that, unconditionally, no matter how much he hurts them?"

I felt like I got her then. I'd gone to school with girls like her, girls with big families who had to take care of other people all the time and who got hard from it instead of soft. I remembered when Todd Hayward had sex with Ashley Lindstrom's little sister and then broke up with her the next day—Ashley caught Todd by the lockers and left bloody scratch marks all down his face and arms, like some kind of tiger. I could see that hardness in CeCe. She'd gotten out of her hometown and come to college and found somebody to take care of who actually made her important, and she wasn't going to let that go.

"He's lucky to have you," I said. "But maybe this time you need to step back, let him handle his shit himself."

She rolled her eyes. "Oh, fuck you," she said. "Don't fucking condescend to me."

She picked up her purse. "I'm going to tell your sister I tried to talk to you but you didn't listen."

"Tell her when?" I asked, but she turned and walked out the door.

WHAT CECE SAID stuck with me, and I meant to tell Sophie about it, but the next time I saw her, she just wanted to make plans. There was a party at an off-campus house over by the cemetery, the last big party before Thanksgiving, and she thought if we could get some footage of Daniel there, the movie might be finished. I thought maybe I'd see Andrea there, and I was excited for her to see me again in my capacity as co-director. I told myself CeCe was just a jealous girlfriend; I told my sister nothing.

The house was tall and dark and falling apart. It was nice out, one of those warm fall nights that makes you sad because it might be the last one, and guys in suspenders were out on the front porch barbecuing corn.

"Watch out for the loose board," one of them said as I tripped on it and fell into the kitchen.

Inside, people were floating in thick smoke like ghosts. I saw a pretty girl with hair down to her ass stirring wine on the stove. I saw a wedding cake with a fist-size hole punched in it. I saw a tray of brownies labeled "nuts" and a tray of brownies labeled "party." I saw a bowl of water full of rose petals and a guy dip a cup in it and drink. I saw three girls wearing see-through white dresses like nuns from a cool religion. I saw their six nipples and I got embarrassed and turned away.

Sophie was already shooting. People were getting used to her—one guy waved at the camera, and another lifted his beer bottle like a toast, but mostly they just ignored us. I didn't see anyone I knew. I was jealous of Sophie—she always had the camera to put between herself and other people, but I had to talk right to them out of my own stupid face. I found a punch bowl full of something and ladled it into a plastic cup. It tasted sweet and a little bit poisonous, and I drank it very fast.

I didn't have all that much experience with alcohol. My only source of booze in high school had been the liquor cabinet at my friend Tyler's house, but we were always scared to take too much in case his dad found out—Tyler had to go to the hospital sometimes for shadowy reasons, and once when we broke his bike doing gravel races, his dad yelled so hard he cried—so I'd never really been drunk before, but now I could feel whatever was in the punch slamming into my brain. My muscles relaxed. I felt like I was part of the party, like I belonged to it. I started to recognize people. A guy in my English class who had always seemed too cool for everything waved at me, and then I was standing with his friends and actually talking and laughing, although I couldn't really hear anything they said. I could still see Sophie with the camera, but we were drifting farther apart, and then I couldn't see her anymore, and I didn't worry about it.

I was on my second or third drink when I felt a hand on my shoulder.

"Robbie," said Andrea, "I'm so glad you're here."

Her cheeks were flushed; she had dark circles under her eyes. Her hair fell around her face all tangled and pretty. I wanted to stick my hand in it and pull her against me. I thought there probably was a kind of guy who would do that, and girls probably liked him. Instead I was the kind of guy who said, "It's great to see you. You look great."

She laughed, a sad laugh that made her seem older.

"I look like shit," she said. "Will you come outside with me? I kind of need someone to talk to."

"Of course," I said.

The yard was wide and deep and sloped down until it met a stand of oak trees. Close to the lights of the house were clusters of people drinking and laughing, but as we walked farther down the hill, the crowd thinned out until it was just couples half hidden in the shadows. The bottom of the yard smelled like rain and fallen leaves, and it made me think of home, of the green places near the creek where it smelled like rain all year round. Andrea sat down on the grass in a single fluid motion, and I sort of stumbled into a squat beside her.

"What's wrong?" I asked her.

She gave that laugh again. "I'm getting divorced."

She held up her left hand, and now I saw two rings sparkling on it, a gold one and a diamond. I'd never thought to look at anybody's hand before—it had never occurred to me that someone my age could be married. All I could think to ask was, "Why?"

"It's my fault," she said. She wrapped her arms around her knees. "In high school we were so in love. We thought no one understood us. And when we were eighteen, we got married as this, like, fuck-you to everyone who said we couldn't do it, that it wouldn't last. And now, surprise, it hasn't. My parents said I'd want to date other people, and I do. I just want to be a regular girl."

She stretched her feet out in front of her. She was wearing purple sneakers with a heart drawn on the left toe. I had no idea what to say.

"Maybe it'll be good," I said. "I mean, now you can do what you want."

She looked up at the branches above our heads. I saw a bat flick between them. When she looked back at me, she seemed indignant, almost mad.

"Yeah," she said, "but wouldn't I be a better person if I didn't care about that? Shouldn't I just care about the person I love and the promise I made and not anything else? Isn't that how really good, strong people are?"

Right then I got extremely tired. The vodka was turning heavy in my head, and it seemed suddenly very clear that I wasn't going to do anything more than talk with Andrea that night. I thought about her husband and their teenage wedding and how much they must've loved each other to do something nobody I knew would ever think of doing, and I wondered if she was right. Maybe if you loved someone that much, you should do everything you could to defend that love, even against yourself.

"I'm sorry," I said, "but why are you asking me this? I've never been in love. I haven't even kissed a girl."

I hadn't planned on admitting that, and once I did, I knew I'd really given up on sleeping with Andrea that night, or whatever quasi-sexual thing I'd been hoping to do with her in somebody's weird yard. I just wanted to go home.

But she didn't seem upset or surprised.

"I had a class with your sister last year," she said. "Once I asked her how she was, and she just stared right through me like I didn't exist. She was so strange and mean, and nobody liked her. Then you came, and now she's this celebrity. That made me want to be your friend, that you could do that."

"I didn't do anything," I said. "It was her idea to make the movie. I just talk to people sometimes."

"Whatever you do," she said, "you're helping someone else live in the world, and that's more than I've ever done."

I remembered the summer when I was seven and Sophie was ten, and one day she refused to eat and hid in her closet, shivering like our cat right before it died.

"What's wrong?" I asked her.

"My stomach hurts," she said. "Don't tell Mom."

"Why not?"

"I'm not going to the doctor," she said. "They ask all these questions, and then they send you to another doctor, and they ask more questions. I'm never going to the doctor again."

This was around the time of the IQ test, which led to an appointment with a psychologist, which led to an appointment with a psychiatrist who prescribed Sophie a drug that kept her up all night chewing on her hair until she refused to take it anymore. From each visit she came home mad and exhausted, complaining about questions like "How do you feel around other people?"—which to her had no answer.

"I don't think it's that kind of doctor," I told her, but she didn't care.

"I'm not going," she said, waving me away.

That night I tried to bring her dinner, but she was curled in the fetal position with her cheek on the floor. Her skin was a bad color like cooked fish, and her forehead burned.

"I'm getting better," she said, but I knew she wasn't.

"We'll tell the doctor you can't talk," I said, "because it hurts too much. And if he asks any questions, I'll answer them for you."

She looked up at me and her eyes were dull with hurting.

"Okay," she said, and let me lead her out.

I only had to answer a couple questions. Soon they took her away into a part of the hospital where I wasn't allowed to go. It turned out that her appendix had burst and filled her belly with infected fluid— another day and the infection would have spread throughout her body.

She didn't thank me—I'd never seen Sophie thank anyone before or since—but after she came home with her stomach all bandaged up, she did look at me over her bowl of Jell-O and say, "Without you I could've died."

It wouldn't be so bad, I thought, to be the one who took care of Sophie, who made it so the world would know her.

I was feeling warm toward Andrea now. I was grateful to her for making me feel useful, and I wanted to do something to help her.

"You're going to be okay," I said. I tried to think of something smarter to tell her, but she seemed satisfied. She scooted up next to me and laid her head on my chest—her hair smelled clean and sweet. I put my arm around her. I felt peaceful and hopeful, and as I fell asleep with her there against the tree, I didn't wonder where my sister was or whether she'd gotten home safe.

We woke up sometime in the early morning when it was too cold to be outside anymore. It was still dark out, and I walked Andrea most of the way to her house. We were sleepy and still kind of drunk, and we didn't talk much, but it felt easy and right to be walking close to her, brushing up against each other sometimes and not apologizing or moving away. I didn't kiss her because I was afraid of looking like an opportunist, but after we hugged good-bye at the edge of the little creek, she squeezed my upper arm and said she'd see me soon. After that I ate a Snickers I had in my desk drawer, and then I went back to bed to redo the night's sleep, which had been full of half dreams, half hallucinations in which gray figures crossed the yard to tug lightly on my hair and clothes. It was afternoon and I was just waking up when someone knocked on my door.

My sister's left ear was higher than her right. Her mouth sloped down a little to the right side, and her cheekbones flared out of her thin face like wings. I had never noticed any of this before, and I might've gone my whole life without knowing it, if she hadn't come to my door that day with her head completely shaved.

"You cut your hair off," I said without thinking. Then she lowered her head, and I saw it was covered in cuts and pink, raw patches and tufts of leftover hair—she hadn't done it herself.

"What happened?" I asked.

Sophie never cried—I'd seen her do so exactly once, at nine, when a Frisbee we were playing with hit her square in the face. Even that seemed more like a physical reflex than sadness. When we were kids, she would sometimes scream with rage, her eyes crazy, but by the time she was fifteen or so, the only indication she was upset was her breathing, which would go sharp and shallow, her nostrils flaring. She was breathing like that now. She didn't answer my question.

"Here," I said, "come in."

She sat on my bed. She wasn't wearing one of her usual dresses, but a white T-shirt and a baggy pair of jeans. Her neck and shoulders were painfully skinny; her scalp was pale.

"Do you want anything?" I asked. "I have Sprite."

She nodded. I was glad I had something I could give her. She popped the can open and drank, and her breath slowed down.

"I finished the movie," she said.

It was such a left turn that I wasn't sure I'd heard her. "Sorry?"

"I mean, I still have to edit it. That'll take a while. But I finished shooting."

She sipped again, reached up as if to smooth her hair, found nothing, and brought her hand awkwardly down.

"Sophie," I asked again, slower this time, "what happened to your head?"

She shrugged. "It's not a big deal," she said. "I didn't like my hair that much anyway."

I put two and two together, finally. "Did CeCe do this?" I asked.

Sophie scratched her raw scalp. "I still don't get why she's so mad," she said. "I don't want anything she wants. I'm not going to stop her from marrying him or whatever."

I was still trying to make sense of the logistics.

"CeCe found you at the party, and she shaved your head?"

Sophie looked at her Sprite. "More or less," she said.

So while Andrea had been telling me what a great brother I was, CeCe had been taking a razor to my sister's scalp. Or maybe it was earlier, when I was trying to maneuver my way into Andrea's pants. Or earlier, when I was using my status as Sophie's helper to ingratiate myself with people. I hadn't even managed to warn Sophie beforehand, because I was too excited about going to the party. I felt like calling Andrea and asking her to come over. I wanted to punish myself by showing her how useless I was.

"I'm so sorry," I said. "I should've been there."

Sophie shrugged. "She kept saying she warned you. Like that would mean something to me."

"She did warn me," I said. "I could've helped you. Instead I was off being a dumb-ass."

The fact that I'd failed her because I was hoping to get laid was especially gross to me. I was ashamed of myself, like she'd caught me masturbating.

But Sophie looked at me sharply, anger in her eyes.

"I know you think I can't take care of myself," she said, "but it's not your job to protect me."

"I know you can take care of yourself," I said.

"No," she said. "You don't. You're always trying to run interference for me. What do you think I was doing before you came here? Do you think I was just curled up in a ball somewhere?"

I thought of what Andrea had said about Sophie snapping at people in class. Wasn't she nicer now? Didn't people like her more?

"No, but—" I started.

"But what?" she asked. Her bald head made her anger scarier— she looked like a dying person, with a dying person's feverish eyes. "I'm not crazy, and I'm not retarded. I'm not blind. I don't need you to be my guide dog."

Now I was angry.

"All I'm trying to say is I feel bad that you got hurt," I said, "and I wish I'd been there. Sorry if that makes me such an asshole."

She sighed. She reached up to touch her scalp; her hand was already learning to expect bare skin there.

"You're not an asshole," she said. "I just don't want you to think you have to keep me safe. That's my job."

I was still feeling angry, and guilty, and I could tell the second one was only going to get worse. I wanted to push some of the blame off onto Sophie.

"You're not very good at it," I said.

She just shook her head. "I am," she said. "It's just really hard."

She drained her Sprite, scratched at her ankle. She was wearing sneakers with no socks. She looked like a twelve-year-old boy. I remembered a kid I'd played with when I was about that age, a scrawny boy who came around when my friends and I were playing tetherball after school. The kid was wearing a plain T-shirt, which marked him as different, because we all had shirts with our favorite cartoon characters or sports teams on them. He said his parents were spies, which I didn't believe—in retrospect, since it was spring, they were probably migrant farmworkers. As proof he taught us some phrases he said were French—they were actually gibberish, I knew even then, but I remembered them for years and used to repeat them to myself when I couldn't sleep. After that day, though, I never saw the kid again. I wondered if Sophie wanted to be like this, showing up in my life just for a second, asking for nothing.

"If I'm not supposed to help you," I said, "what do you want me to do?"

"Can I sleep in your bed?" she asked. "I didn't get much sleep last night, and I don't want to be in my apartment right now."

It surprised me that she didn't want to be alone, and that she'd admit it, but I was glad to have something to do. I cleared the textbooks off the bed; she kicked off her sneakers and crawled in, but she didn't lie down. Instead she lowered her head.

"Can you?" she asked.

I put my hands to her scalp. It was hot and smooth. I couldn't remember the last time I'd touched her bare skin. As a kid I'd imagined I could read her thoughts through her head, but now I couldn't even guess. She shut her eyes, and I took my hands away. As she slept, her face got calm—even with her shaved head she looked so normal, somebody's twenty-one-year-old sister who needed a place to stay.

Sophie slept for hours with no sign of waking up, and I couldn't stop myself from going to find CeCe. I knew where she lived—she and her two equally high-maintenance roommates, both of whom were dating slightly-less-popular versions of Daniel, had exclusive pre-parties there on Friday nights, and even people too cool to want an invite or too uncool to ever get one (until recently I'd been the latter) knew where they were held. I didn't know what I'd do when I got to her—I knew I couldn't hit her, even though I wanted to. I thought maybe there was something I could say that would make her cry, and then Sophie, sleeping soundly in my bed, would have the upper hand.

CeCe's roommate Leigh, a tall girl who was dating the heir to a pesticide fortune, answered the door. I could see behind her into the living room—there were actual framed pictures on the walls, landscape prints and photos of the girls laughing. Leigh's hair was wet. The air around her smelled like shampoo and perfume.

"CeCe's not here," Leigh said. "She went home to see her family."

"When will she be back?" I asked.

"I don't know," she said. "It might be a while."

I felt stupid and powerless. What was I supposed to do, leave a message? I looked down at my empty hands.

"Look," she said. "We're all sorry about what happened. If we'd been there, it wouldn't have."

"Well, you weren't, were you?" I shot back.

She looked hurt and embarrassed, and I immediately felt guilty.

"Sorry," I muttered as I turned to go.

Before she shut the door, Leigh said shyly, "I think your sister's cool."

For the next month, Sophie barely spoke. She spent as much time as she could in the editing room, and when they kicked her out to lock it for the night, she'd either go home or come to my dorm, where she'd eat my snacks and resist my attempts to talk to her. She didn't seem angry. She just seemed checked out, like she was trying to pretend she wasn't at school anymore.

When she got the fellowship in New York, I couldn't be happy for her. At first I didn't even understand what it was.

"How can you go to grad school when you haven't graduated yet?" I asked her.

"It's not grad school," she explained. "It's a fellowship. They teach you how to make a movie."

"And you hate it here so much that you're just going to leave with a whole year left?" I asked.

"I don't hate it here," she said. "I might come back and finish my degree later."

I didn't believe her.

"This is my fault," I said. "I let you get hurt, and now you're just going to leave."

She smiled at me then and shook her head, like she was just a normal big sister and I was a kid who was being silly. Her hair was growing back in; she had a quarter inch of dark fuzz on her head now.

"Not everything has to do with you," she said, still smiling.

SOPHIE SCREENED *DANIEL* the last week before winter break. She reserved a room and a projector from the film department without my help. The room was packed—Andrea and I sat in the front and watched it fill in behind us, people standing along the walls. CeCe didn't come, which didn't surprise me. Neither did Daniel.

The first few minutes of the movie were familiar. I saw the footage I'd shot in front of the row house—it looked jerky and amateurish, and I was embarrassed, but Andrea squeezed my arm and whispered that it was great. The first few scenes Sophie had shot looked shaky too, and I started to relax, thinking that was just how the camera was. But the scenes she'd shot later—Daniel practicing and people talking about what they thought of him—looked like a different person had made them, somebody older and more confident. About ten minutes in was a scene I didn't remember, Daniel in the park all by himself, spinning around and shouting like a little kid. It was funny to watch, and a couple people laughed, but the footage itself was beautiful—the blue-gold light, the swings squeaking in the distance. Even Daniel looked different, his breath in the cold air like a halo around him.

I remembered when I was five or six and Sophie taught me to draw. We set out my Batman action figure on the kitchen table, and both of us sketched him in pencil. I started off okay—the cape, the double-pointed hood—but then I got off course. Batman's arms ended up too long, his legs too short, like he was a crime-fighting orangutan.

Sophie shook her head. "You drew Batman like he looks in your head. You have to draw what you see. Just think of it as shapes. Don't even think of it as Batman."

"Then it won't look like him," I said.

But I looked again at my drawing—I'd tried to draw Batman leaping in the air, even though the action figure was just standing on the table. And Sophie's Batman was perfect, down to the dents where his plastic joints came together. I never learned to draw as well as she did; I realized I probably wasn't going to be as good at making movies either.

Then I saw my sister's face. She was on the screen, her head freshly shaved. The camera jerked all over the place—whoever was shooting didn't know how to work it.

"Say it," a male voice said.

Sophie just looked around her. She was in a badly lit room with a flowered plastic curtain behind her—a bathroom. She looked scared.

"Say it," the voice said again, louder.

Sophie stared down at a piece of paper in her lap. She read in a monotone.

"'My name is Sophie Stark,'" she said. "'I am a worthless nobody. No one gives a fuck about me or my ugly, rotten cunt.'"

Then a female voice spoke. I recognized CeCe.

"Don't just read it," she said. "Say it like you mean it."

Sophie looked up at the camera then. She didn't look scared anymore. She looked like she had when she was nine years old, examining Batman.

"'My name is Sophie Stark,'" she said again. "'I am a worthless nobody. No one gives a fuck about me or my ugly, rotten cunt.'"

"Say it again," CeCe hissed.

Sophie lifted her chin high. Her bald head looked regal now. Her voice was loud and strong.

"'My name is Sophie Stark,'" she said. "'I am a worthless nobody. Nobody gives a fuck about me.'"

She paused there and looked away from the camera. I assumed she was looking at CeCe, and I imagined her standing there, digging her fingernails into her skin, trying to figure out why she wasn't getting what she wanted.

"Say the rest of it," she said.

"'Or my ugly, rotten cunt,'" Sophie said, and the movie was over.

I immediately shoved my way to the front to talk to Sophie. I was angry—at CeCe, at Daniel's friends, who I now knew must've been with her, but at Sophie, too. I didn't understand how she could put something so gross and humiliating in her own movie and seem so happy about it.

Sophie was surrounded by people—at least ten girls and a few guys, too, were crowded around her, asking questions and trying to get her attention. She didn't seem panicked; she was answering, even smiling.

"How did you get the courage to put yourself out there like that?" a girl with purple acne asked.

"I don't really think of it as courage," Sophie said. "I just wanted to make an interesting movie."

I realized then that Sophie did care what other people thought—at least, she liked to be praised. I shouldn't have been disappointed—I'd kept glancing over at Andrea during the movie to see if she was impressed—but I was. I waited awhile for the crowd around Sophie to thin. When it didn't, I went home.

A FEW DAYS LATER I helped Sophie ship her things to New York. She'd gotten rid of almost everything—her apartment was clean and empty, and four boxes were stacked neatly on the floor. We borrowed her roommate's car and drove to the post office without talking. It was a beautiful winter day—perfectly clear, face-burningly cold. In line at the post office, everyone else was shipping Christmas presents and grad-school applications. When we took our spot all the way back by the entrance, I asked Sophie, "Why would you want to put something like that in your movie?"

"Oh," she said, "that was my plan all along."

The line moved forward, but I didn't move.

"You planned that?" I asked her.

"Well, not the shaving part. But as soon as they started filming, yeah, I knew I had to use it."

A guy with a stack of manila envelopes had lined up behind us, and now he was looking nervously at the gap that had opened in front of us. I still didn't move.

"Why?" I asked.

"I needed something big to happen. I had all this good footage of Daniel, but I needed something more to make it a real story. I don't know how people do that, like how screenwriters make a story out of nothing. I was kind of worried. And then they just stepped in and made a story for me."

"So the whole time, while they were making you say that awful shit, you were just thinking what a great ending this would be?"

The guy with the envelopes cut ahead of us.

"Basically," said Sophie. "I mean, they weren't holding me down or anything. I could've run, but I waited so they could finish the scene."

"Weren't you scared they'd keep the tape and show it at frat parties or something?"

"Oh, yeah," she said. "I was definitely scared they'd keep it and I wouldn't get to use it. But luckily all these girls were lined up outside the bathroom, banging on the door and stuff. That Steve guy put down the camera so he could answer the door, and the girls all started yelling at him, and then everybody was arguing and distracted so I just grabbed the camera and ran."

All this time I'd been feeling terrible for leaving Sophie alone, she'd been enjoying herself. I thought about walking out and leaving her to deal with the boxes on her own.

"Why didn't you tell me this before?" I asked.

She shrugged. "You didn't ask."

I started pushing the boxes forward, finally. I didn't want to look at her anymore.

"You knew how bad I felt," I said. "You just let me feel that way even though you planned it all along."

People were staring at us openly now. Sophie turned to me, and I could tell she was angry.

"I told you not to," she said. "You wouldn't listen. You think everything I do is some judgment on you."

"Come on," said the girl who was behind us now, staggering under a giant box.

We both pushed our boxes forward. When Sophie turned to me again, she looked less mad. She looked like she was proud.

"Listen," she said, "I was upset that night. I was really scared of them at first. I didn't know what they'd do. They cut my scalp, and I was bleeding. Making it part of the movie, that was the only way I could fight back."

"It's a weird way to fight back," I said.

"You were at the screening," she said. "People wanted to talk to me, and I could actually talk to them because of the movie. I think I can be really good at this. Please don't make me feel bad about it."

I didn't say anything. We reached the cashier, who grumbled at us for taping the boxes wrong, then retaped and labeled them and sent them off to New York. The next day I drove Sophie to the airport in the early morning, and I helped her with her tiny suitcase. Then I watched her walk into the crowd of people, and I remembered how small she was, and I was afraid. I worried she'd meet someone in New York who could hurt her much worse than CeCe had. And then beneath that was something else, something vaguer: I thought of her proud face at the end of the movie, and I was afraid of what she was capable of, what she might do without me around to watch. I thought of running after her and demanding to come along, but I didn't move, and then the crowd closed around her and I couldn't see her anymore.

GRIMBLE BAY DAILY HERALD

Local Theater Shows Independent Film

R. Benjamin Martin

I watched *Daniel* with three other people. For the Ocean View Theater on West Grimble Drive (which does not have a view of the ocean, though it does, as its marquee proudly states, now boast a working heater), this is a rather impressive crowd. That they turned out to see a medley of short films by independent directors was doubly unusual. I was glad to see Grimble Bay townsfolk exposing themselves to something new and untested, especially since the Ocean View typically shows, inexplicably, revivals of such nonclassics as 1977's *Slap Shot*.

My three fellow audience members all appeared to be residents of our local retirement home. Two complained loudly throughout the film's opening scenes that it was "hard to understand" (which it would not have been, absent the complaining) and left after the first five minutes. The third, like me, remained riveted as the film unfolded.

Daniel was Sophie Stark's first film, a college effort that hadn't seen release until now, when the critical success of *Marianne* has drawn some modest attention to her work (though less, I would argue, than it deserves). If *Marianne* was imperfect, then *Daniel* is a total mess—it's clear that at the outset Stark didn't actually know how to work a camera. But what the film does, as well as most better-known films on the topic and better than some (the overrated *American Beauty* comes to mind), is convey the experience of obsession.

At the beginning of the film, Stark's desire to worship her subject—a frattily handsome college basketball star—clearly outpaces her skill at doing so. Early scenes of fans extolling his greatness from the stands are dull—I surely cannot be alone in attending movies in part to escape the tedium of sporting events—but over the course of the film her technique seems to evolve to catch up with her devotion. An extended shot of the title character spinning around and around like the child he no longer quite is warmed the heart of even this jaded viewer, who in the past thought himself profoundly allergic to anything remotely heartwarming.

And then, in the final scene, whose substance it would be unfair to reveal here, the obsession takes on a life of its own. Freed from its object, it suffuses the face of the filmmaker herself. Daniel is gone, and now Stark is obsessed with her own image, or rather the power that image has to disturb, to enchant, to enthrall.

And despite my reservations, I—along with my elderly fellow viewer, whose name turned out to be Violet—did find myself very much enthralled.

Jacob

I DIDN'T KNOW ANYTHING ABOUT SOPHIE STARK. MY PRODUCER, Gary, was the movie geek; he'd seen *Marianne* and said we had to get her to do the video. I didn't care. I didn't want to make a video anyway. The label thought it would sell records, and it didn't, and I've never done another one, and I'm glad. But I was younger then, and I was still doing things because I thought they might help my career somehow and because deep down I didn't like saying no to people. So the label execs, who were really just these guys four years older than me with an office in Brooklyn, said do a video, and Gary said Sophie Stark. And I picked the lake, because a masochistic part of me had always wanted to go back there.

We didn't rent the same house my family used to stay in—that would've been too weird—but the one we got across the lake looked a lot like it. And it had the same smell, like if you made a dent in the floor, the lake water would well up. I thought about the ghost stories my dad used to tell—the little girl who drowned in the lake and left wet footprints on the stairs, the old lady floating from room to room with her feet a few inches above the floor.

Ghosts or not, the shoot didn't go real well. I can see now that the song wasn't actually very good—"Deep" is the kind of fairy-tale-knockoff ballad that was sort of popular at the time but that now just sounds sort of twee and annoying. Sophie ignored a lot of the lyrics. The final video is mostly just this eleven-year-old actress she hired sharpening a knife and then rowing out into the middle of the lake. Now I recognize how good it is—it's not dreamy or old-timey at all, like I wanted back then. Instead, the way she shot it makes it look almost like a documentary, even though some of the things in it couldn't happen in real life, and that makes you want to watch it over and over, like you're going to find out more about these people, even though they're not real people and of course you aren't.

At the time, though, I wanted her to do it my way. I didn't get why she couldn't put more scenes of me and the band in the video. I mentioned a verse where I sang about following the girl with the red shoes all the way through her life, from childhood to her death. We could shoot that in the forest, I thought. I could play the guy following her. This was during the time I thought I could be a real rock star, and it made me forget a lot of things about myself, like that I was a weird schlub who should not star in videos.

"Sorry," was all Sophie said, "I just don't think that part is very interesting."

By Saturday night, the end of the three-day shoot, we were all pretty sick of one another. My bandmates were mad at me for roping them into this, I was mad at Sophie for ignoring all my ideas, and I wasn't sure if Sophie was mad at anyone, but she looked depressed, and then she went outside to call her fiancée. The guys in the band went into town to get drunk. I stayed at the house, allegedly to write more songs but really just to lie on my bed and think about how shitty my existing songs were and rhythmically stuff Doritos in my mouth. I'd suspected for a long time that the music I was playing was a crappy imitation of other people's better music, and I was worried other people were starting to catch on. As I fell asleep I was thinking about my first piano lessons in third grade: the cold quiet room, the pretty Russian teacher with her thick low voice, the way the music cut through my brain and left it clean and bright and open.

Later that night I woke up to a loon calling on the lake. I remembered that sound from when I was a kid. I used to be able to make it myself—the grown-ups would turn to scan the water and I would let them squint with their grown-up eyes until I got too excited and had to laugh and scream that it was me. When my voice changed I couldn't do it anymore, and since then the sound had always put me on edge. It was a warm night; the cameraman in the bed next to mine had a loud fan blowing across his face. I'd always slept so well in our old house, but here the night felt bent out of shape somehow; the loon's voice shook me up and I couldn't settle. When I heard it again I got up to look for it.

The view out the window calmed me down a little bit. The moon was high and full, and the lake was glass, and the light at the end of the general store dock was just where it always had been, and for a minute I could pretend I was back in the old place, and Mom was alive, and my sister, Jenna, was ten years old with Band-Aids on both knees and no thought in her head of marrying an evangelical minister and homeschooling their kids, and Dad still looked like some of his life might be ahead of him. And then I saw someone on the dock, a black outline on the water, and I knew it must be Sophie.

I told myself I was going to have a talk with her, get her to explain what was wrong with my song, but as I pulled on pants and walked down the path to the dock, I was thinking about fighting. I'd never been in a real fight—growing up, I was always the chubby, wimpy kid who said sorry before anyone could kick my ass. But for some reason I kept thinking I'd tap her on the shoulder and then she'd wheel on me and slug me in the face, and I'd fight back, but she'd fight harder and dirtier, biting me and kneeing me in the balls. I was getting mad as I walked down there, thinking about how she was cheating in the fight we weren't having.

I stopped a couple of paces behind her. I was barefoot, and she still hadn't heard me, and I realized I didn't know what to say. Just "Hi" sounded weak, but "Hey!" sounded too angry, like she'd gotten to me already. Finally I decided to start with just her name, "Sophie," just like that, but before I could say it, she turned around, and her face was covered in tears.

"You couldn't sleep either," she said.

She was all wrapped up in an afghan from the couch inside, and it made her look a little bit crazy, like somebody who didn't know how to put on clothes. Her voice was thick and hiccupy with crying, and I felt kind of cheated, like I'd gotten all ready for something that wasn't happening, but I wasn't going to fight with her now.

"What's wrong?" I asked.

"Nothing you have to worry about," she said. "After tomorrow you never have to deal with me again."

I was curious—I hadn't pegged her for somebody who cried. But if she was going to be a dick, I couldn't let myself stand there and take it. I used to worry about my dignity a lot then.

"Fine," I said, and turned to leave. I'd walked halfway back up to the house when I heard her voice again, completely different this time, all high and teary.

"Wait," she called. "I'm sorry."

I turned back. She was standing in the porch light's beam and her face was so puffed and red from crying that it looked almost soft. She was twenty-six then but I'd pegged her for older because of how bossy she was; now she looked young and scared.

"I'm not usually this bad," she said. "I mean, I'm not great. But I've had some difficult things recently, and I think it's made me especially bad."

I didn't want to feel sorry for her, and I might not have, except that she sucked so hard at playing for sympathy, like she didn't get how people talked about their problems. Still, I didn't move.

"I'm sorry," I said.

"No, it's fine. I'm going to be fine. It's just—you know when someone leaves you and you realize that person was responsible for all the best parts of you, and now those parts are gone and you don't know how to get them back?"

I remembered Tessa, five years before, the way her long back looked the day she said it was time for her to find a husband. I was twenty-three and she was thirty-five, and she said it the way she always said things to me, kind of offhandedly, like everything that happened between us was a joke to her. I said I'd be her husband, and she looked at me with a little pity-smile and said I hadn't been listening—she wanted kids, a house. I said I'd get her a house, we'd have two kids—we'd even picked out their names together, I said, and right then I realized she'd just been playing the whole time. She cupped my chin in her hand and said, "Oh, honey, you'll be a wonderful father someday," and then left as easily as if I'd never existed.

I still missed the daydream of those kids—how I'd learn to braid Rebecca's hair so Tessa could get an extra few minutes of sleep, how I'd tell Isaac I loved him every night so he'd never forget it, even after I was dead. And I missed Tessa—the way she got dressed in the morning, her hands, her straight, no-bullshit mouth. Since she'd left, all my relationships seemed to last about six months. The girl would start thinking she understood me, and I wouldn't correct her, and then what she thought was going on between us and what I thought would get so far apart that when I broke up with her, she'd think I was proposing. It had gotten so regular that I could see all the stages before they happened. I'd meet someone and hear the clock start ticking.

"Sure," I said. "You and your fiancée . . ." I started, not sure how to finish.

She shook her head. "We were never engaged. I just say that to make myself feel better. I made up this life where I ask her to marry me and she says yes, and then she gets really girly and traditional and buys all these bridal magazines and calls me a million times a day with questions about centerpieces, but none of that is true. She left in March."

For years after my mom died, I sometimes told people she was still alive—mostly people I didn't know very well, but sometimes even close friends like my college roommate, who acted like I was crazy when I finally told him the truth. I wasn't crazy. I just wanted to skip the moment when people got all quiet and awkward trying to figure out what to say. And I wanted to forget those bad last years when Mom became someone none of us knew, and then not someone at all.

"What happened?" I asked.

Sophie gave the biggest shrug I'd ever seen. She threw her shoulders back and her face upward like she thought the sky might open and send her down an answer.

"I don't know," she said. "That's not true. I know. I'm hard to be with."

I couldn't stop myself from laughing, thinking about how she'd insulted me. She smiled a little bit, then got serious again.

"I don't mean I'm a bitch. I mean, that's a problem, too, but less so, most of the time. I just mean I don't understand other people that well, and sometimes they don't understand me either. It leads to trouble."

"I can see how that could cause trouble," I said, "but it doesn't mean there's something wrong with you."

"Well," she said, "I haven't been alive all that long, but I've had enough breakups to know that the common element is me."

This last part sounded like she'd read it in a self-help book, and I had a mental image of Sophie sitting cross-legged on a bed somewhere, paging through a pink paperback with a pen in her hand, trying to figure out how normal humans had relationships.

"Listen," I said. "My mom was sick for a lot of her childhood and her teens, and she had a lot of surgeries and a lot of scars. When she got to college, she didn't really know how to act with people her own age, and she was so sure nobody would ever want to date her that she didn't know what to do when people did. And so she had a lot of bad boyfriends and boyfriends that hurt her. Then when she was twenty-five, her dad died, and she decided to stop dating and build a house on this lake and live here alone. And my dad was the guy she hired to help build the house. And when the house was done and my dad asked her to marry him, she asked him why he wanted her when he could have someone with nothing wrong with them. My dad didn't give her a bunch of compliments or anything like that. He just said, 'No I couldn't. That person doesn't exist.'"

I didn't tell her the rest of their story, how they married and loved each other for twenty years, and then in less than two years she went crazy and died. I didn't think there'd be any need to tell her, because after we said good-bye the next day, I thought I'd never see her again. She was smiling now, her face still wet. I wanted to touch her, not even to kiss her necessarily but just to feel her skin, which I for some reason thought would be hot and thin and fragile like the skin of a mouse. I took a step toward her, and I could feel the heat coming off her. Then she brought her arm up between us and wiped her eyes with the afghan.

"Why did we come here?" she asked.

The night snapped back into focus. Frogs were singing in the woods; the moon was starting to set.

"What do you mean?" I asked her. It was the kind of question people back in the city would ask me at parties, meaning *What is our purpose in this world?* But Sophie didn't seem like the type to get existential.

"I mean, why did you want to shoot here? I can tell you've been here before. What happened here?"

Her face was dry now, and she was looking at me hard with her big eyes, sizing me up. I remembered that I barely knew her at all.

"I used to come here when I was a kid," I said, turning away. "I'd better get some sleep."

"Good night," she said. And she put her hand on my arm, just for a second, and her skin was just like I'd imagined.

．　．　．

THE NEXT MORNING the guys were loading up the van. I put the amps and guitars on board, but when I tried to help Sophie's crew with the lighting equipment, they gave me a look like they didn't know who I was, so I just stood around in the driveway, staring at the trees and my feet. I was thinking maybe this weekend would be good for me. I was feeling clear and alert. When I got back to the city, maybe I'd be able to write songs again. Then I felt skinny arms wrap around me from behind.

"Let's not go today," Sophie said. "Let's stay."

At first I thought we wouldn't be able to do it. When I called, the owner said it was rented to someone else starting Monday, and when I asked if there was any way they could switch, he gave me a lecture about city people and the things we needed to understand. I thought of telling him I'd come here every summer for fifteen years, but I was worried he'd tell me bad news about the house, like the new owners had torn it down and put up a big new ugly house in its place. Instead I just hung up. But when I told Sophie it was a no-go, she called him back, and within fifteen minutes he had changed his mind.

"I just told him we needed it," she said, blank-faced.

And then we were alone with that whole house around us, just staring at each other. I admit that I thought we'd have sex; it seemed like the next step. But we were just standing together in the empty living room, and I had no idea how to get started. I couldn't tell if she even expected me to do something—she was looking at me out of those eyes like a cat or a bird of prey. I was embarrassed, and

I didn't know why. Finally I went to the kitchen and got my guitar, which was still right by the door, ready to get loaded into the van.

"Want to hear some music?" I asked her.

She nodded and sat down on the daybed. I sat next to her, close enough for my leg to touch her a little bit but far enough that if she asked if I was hitting on her, I could deny it, maybe. I felt twelve years old. I thought I'd play something romantic, so I started in on "Walking After Midnight." But once I finished the first verse she stopped me.

"Will you play one of your songs?" she asked.

"I thought you hated my songs." I tried not to sound like I was pissed off about it, but I'm pretty sure I failed.

"I didn't say that."

"You did say they weren't interesting."

"Oh," she said. "I just meant the words."

It was true I'd never been much of a lyricist. I heard the music in my head first, and later I'd kind of match some words up to it and hope it all fit together. My favorite songs of mine, the ones that came closest to the feeling I'd had writing them, were the ones with no words at all. But I wasn't playing those songs in public much then. People liked a story, I thought; they liked to sing along.

So I launched into "Luella." Like a lot of the songs I was writing then, it wasn't really about anything in particular. It had a girl with broken hands who stays inside a lot, and people wearing blue in a white room, and some stuff about sadness. When I finished, she asked me, "Is that about your mom?"

"I guess so," I said. "A lot of my songs are about her, a little bit."

"What happened to her hands?"

A lot of things happened to my mom's hands. When she was born, my grandma thought she was making fists, but the fists wouldn't open. The doctors X-rayed them and found dozens of tiny bones, all in the wrong places. I've seen the X-rays. For some reason my grandparents put them in her baby book, next to the first photos of her, a wide-eyed baby in a knit hat. Over the next fifteen years, she had ten surgeries to make fingers. She spent a lot of time in the hospital, and she told me things that only people who have been sick for a long time know, like that there is school in the hospital, even for kids who are going to die. My mom learned long division in the hospital. She read *To Kill a Mockingbird* and *Jane Eyre*. She told my sister that she got her first period in a hospital bed, and my sister told me that years later, when we were drunk together for the last time before she got born again and quit drinking and everything else.

And then it was over. She was in the tenth grade, and her hands were as good as they were ever going to be. They turned out to be pretty good. She could write and draw and braid hair; she could count change and wear gloves and use chopsticks. She could even play the trumpet, and she was in the school marching band for a year until she quit, not because the fingering was hard on her new hands but because she was tone-deaf. There were only a few things she couldn't do, like play cat's cradle, fasten a necklace, give someone the finger.

Once, in high school, a boy put her left hand on his erect dick while they were at the movies. My sister told me this one, too—she said he told our mom he just wanted to see if she could feel things. In college a boy told her that her hands looked like bound feet. Another called them his little meat puppets. A third gave her some expensive cashmere gloves, then asked her to keep them on during dinner with his parents. Once my mom slapped a man across the face with her right hand.

"Did it hurt?" a friend asked her, concerned.

"Him?" she said. "It sure looked like it."

My mom got a wedding ring specially sized for her little finger, since she didn't have a ring finger on her left hand. When my sister started first grade, my mom bought her five different kinds of nail polish and let her pick a new one anytime we went to the drugstore. When we were in Little League, she couldn't play catch with us, but she could play Ping-Pong. Her hands ached sometimes, and when they did we fought to be the one to put her special heating gloves in the microwave for her. Once her mind started to go, she forgot about her hands and started doing things that she knew were dangerous for her, like hammering nails. We came home to find ugly pictures of flowers hanging all over the living room wall and her calmly watching *The Wonder Years*, and after that we weren't sure if it had ever been dangerous in the first place.

I didn't tell Sophie any of this. The more I thought about my mom, the more I realized what a stranger Sophie was and what a weird idea it had been for us to stay in the house together.

"She was born with a condition that made her hands deformed," I said. "So she had to have a lot of surgery as a kid."

Sophie nodded. "Did it work?"

It was a funny question, like there was a switch somewhere, and if the doctor flipped it just right, Mom's hands would just turn back to normal. But even though she talked about how hard the hospital was and how hard it was to get used to life when she finally got out, she was always really upbeat about the hands themselves. She was always up for answering questions about them, especially if a kid asked. She didn't sugarcoat—I once heard her tell a boy in my sister's class that her hands would get older faster than other people's and that for her fiftieth birthday she was going to ask for Velcro shoes. But mostly what she ended up telling people was that even though they looked different, her hands were a lot like theirs.

"It worked," I said. "All things considered, it worked pretty well."

Sophie nodded again. "Is she dead?"

It shouldn't have been such a slap in the face. After years of being the only one, I'd finally gotten to the age where some other people I knew had dead parents. And it wasn't like I'd been talking about my mom's book club, or her golf handicap, or her retirement plans, things I sometimes did make up when talking to strangers. Still, I felt like I'd been giving Sophie the happy version of my mom, and I didn't like getting jerked back to reality.

"How did you know that?" I asked.

"You talk about her the way people talk about their dead relatives," she said, "not their living ones."

It bothered me that she could see through me that quickly. And that phrase "dead relatives," like my mom was some cousin in a black-and-white photo with her name written on the back because otherwise everybody would forget her. The urge to fight came back in me. Instead I said, "Well yeah, you're right. She's dead."

I didn't look at Sophie after I said it. I figured anything I saw on her face would make me mad. I thought of how late I would get back to the city if I left right now. I wondered what I would do when I got there all snarled up inside. I thought about calling Tessa, which I sometimes still did, even though she was married now with a daughter and a baby son. Then Sophie said, "Will you do something for me?"

I couldn't believe she would ask me for a favor. I looked up at her; her face was unapologetic and completely serious.

"Will you teach me how to swim?" she asked.

I stared. For a second I wasn't mad anymore; I was just mystified.

"You can't swim?" I asked her.

She shook her head. "I never learned."

I remembered how her skin had felt the night before. I decided I wasn't ready to give up yet. I wanted whatever was between us to play itself out in a way I could understand.

"I'll teach you," I said.

She didn't have a bathing suit—she wore a pair of jean shorts and a black T-shirt. She walked ahead of me into the water until the hem of her T-shirt was wet, and then she turned around, hands on her hips.

"Okay," she said. "I'm ready."

I realized then that not only had I never taught anyone how to swim before, I didn't actually remember learning to swim myself. All I remembered was doing it—the water like liquid pine in my mouth, the way the cold tightened the flesh against my bones. I remembered being afraid of it sometimes—at night I used to think about something big and cold and ancient with no eyes and no name, slowly rising up from the bottom. But not being able to do it was as impossible to imagine as not breathing.

"Watch me first," I said, buying time.

She crossed her arms. I walked to the edge of the dock and jumped in. I remembered how I used to feel as a kid in the water, like my body was smoothed out, like I was even a little bit graceful. I took a few strokes as easily as walking. When I came up, I had no better idea of what to tell her, but she was still watching.

"So that's what it looks like," I said. "Want to try now?"

She put her hands in her wet pockets. "I know what it looks like," she said. "That's not really the problem."

"So what is the problem?"

"The problem is my feet. I don't like to move my feet."

I imagined her feet planted in the lake mud. I imagined them red and raw, like her hands. "Didn't you ever float or just paddle around, when you were a kid?"

"No," she said. "I was too afraid of the water."

"What were you afraid of?" I asked.

She looked past me at the other side of the lake. For a second I worried she could see the old house, even though it was over in the cove, totally hidden from view.

"Does something ever just feel bad to you?" she asked. "Like it makes your hair stand on end?"

I thought of our dog growing up, how late one night he'd stood by the front door, every muscle in his body tense, making a sound in his throat we'd never heard before, and how even though my parents said everything was fine and called him a crazy dog, I could tell they were a little scared of whatever it was he knew that we didn't. I wondered if Sophie could see or hear or smell things nobody else could. For a second I was afraid of the water too.

Then I had an idea. "Why don't you try jumping?"

"What, like jumping in?"

"No, jumping up. Straight in the air."

She smiled then, the first I'd seen her smile all day. "Roguish," my mom would've called that smile. Then she launched herself out of the lake and came down right next to me, sending a sheet of cold water smack across my face.

"So you can jump," I said.

"Of course I can *jump*," she said. "What I need to do is *swim*."

"Well I can see why everyone was so excited to teach you," I said.

But I wasn't mad. The splash had soaked her too. Her T-shirt stuck to her chest and I could see her little ski-slope breasts. I'd always liked curvy girls, girls who made me feel like I was normal-sized and not a weird, lumpy giant. But something about Sophie felt big even though she was small. I could see her belly button press against her shirt as she breathed.

"I have another idea," I said. "Let me hold you by the waist. Then you can feel what it's like, but I'm there if you need me."

"How do I know I can trust you?" she asked.

"I have never once drowned someone," I told her.

Then I saw she was serious.

"I promise," I said. "I won't let anything happen to you."

"Okay," she said. "You hold on to me first. Then I'll let go."

I held her at the waist. She was hard there, muscly. I thought of a mink, something quick and stealthy, a hunter.

"Ready?" she asked.

"Ready."

I felt her lift one foot, then the other. Then she leaned back, kicked her legs, and dropped her weight into my hands. She thrashed at first, and looked up at me for a second like what had I gotten her into, but then she found her balance and let me and the water hold her.

"That's great," I said. "Now you're floating."

She looked up at the white sky. She was scared but smiling.

"Now try kicking a little bit," I told her.

She churned the water with her legs. Her feet were nothing like I'd imagined. They were long and pale and pretty with tiny toenails like a kid's.

"My mom told me you can tell if someone's healthy by their toe-nails," I said. "If they're too dull, you're not getting enough protein."

She ignored me and kept kicking.

"Now your arms," I said.

"Do what with them?"

What *did* you do with your arms? I tried to think of words to describe it, but all I came up with was "swim." Then I remembered the first snow some November when we were little, my sister rushing out in her footy pajamas and red mittens and flopping right down in it.

"You ever make snow angels?" I asked.

She looked at me like I was crazy. "Of course I did."

"So do that," I said. "Do that with your arms."

And she did, like she was born doing it, her shoulders moving smooth and easy.

"You're doing great," I said, and she looked at me with total wonder.

"Am I?"

"You are. Now let's try it on your stomach."

She looked scared.

"It's okay," I said. "I've got you. It'll be the same, just flipped over."

She nodded, and I loosened my grip on her just enough that she could roll her body over. She did a quick flip, and her shirt rode up, and I saw a slice of pale skin right above her ass. She kept her head out of the water, turned it toward me and asked, "What now?"

"The same thing," I said. "Just kick and do the snow angel. Do it until it feels natural."

On her stomach she was clumsier—her legs went fast and her arms went slow. I heard her breath come quick and shallow. I was about to say we should take a break and try it again later when I felt her start to click into a rhythm. Her body had learned something.

Her legs synced up with her arms, and her snow-angel strokes got deeper, stronger, more like real swimming.

"You're doing it," I said, and she didn't answer, she was so deep in the movement. I could see her thighs and shoulders working. I wanted to see her take off, shoot across the lake. I let her go.

She took two more perfect strokes. Then she felt the water where my hands had been, and jerked, and spluttered, and came up snarling. She moved so fast I could barely see her. She was scratching me on the side of the face, punching me in the gut with her pointy fists. She was clawing me all over, and I couldn't catch her hands. She was shockingly strong. She was yelling, "You promised! You promised!"

Finally I found her arms in the water and pinned them against her sides. We were both standing on the bottom. Her face was covered with water and tears, and her eyes were wild. What did I have in my hands?

"I'm sorry," I said. "I'm sorry."

And she broke free and mashed her mouth against mine.

SOMETIME LATER, when it was dark outside and we were lying in the narrow bed closest to the lake, she asked me how my mom had died. It wasn't the first time a girl had asked me that in bed. It was the kind of question they liked to whisper when they wanted to feel closer to me, like after we had sex or when we were going on a day trip together for the first time. They always asked really slowly, telling me it was okay if I didn't want to answer, like part of the point of the question was showing how sensitive they were being about asking it.

Tessa hadn't asked—I'd just told her the first day we met, and the way she nodded and looked right at me the whole time, like nothing I could say would be too much for her, made me fall in love right then. That was one reason I didn't usually tell the whole story anymore.

"Congestive heart failure caused by metastatic brain cancer," I'd say, which was what the coroner had written on the death certificate I'd snuck a look at once when my dad was sleeping. Then, if they still pressed, I'd say it was a long time ago (true) and my mom and I hadn't been close (not true), just to stop them from forcing me into a closeness I never asked for. But Sophie just asked the question flatly, and her hand was on the weird hip flab I always tried to hide by leaving my shirts untucked, and I felt like here was someone with no agenda, who wasn't trying to get anything out of me, and I wanted to give her everything I had.

It was in the other house, I told her, the one across the lake where we used to stay in the summer. It was August; I was thirteen. I'd gotten my growth spurt and turned from a fat kid into a doughy taller kid, and I (wrongly) thought this was just the beginning of me getting good-looking. I wanted summer to be over because there was a girl at school, Denise, who I'd never talked to but who I was sure was going to be impressed that I'd learned to play jazz on the piano. Jenna was nine. She liked a TV show about little animals who battled one another, and since we didn't have TV at the lake, she had entered withdrawal and started recapping previous episodes in way too much detail. That night at dinner she was describing one where an evil cat-dragon character is introduced for the first time. She'd been going on for several minutes, and I'd been trying to imagine what Denise's breasts looked like under the pink tank tops she always wore, when I heard Mom say, "Jesus Christ, can you shut up for even a second?"

We all stared at her. My sister's eyes filled with tears.

"Lizzie," my dad said, his nickname for Mom. He sounded more confused than mad. My mom jumped up to put her arms around my sister, tell her she was just tired and not to pay any attention, but before she did, I saw something on her face, this flash of pure anger.

For months after that, everything seemed normal. We went back to school, Denise had no interest in my piano-playing ability, Mom started teaching German to Jenna in the evenings. They were closer than ever—they'd whisper together on the couch or tell each other German jokes across the dinner table. I still thought about that night in August all the time, and then I thought about it less.

Then one night my parents had a big fight. This wasn't that unusual—they yelled at each other sometimes, especially about money. What scared me was the way my dad looked at my mom the morning after, like he was scanning her surface for cracks. Much later I learned they'd fought because Mom's officemate had called my dad. Her name was Eileen, and she'd worked with my mom for ten years. She told Dad that Mom had started snapping at her, calling her an idiot and a bitch. She said Mom accused her of stealing from her office, when she didn't even have a key. She wanted to know if Mom was okay, if something was going on at home.

When Dad told her what Eileen had said, Mom accused Eileen of lying, and even suggested that Dad and Eileen might be having an affair. After a long time, he managed to calm her down, and she admitted that she hadn't been feeling like herself lately and she might be getting depressed. He convinced her to see a therapist, and so Mom started going to appointments every Thursday night and coming home with a weird new way of talking to us, every sentence starting with "I."

But she didn't get better—she got worse. At first it was just every now and then—she'd say, "This fucking TV" (she never cursed), or she'd ground Jenna for dropping a bowl of beans. She'd always been such a patient driver that we'd whine at her for not passing people on the highway; now she started yelling at other drivers and cutting them off. She stopped giving Jenna her German lessons because she needed alone time to recharge her nerves. Then she started accusing us of things. She said I was trying to make her cut herself by leaving a knife out on the counter, my sister was talking about her to her friends from school, my dad thought she was ugly.

One night she and I were alone in the house. I was practicing piano. It was one of the few things Mom really couldn't do, and she'd always loved that I could. She called me a genius and a prodigy. I knew that wasn't true, but I knew I was better than the other kids in my piano class, who got nervous at recitals and choked on the hard parts, turning red and banging one wrong key after another. I liked the hard parts best; the more I had to concentrate, the lighter and freer I felt. That night I was working on one of my own pieces— I'd just started composing, and I could tell that I wasn't good yet, but that I would be—when I heard her come down the stairs. Already the sound of her footsteps made the back of my neck tense up.

When she came into the living room she was calm enough. She'd started doing exercises where she took a deep breath to keep her from saying something angry, and I saw her chest expand before she opened her mouth.

"Can you please do that more quietly?"

She said it really slowly, which was another thing she'd learned. I didn't argue; I kept hoping that if I did everything right, she'd go back to the way she was before.

"Sure, Mom," I said, and I shut the living room door and started playing as quietly as I possibly could. After a few minutes I got into the flow of it again. Sometimes when I play the piano, I have no thoughts in my head and no memories. I think it's like being an animal, just moving toward the scent of food without knowing how or why, without even the concept of knowing. That day I was deep in that feeling, and I forgot about my mom—the second time she came down the stairs, I didn't hear her.

"What did I just say?" she yelled.

She caught me off guard and I forgot to be polite. I said the first thing that came into my head:

"I *am* being quiet."

"You're even louder than you were before. I'm trying to write a report up there, and I'm typing the same word over and over because I'm so distracted by your noise."

Now I was angry. I thought of my friend Evan and how I'd always felt sorry for him because his parents yelled at him in front of me and called him a little jerk and a liar. Now my mom was worse, because Evan actually was a liar and his mom and dad were just mean and loud about it, but I hadn't even done anything wrong. I never had friends over to our house anymore, because I was worried they'd see that my mom had turned crazy and that I was scared of her.

"Why can't you just leave me alone?" I asked her. My voice was louder than I wanted. "I'm not doing anything to you."

Her face was turning a bad color, like meat. She was no one I recognized.

"You're trying to drive me crazy," she yelled.

I could feel myself starting to tear up, and that made me even madder.

"You don't need any fucking help with that," I yelled at her. "You're going crazy on your own."

For a second I felt a big weight lifted off me—I'd said the worst thing I could think of, and now I didn't have to keep anything inside anymore. Then Mom hit me in the face.

By the time Dad and Jenna came home, my cheek was only a little red and Mom was downstairs holding an ice pack and drinking tea. Part of me hoped Dad wouldn't believe me, so maybe I could convince myself that Mom had slammed her hand in the car door or even that I'd hurt her, grabbed her little fingers and bent them back, something that recently I'd fantasized about doing. Instead he just nodded, and then he put his arms around me and hugged me for a long time. The next day he took Mom to the doctor, and three days later they found the tumor in her brain.

SOPHIE LISTENED to all this silently. She didn't make any of the little noises people usually make when they listen to you, and a couple times I thought she was asleep, but every time I looked over at her, she was paying perfect attention, lying there wide-eyed in the dark. When I stopped—I was out of breath, I realized, and my heart was kicking in my chest—she asked, "Why did you start playing the guitar?"

I was annoyed with her; I was trying to tell her something important, and now she was asking me the kind of question people ask at bad parties when they're just casting around for something to say to each other.

"What does that matter?" I asked her.

She didn't look offended, and she didn't look sorry. She stared at me with those big eyes. "I'm curious," she said.

Something about the way she didn't even register my anger made it fall away.

"I wanted to impress people," I said. "Nobody sleeps with you because you're good at the piano."

She nodded. "But you don't like it as much."

"That's not true," I said, but it was true. "With the guitar I'm always thinking about how it sounds and whether people will like it. I'm self-conscious. But when I play the piano, it's like I'm lifted out of myself. Sometimes it's like I don't even exist."

Her eyes were confusing me. Usually girls didn't look at me all that closely. I'd be talking, and I could tell they weren't really listening to me; they were just thinking about where I fit into their lives. I'd see it playing across their eyeballs—"A musician, but a good guy, seems like he'd be a good dad"—and around then I'd usually take off. So I liked having Sophie's full attention. I wanted her to tell me I was okay, that everything I was telling her was normal and good and right.

"Don't you ever feel that way?" I asked. "Like you're sick of all your thoughts and feelings and you just don't want to deal with them anymore?"

"No," Sophie said, "but it's interesting."

Her voice was cold, but when I laid my fingers across her wrist, her skin was hot, her heart pounding. I could feel the sore spots in my back where she'd clawed at me. Another thing girls didn't usually do was touch me like they really wanted me; a lot of times my body felt like something they were going through to get to something else. Sophie had gone after my flesh like it was food. I put my arm around her waist.

"Why do you make movies?" I asked her.

"I don't know," she said.

She was quiet a long time, and again I thought she was asleep, and then I might have fallen asleep myself. Then I heard her say, "I think I'm like one of those crabs, where it builds itself out of parts of other animals."

She might have said "its shell," but in any case it didn't make a lot of sense, and I was worried I'd drifted off and missed something important.

"What do you mean?" I asked.

"Forget it," she said.

"No, please, I'm curious. What do you mean about the crab?"

"Seriously," she said, "forget it. I just say stuff sometimes. You were in the middle of your story."

And I wanted to keep telling her, so I did.

When we knew what was wrong with Mom, we all got busy. Dad scheduled her chemotherapy treatments and called her friends and family, I took over dishes and vacuuming, my sister made "Get Well" drawings and put them all over the house. My dad learned about how cancer treatments worked and explained them to me, with diagrams. I remember feeling almost excited, like we had a mission now.

At first the treatments shrank the tumor, and for the next year we had Mom back. We had a normal Christmas, except that all our presents were way too extravagant. I got an electric keyboard, and Mom got a bicycle. It was a stupidly optimistic gift, but she rode it once, around the block, while my sister and I watched nervously like we were the parents. Mom went to my sister's dance recital and the high school talent show, where my band, A Gooseless City, played a song I'd written about a man who worked in a coal mine, and she clapped and cheered even though we were awful. She started teaching my sister German again.

Once that year my mom took me to the aquarium. I don't remember where my dad and sister were, but I know it was just the two of us. I felt embarrassed and too old to go look at fish with my mom, but the aquarium had a giant octopus on loan then, and Mom really wanted to see it, and that year I never said no to her. We looked at a bunch of tropical fish first, and a pancake turtle, and a moray eel that looked like an evil log, and then there was the octopus. It was in a dark room and lit from above, and it moved like no living thing I'd ever seen. Its arms and its weird pale underbelly were against the glass, and it was straining and sucking and writhing; when the arms moved apart I could see its pointed monster head. It was the size of a three-year-old child, and it seemed awful to me that something could be so big and have no bones, that something could be so far from human and obviously want something as badly as it wanted to get out of the tank. I heard a black sound in my head. I wanted to go home, but my mom put her arm around my shoulders and squeezed— she was touching all of us a lot then, stroking our cheeks, ruffling our hair. When I turned to her, she had on the funny tight smile she got when she was trying not to cry.

"I know you know this already," she said, "but I have to tell you anyway. When I get—" She paused. "When I get mean, when I say nasty things to you or your sister or your dad, I want you to know it's the cancer talking and not me."

"I know, Mom," I said. All my scariest thoughts were rushing into that dark room, and I wanted to go back out into the light where we could laugh and get a soda.

"I know you know. But I just want to tell you, because even though I hope it never happens again, I think it might. And I want you to be ready and know that your real mom would never say those things, not ever."

I nodded and we hugged, and then we went to the food court, where she bought me starfish-shaped chicken nuggets, which I was definitely too old for but which I ate with barbecue dipping sauce. Mom laughed and chatted like she was glad she'd reassured me and like she'd reassured herself, but all the time I kept thinking that if she knew that the meanness came out when she was sick, and if she knew that it would again, then it had to be somehow part of her.

It was late spring when she started getting worse again. It was more unpredictable this time. She'd be talking about our dog getting into the trash, and then her voice would drop an octave and she'd say he should be put to sleep, and then she'd laugh and say she was only kidding, why was I looking at her like that? She started hiding things from us—small, worthless things like the dog's leash or the salt and pepper—and when we confronted her, she'd say she was just rearranging. At first the doctors said her scans were clear, and I thought maybe we were being paranoid, maybe she was cured now and we were the ones who were crazy. Then they did another scan and found the cancer back after all, crawling through her brain. The doctors offered her an experimental treatment, a new chemo drug they said could extend her life by as much as a year. She said she'd take it, but that night she asked to talk to my dad alone. Jenna and I left the hospital room, but instead of following my sister down to the cafeteria I stood outside and listened.

"I can't be in the hospital anymore," she said.

"I know it's hard," my dad said. "But it's like you used to say when you were a kid—'That's where they make you better.'"

Mom laughed then, and the way she laughed made me afraid. I thought of leaving, but I didn't move.

"Listen," she said, "when you're a sick kid, everyone has a certain way they want you to act. They want you to be all sweet and positive, so they don't get too fucking depressed about the fact that you've had fifteen operations and you're only eight years old. And you learn to give people what they want, because it's just easier. But I'm an adult now, and I'm going to die, and I'm done giving people what they want."

I did follow Jenna to the cafeteria then. And when she asked me what was wrong, I told her to shut up, which I never did, and when Dad came down to get us, he explained the meaning of "palliative care."

It turned out that what Mom wanted was to go back to the lake. The doctors okayed it—she was weak but she wasn't on chemo anymore, and they said we should do what made her happy. Mom wouldn't let me help her pack—she said she hated how I was always sticking my nose in her business. But when we got to the lake, she seemed calm, even happy. We sat with her on the dock, and when she saw a loon, she jumped up and pointed and made sure we saw, just like she'd done when Jenna and I were little. She offered to help Dad cook, and she did it without fighting, washing the lettuce and slicing the hard, unsalted bread from the bakery in town, smiling at us over dinner in a way she hadn't in months. She ate, too—the bread and salad and even meat. We went on a short walk down the road one morning, and she took her scarf off, and I saw white-blond hair growing from her scalp, like a baby's. I let myself think maybe she would get better after all.

On the warmest day that summer, Jenna and I wanted to go to the little beach by the general store—I wanted to look at the girls, and maybe Jenna wanted to look at boys, too. She was eleven by that time and so quiet I had no idea what went on in her head. We tried to get Mom to go with us, but she said she was tired.

"You should take them," she told my dad. "Get some exercise. I'm going to stay here and read."

So he took us, and I watched an older girl with long beautiful legs and angry red pimples swim lap after lap, butterfly style. Then my sister and my dad and I raced to the marker buoy, and I won, and then we all went to the store and got chocolate-and-vanilla-swirl soft-serve ice cream, and Jenna got it on her swimsuit and waded back into the water to wash it out. I remember all this very clearly, because when we got back to the house, my mom was gone.

It took the police and the dogs three days to find her. She wasn't in the lake, although they did drag part of it. She was in the woods, north of the house, just over a mile from the road. She had cleared the leaves away from a space under a beech tree and lain down there with her head pillowed on her hands. The coroner said she'd been dead just over a day.

After the funeral, after that first hard year when we didn't have to go to school if we didn't want to and we ate cereal for dinner most nights of the week and all slept in the living room because we couldn't fall asleep alone, my dad started to feel better. He still teared up when he talked about her, and on her birthday and their anniversary and the day she was diagnosed and the day she died, but he started disciplining us again and playing Frisbee with the dog instead of taking him on short sad walks around the block, and he shaved the beard he'd grown because he was too miserable to look at his own face. My sister started having friends over again and going to the mall and buying the ugly clothes girls her age wore to try to look older. I was the only one who didn't start to get happier once the first bad grief was over, because all I could think about was that when my mom knew her life was ending, what she wanted was to get away from us.

When I was done telling Sophie all this, the sun was coming up. I could hear chickadees and white-throated sparrows waking up outside. Sophie lifted herself onto her elbow and turned her face toward me.

"Can we go there?" she asked.

This was so far from what I'd been expecting that I didn't even understand. "Go where?"

"Where your mom died."

After the police found my mom, my dad had her cremated. Then we took her ashes back home and had the funeral. In between were two days where we stayed in the lake house without her. Dad didn't let us out of his sight then—he didn't say it, but I knew he was worried he'd lose us, too. So I spent those days walking from room to room, not seeing anything or saying anything, just trying to stay ahead of the panic that caught up with me whenever I stopped. I definitely never thought of going to the place where she died—I didn't even really think about it as a place. When I thought about her death, I thought about where I'd been when the officer knocked—sitting on the wicker couch by the front door, trying to practice my guitar, trying to think of ways it could all still be okay.

"I don't know where it is," I said.

"Haven't you ever tried to find it?"

She sounded disappointed in me, and it made me defensive, even though I didn't know what I was defending myself against.

"How would I find it?" I asked. "It's not like it's marked or anything. It's just forest."

"But you know how far it was from the house. You know it was a beech tree. At least you could probably find the general area."

I don't know what I'd wanted her to say; because she listened so closely and didn't try to offer the kind of comfort that never comforted me, I thought maybe she'd give me something that would change the story somehow, make it easier to think about. Instead she was just grilling me.

"Why would I do that?" I asked her.

Sophie rolled onto her back, pointed her wide eyes at the ceiling.

"I just thought you might want to see what she saw."

I could have gone looking for the place where my mom died; maybe other people would have. But I was afraid to, and not just because it would bring back the memory of that last day before they found her, the phone not ringing, dread hanging in the house like smoke. The truth was I was scared she saw something in me. She was mean to everybody when she was dying, but she was especially mean to her family, the people she knew best. I was scared that she saw us for what we were and that what we were was crappy, pathetic, worthy of hating. As long as I didn't think too much about her last days, this was just a possibility I could mostly ignore. But if I really understood what she'd felt at the end of her life, I was worried I'd be sure of it.

At the same time, I wanted to hold Sophie's interest. I felt like I was performing for her—I didn't know whether it was a good performance or a bad one, but I didn't want to stop. And I didn't like the way Sophie was looking at me, like she'd given me a challenge I was failing to rise to.

Sometimes I think about what would've happened if I'd said no to her—if things would've moved slower, if we would've been more like a normal couple who date for a while and fight and make up and only get married when they know what they're getting into. Or if she would've just left the next morning and found somebody else. But I didn't say no.

"We can go," I said. "I don't mind a walk in the woods."

WE SLEPT AND ATE, and by the time we got going, it was late afternoon. We drove through town, past the chicken-wing place and the general store with the old wolf-dog sleeping under the steps. As we slung around the cove to the northern side of the lake, I could feel my shoulder muscles creeping up the back of my neck. I was worried the new owners had razed the house to the ground; I was worried it would look exactly the same, like I could walk right in and Mom would be there making potato salad. Neither of these things turned out to be true. The house was still standing, it was the same in all major aspects, and it had clearly been taken over by strangers. They had replaced the broken shutters with bright red ones; they had set up a picnic table in the back. They had gotten rid of the old motorboat my dad had let rust by the kitchen steps and planted some kind of purple flower in its place. Their lights were on; we could see a gray-haired lady in the kitchen, someone's mom who'd been allowed to grow old. I turned and made straight for the woods.

Sophie saw the signs first.

"Who's Wolford?" she asked.

PROPERTY OF WOLFORD, the signs said, one on each of three pine trees. TRESPASSERS WILL BE PROSECUTED.

"I don't know," I said. "This was always state land."

"No one will mind if we just take a look," she said, and then she did something she hadn't done before, which was to reach out and take my hand. We walked like that into the forest. I had forgotten how strong it smelled. The lake was all cold and clean and sharp, a smell that made you feel cleaned out inside. But the forest smelled like rot and moisture and secret growing. Clusters of yellow mushrooms sprouted from the undergrowth; shelves of fungus stuck out from the trees. The light turned deep green. My sister and I had always been scared of the forest. Our uncle had told us the story of a creature there, something that watched you from the trees, and even though we didn't believe him, we did. There was only the narrowest path to follow, and then there was no path. I held Sophie's hand tightly, and she held mine.

We walked for a long time, much longer than I thought a mile could take, and all the way the oaks and pines and firs crowded in on us. Beeches, too—any tree could've been the one my mom chose, the place that felt right or that was just the farthest she could reach. I hoped it was the former, that she was looking for something specific and not just desperate to get away. But what would she have been looking for? What my dad and my sister never understood was the lesson of her death: We didn't know her at all.

We walked and walked, and the forest closed in, and I was scared and ashamed to be scared; it made me sad to think of Mom giving herself up to a place that felt so alien. And then the trees opened out in front of us, not much but just enough to make a small space where you could sit, or lie down.

"Do you think this is it?" Sophie asked me.

"I don't know," I said. "It's about the right distance, but there's no way to know for sure."

A little light fell into the clearing, brightening the leaves at our feet. A chickadee sang. Somewhere behind us a dog was barking. I felt disappointment slam into me. I'd let myself expect something out of this—some kind of revelation, good or bad—and now I realized how stupid I'd been to imagine I'd get anything like that. I was angry at Sophie for making me think it was possible.

"Let's just go," I said. "We shouldn't have come out here."

"Are you sure?" she asked. "This could be it."

The dog barked again, closer now. Sophie and I looked at each other; I was thinking of the signs we'd seen, and how much the police there hated summer people, and how if we got caught we'd probably spend the night in jail. Sophie took my hand again without a word, and we started to run. The clearing closed at our backs and the trees rushed in again; we trampled wet ferns. The dog was loud behind us; we pushed deeper. Finally we found a place where the brush was thick and wild and the roots of a cedar made a hiding place against the ground. We crouched there. The smell of the forest was strong, and the air was colder than before. I listened to Sophie's breathing; her skin was hot. For a long time, I had no thoughts in my head. When they came back, finally, I thought of how unalone I was, with her chapped hand still wrapped around mine.

We heard the dog bark, softer and farther away. I knew this was not where my mother had lain down—no clearing, no beech. But still I tried to picture her there, the way she was at the end of her life, slow and old from the drugs and pain but also pretty like a baby, with pink cheeks and that soft hair. I tried to picture what would make the mom who sang us "Michael Row the Boat Ashore" and let us take turns warming her hands between two of ours crawl out into the woods to die alone. I tried to see what this place would offer. The dark trees and the blackberry thorns and the cold dirt gave me not a single clue.

"I can't imagine it," I said to Sophie.

Her eyes were shut. "I can," she said, and then she smiled in a way that wasn't very happy but was completely and totally sincere.

And when people ask me why I married her that September, even though I'd only known her for three months and I knew it wouldn't last, I tell them that a life is a heavy burden and imagine if someone just carried it for you for a while, just picked it up and carried it.

A Music Video That Doesn't Suck

R. B. Martin

We don't usually write about music videos here, especially not ones by artisanally bearded purveyors of indie faux-etry like Jacob O'Hare. We're making an exception for the video for "Deep," because its director, Sophie Stark, is rapidly making a name for herself among people who still know and care about good movies. Seriously, turn the sound off on this video and just watch it.

It's easy to feel like all the good art has already been made, like everything you grew up loving was gone before you got there. It's especially easy to feel this way if you always wanted to be a writer and then, by the time you finally started to become one, writing was valued so little that you were apparently supposed to give it away for free. And you saw the same thing happening with music, and you realized that movies would probably be next, until the only things assigned any worth anymore were the shittiest, schlockiest, most actually worthless. If you've seen all this, then it's hard to understand why smart people would keep trying to make good work, why they don't burn their laptops and their guitars and their cameras and move to Antarctica or something.

And then you see a three-minute video of a girl sharpening a rusty knife, drawing it across a whetstone with tiny chapped hands, then kissing her sleeping grandfather and canoeing out into the middle of a still lake in the dead of night and stepping splashlessly into the water. And the lake closes over her head, and you wait while the canoe bobs, and a bat flicks across the sky, and the trees shiver in the light breeze, and you wait some more, past when you think it's a joke, past when you think the video is broken, past when you think this is some bullshit arty thing where nothing happens, past when you start to get actually sort of mesmerized by the tiny, tiny movements of the waves, and then you see her head, her shoulders, her arms. She's coming ashore, and she's dragging something: a fat, glittering fish the size of a man. And as soon as you have a chance to see it, it's over, and you have to play the whole thing again just to be sure you didn't imagine it. And then you remember that making something like this is its own reward and that isn't enough, but also it is.

Daniel

IN A WAY I GUESS I FORGOT ABOUT SOPHIE. IT'S TRUE THAT I didn't think about her much for a long time—there were years in there when her name probably didn't cross my mind at all. But it wasn't the kind of forgetting where you lose something forever, like the capitals of all the countries in South America, where if you want to know it again you've got to relearn it from scratch. It was the kind where something's just hidden below the surface a little bit, but it's there. I know that because in 2008 her movie *Marianne* came on the indie-movie channel, and my wife, Lauren, and I watched it. We were trying a lot of new things then. Lauren liked the movie and thought it was beautiful but hard to understand. I told her I liked it too, but really it got under my skin. It wasn't the plot so much as the way everything looked, all closed up and closed in, like when Marianne was cooped up with her family and she couldn't get a breath of fresh air or enough space to lie down safe in, even. And the only time you get a break is at the very end, when she stabs Bean and then you see the whole empty parking lot and the trees and the street, nobody on it anywhere.

That feeling stuck with me and bothered me, so finally I looked up the movie on the Internet, and that's when I recognized Sophie's name. At first I was just so surprised I had to tell somebody, so I called Lauren in.

"Look," I said, "we went to school with her."

Lauren didn't remember. "How did we know her?" she asked.

"She was that kind of alternative girl with the camera. She's a director now."

Lauren looked at me funny. "I don't remember anybody with a camera," she said.

That's when I remembered that Lauren wouldn't have known Sophie, that the only way I knew her was because she made that movie about me and then we dated—or hooked up, really—for a couple of weeks our junior year, before I ever dated Lauren. And I couldn't really tell Lauren that, because I was cheating on CeCe at the time. I treated CeCe like shit, I'll admit it; I went behind her back with so many other girls I can't even remember them all now. I kept telling myself I would stop, but every time there was a new reason to keep going, mostly that CeCe would never find out, and so it would be like it hadn't happened, except that she did, and it did. I'd never cheated on Lauren in seven years of marriage, and I'd managed to keep her from knowing about that side of me. So I just said, "She had a crush on me when we were juniors."

"Yeah?" Lauren asked. "Did you like her back?"

"No," I said quickly, and it wasn't completely a lie—at first I hadn't liked Sophie. She wore weird clothes and she wasn't pretty, or at least not the kind of pretty I liked back then, the kind CeCe was and Lauren was and is. And believe it or not, I didn't really like attention. Don't get me wrong—I liked being on the court, people cheering, girls flirting with me. But someone asking me questions about myself, with a camera right there—I didn't want that. I didn't want her listening to me so closely, staring at me with her big eyes. I did like her later, more than I knew what to do with, but I didn't tell Lauren that.

"She was pretty weird," I said instead.

"Like her movie," said Lauren, and I laughed and nodded, but I was thinking about the other movie, the one she made about me. I'd never seen it, and now I wished I had. I wanted to know how I came off.

Lauren went to bed early that night. We had sex first—after the accident I'd been afraid she wouldn't want to anymore, but as soon as I was off the hardest painkillers she started reaching for me, maybe to prove to both of us that she could. I knew she was probably scared of my left leg, of the stump below the knee that still freaked me out every morning when I got out of bed. She never looked at it or touched it, but I didn't want her to anyway. I was glad she'd still touch the rest of me. But I sometimes felt like I was far away when we had sex, like I couldn't feel it the way I used to. That night I couldn't go to sleep, so I stayed up at the computer reading sports blogs.

It was after two a.m. when I had the idea to e-mail Sophie. I wasn't drunk—I never drank much, especially after the accident— but I was in that weird kind of mood you get sometimes late at night, like the world isn't real and nothing you do matters. Once I started

Googling her it was easy to find her website. It had a still from the movie—Marianne looking out the bus window at the beginning—and when I clicked through to the "About" page I saw a picture of Sophie. She was wearing a man's suit, and her hair was slicked back from her forehead, but her face was just like I remembered: chin up, daring you to fuck with her. That's how she looked at school when I started liking her, how I started to get curious. The second and third and fourth time she came around, after I told her I didn't want her and I never would, she had that face—shoving that chin at me, those eyes. She reminded me of a kid I once beat up in the fourth grade. I wasn't a bad kid, but sometimes something bad would get into me. I'd see a kid who was so little and scrawny and I'd just get this rage, this urge. And this kid Eldon was always asking for it, sitting in my seat on the bus, refusing to move. The first time I waited until we were off the bus and I gave him a wedgie in front of everyone. While they laughed, his little face got all red and angry, but he didn't cry. The next day he was back in that spot again like nothing had happened, so I shoved him into the big pothole in front of the school, full of motor oil and freezing water. The third time I was starting to worry that he was making me look like an idiot, so I found him during recess, in the cafeteria, and punched him twice in the stomach and kicked him in the nuts. I told him if he ever sat in my seat again it would be like that, but twice as bad. It worked—after that he never sat in my seat again. But he did something that was almost worse—he started being really nice to me. He always said hi to me in the hall, asked me how I was doing, offered me pieces of his fruit roll-up—and always with that expression, head up, eyes wide, like I hadn't really beaten him at all. It got so I was kind of scared of him, and then at the end of the year his family moved and I never saw him again. But he stuck with me, and when Sophie kept coming around acting like I hadn't just treated her like shit, I thought of him.

"*Sophie Stark is the writer and director of the film* Marianne," her bio said. "*She is the recipient of a James Award and a Cleveland First Feature Fellowship. She is currently at work on her second feature. She lives in Brooklyn with her husband, the musician Jacob O'Hare.*"

I looked him up on Google Images. He looked uglier than I expected, kind of overweight with a stupid beard. I couldn't find any pictures of them together, so I couldn't see what they looked like—if they loved each other, if they held hands, if they had that sort of surprised expression I sometimes saw in photos of Lauren and me, like we'd been dropped off suddenly in a place we'd never been.

The site didn't list an e-mail for Sophie, just a contact form with big white boxes. I figured she probably didn't even read what people wrote in there—she probably got a lot of crazies who thought her movie explained everything about them—and maybe that's why I started typing instead of getting embarrassed and going to bed.

Hi Sophie,

How's it going. I'm the guy you made a movie about back in junior year, Daniel Vollker. I want to let you know that I saw "Marianne" last weekend, and I didn't even know it was by you. Now I do obviously. I thought it was really interesting, but I didn't understand why Marianne didn't change her name when she went to New York and why she put back the hair dye in the store, unless she wanted to be found.

Anyway I know you're really busy but if you have a chance to

write back sometime I'd love to hear what you're up to and what
your new movie is about, if you're allowed to talk about it.

Talk soon (maybe),
Daniel

Every day that next week I got up excited, hoping I'd hear from her. I'd even get excited whenever I got a mass e-mail from Sophia Clayburn, my boss's boss, because for a second I thought it might be her. I was checking a lot of e-mail then, because I still wasn't back at work, so it was easy to get kind of obsessed. It was a weird feeling—it had been a long time since I'd really had something to wait for.

I was at the physical therapy clinic when I saw Sophie on TV. They had one up above the leg machine, and I was watching it to distract myself from how I had to wear a plastic leg with a fake shoe for the rest of my life and I didn't even know how to use it yet.

"I know that lady," I said to Phil.

Phil was the guy who worked with me. I didn't like him because he was sort of spacey and talked about positive energy a lot, and because he was clearly in way better shape than I had been even when I had two legs. Since I hurt my knee and had to quit basketball I hadn't really felt like working out; going to the gym just wasn't the same as playing.

"Who?" he asked, and then he looked at the door to see if someone had come in, which made me like him even less.

"No, on the TV. That director. I know her."

She was getting interviewed on some cable channel, but there was no sound, so I had to read what she was saying on the captions.

I MAKE MOVIES BECAUSE I CAN'T——, the caption said, but it was messed up like they always are, and even though her mouth kept moving, there were no more words. I didn't remember Sophie ever explaining why she wanted to make movies, but then she didn't say much about herself in the time we were together. Now I wished I'd asked more questions.

Phil was watching the TV now.

"You know her?" he asked.

"She was my girlfriend in college," I said.

Immediately when I said it I imagined what it would've been like if it had been true. One thing I know about Lauren, and about anyone you meet when you're pretty young and manage to love and stay with, is that they affect the kind of person you become. Lauren definitely made me a better man—harder-working, more humble, better at thinking about other people. I wondered what kind of a man I would've turned into if I'd been with Sophie in those early years instead. It was like trying to imagine having different parents—everything goes blank, with a question mark where your face should be. I did remember that Sophie was always looking at me—she'd stare not just when I took my shirt off but when I was doing normal, boring things like tying my shoes. It was like she recognized something great in me, and maybe if we'd stayed together, that thing would've come out.

"Huh," Phil said, like he wasn't impressed. That made me angry, even though I'd just lied to him.

"She's really famous now," I said. "She might win an Oscar."

"Yeah?" he asked. "You still in touch?"

"We e-mail," I said.

THAT NIGHT I wrote Sophie again:

I know you probably don't have a lot of time for e-mail but I realize I didn't tell you that much about myself last time, so I thought I'd fill you in. I did not go on to become a professional basketball player, which maybe will not surprise you haha. Instead I got my master's degree in communications and now I work for a company that makes farm equipment. I know that probably sounds boring to you but I do get to travel and talk to farmers all over the Midwest. I'm not working right now because I was injured in a car accident, but I'm looking forward to getting back to work soon.

I have a wonderful wife (Lauren) and a beautiful daughter (Emma) who is five and shaping up to be a big soccer star I think. They have been great helping me recover from the accident and are my biggest joy in life. Well that's pretty much all the important stuff about me. If you get a chance, I'd love to hear how you're doing and if you remember the good times we had, like when you showed me your photo collection. I still think about those photos all the time.

Talk soon, I hope,
Daniel

Sophie showed me those photos the first time I ever went to her apartment. She'd been stalking me with her camera for weeks by that point, and then she just stopped all of a sudden. I figured she was probably playing hard to get—I'd had some girls freeze me out like that before, just to get me to call them—but after a couple of days I really missed her. I caught myself getting excited when I saw her out of the corner of my eye, then getting disappointed when it was some more normal girl. I found out where she lived from this girl Andrea I knew who dated her brother. When I knocked on her door I thought she wouldn't be there—I was sort of surprised she even lived in an apartment at all. I always imagined her in a weird old house or a tent or something. But she answered, and she looked surprised and maybe sort of annoyed to see me, but when I asked if I could come in, she said okay.

Her room looked like the kind of nest my sister's hamster used to make out of shredded newspaper. Her bed was covered in clothes— these weird dresses she used to wear and jeans and T-shirts and some plain white panties that looked like a little girl's. There were papers and old food wrappers and magazines with the pages torn out all over the floor, except for a narrow little path to the bed. The only thing that wasn't totally buried in crap was the desk, which had some kind of a diagram or comic strip on it and nothing else. As soon as I came in, Sophie shoved it in a drawer.

"I haven't seen you around lately," I said. I was trying to sound casual.

"The movie's finished," she said.

"That doesn't mean you can't come say hi sometimes," I told her.

"That doesn't seem like a good idea," she said. She ran a hand over her head—her hair was just starting to grow back in. I'd heard what had happened to her at the party, or part of it anyway—a couple of the guys had told me they played a trick on her by shaving her head. I didn't find out CeCe was in on it till much later; I guess they were covering for her. I told them I thought it was a shitty thing to do, but they just said it was a joke and what, did I *like* Sophie or something? I let it go. I used to put up with people being dicks then; we all did. I'm not proud of it.

"I'm sorry about those guys," I said. "They're assholes to everyone, but they don't mean it."

She just looked at me. I didn't know what to say, so I said the first thing that came into my head, which was, "Why did you make a movie about me?"

She didn't miss a beat. "Because I had a crush on you."

"Do you make movies about everyone you have a crush on?"

She looked at me like that was a stupid question. "No," she said. "I just learned how to make movies this year."

"What did you do before that?" I asked.

I realized I was flirting with her. I wasn't sure if I was into her, but I could hear that tone in my voice that I used on other girls when I decided I wanted them to go home with me. But that was one thing that was different: I always took girls to my room, even though I knew CeCe could come by unexpectedly and catch us. I just liked being in my bed, with my Michael Jordan poster on the wall and my coat over the chair and all my other stuff in the places I liked to keep it. It made me feel like I could leave them easily. I felt like if I went to their rooms they'd have a hold on me somehow. I hadn't been in a girl's room that wasn't CeCe's since high school. I didn't know how to act. I sat down on the edge of the bed and then stood up again.

"If it was a boy," she said, "I gave him a blowjob. And if it was a girl, I just stared and stared."

She said it the same way she said everything, just facts. I'd never heard a girl say "blowjob" like that—not sexy, just plain. Most girls didn't use the word at all, just kissed down your stomach until their mouth was there, and all you had to do was not stop them. Most girls didn't admit to liking girls either—sometimes at a party when it got really late, two girls would start making out on the dance floor, but usually you could see them looking off to the side the whole time, making sure the guys were watching. I couldn't imagine Sophie doing that. I realized something else that made her different: I didn't think she cared how she looked to other people. I thought about game nights, how I got so embarrassed if I missed a free throw, thinking about all the girls shaking their heads, looking around for someone better to root for. I couldn't imagine being like Sophie.

"Do you still have a crush on me?" I asked.

I knew it sounded like I was just angling for that blowjob, but I wasn't—or at least it wasn't just that. Her plain voice and her warm weird messy room were doing something to me, and I didn't know if I even wanted to take my clothes off. I really wanted to know what she thought of me.

"I'm not sure," she said. And then, "It's nice that you came over."

It sounded wrong coming from her, a polite thing normal people said. It was the kind of thing CeCe might say to my mom or some other person she was supposed to be nice to, but when Sophie said it, she sounded like she was reading off a script.

"I think you're good-looking," she went on, "and I like watching you play basketball. But I guess I don't know if you're really that interesting."

I was mad, of course. I'd never thought about being interesting before, but hearing Sophie say I wasn't made me feel like nothing, worse than when my high school coach told me I had shitty instincts or when the first girl I ever slept with called me a year later and told me she'd just had her first orgasm.

"I think I'm pretty interesting," I said.

I hated how it sounded, like I was begging, but I wanted her to believe me.

"Yeah?" she said. "Show me."

I felt like I was on a game show and the host had just asked a question I didn't know the answer to, a question that wasn't even a question. I looked around the room, desperate for something to jump out at me. I saw some balled-up socks on the bed.

"I can juggle," I said.

"I don't care about that," she said. "Tell me the scariest thing that's ever happened to you."

For a minute my mind blanked. I thought about saying, "This," but I didn't want Sophie to know how much she rattled me. Then I thought of a story I could tell.

One day when I was eleven, I was playing with my sisters and my brother down by Gormans' Pond. The pond was all slimy with algae, and our mom always made us promise just to play along the bank, never go into the gross water. But I always had to be doing things my sisters and brother wouldn't do, so that everyone would remember I was the oldest and the best, and when I was eleven I was starting to worry because my brother was getting tall and good at soccer, and my sister Cassie was getting a reputation as scary for stealing things and hitting other girls. So that day I told them the new game was jumping right in the pond, and I got a running start and cannonballed in.

The water rushed into my nose and mouth and it tasted bad, not just normal bad but like rotten dead things, and I knew my mom was right that this was a place we shouldn't be. Cassie and Brian and my shy littlest sister, Emmeline, jumped in after, and I felt guilty for making them all do it, but I was the only one who got sick. It started with a fever that made me sweat all over and see things that weren't there, and then when my mom called me from another room, I realized I couldn't move my head. They took me to the hospital that night and even though the doctor talked to my parents in a low voice behind a curtain, I heard "meningitis" and that if they weren't able to bring the fever down I could die or be paralyzed for life.

The first one didn't bother me that much. I didn't lie awake worrying about death like Cassie, who had to go to special meetings with our pastor because she couldn't make herself believe in heaven. I didn't think about things like that. But already everything I cared about in life was about moving, being strong and fast, and I knew if I couldn't move anymore it wouldn't be worth being alive. I was weirdly calm, and while my mom was crying behind the curtain I made a plan. If I couldn't walk, I wouldn't be able to jump off the bridge like Trevor Dunston's uncle or walk onto the railroad tracks like the Whites' alcoholic oldest kid. But I knew my dad liked old-fashioned razors with replaceable blades, and when I went to the bathroom (I guessed my parents would have to wheel me there), I'd lock the door and slit my wrists.

After a couple of days my fever cleared, and after a week I went home. My parents were relieved, and nobody really talked about my meningitis after that, but it still came back to me late at night sometimes, how easy it had been to decide to end my life.

As I told Sophie the story, I tried to see if I was passing her test, if I was being interesting. I still don't know what the answer is—I know that afterward she just nodded and looked at me until I got so embarrassed I wanted to hide in the dirty clothes piled on her bed, and finally I just stood up and said that I should go. The only hint I got that she didn't think I was boring or crazy was when she said, "You can come back tomorrow if you want to."

Now I have a different story to tell her. One night I was driving home from a meeting with some suppliers and thinking about what I'd say in my follow-up e-mail to them to get a lower price. I remember it was a clear night in November, that part of fall when you can smell winter coming. I remember that I was annoyed about the suppliers who talked to me like I didn't know anything about manufacturing, about how I didn't actually know much about manufacturing, about how Lauren wanted me to spend more time with her parents even though her parents always acted like I wasn't in the room. The back of my neck was tense and I was doing this singing thing I sometimes do to calm myself down. Then I saw a pair of headlights move in a way that headlights shouldn't, veering across the center of the road and lining right up with my eyes.

Afterward they told me that I probably had retrograde amnesia, where you lose your memory of the minutes or even hours before you were knocked out, but that's not exactly true. I remember the moment when I knew we were about to hit, when I felt weirdly, totally calm. I remember a scraping sound that seemed to go on and on. I remember I saw white lights shining in on me from everywhere, and then the lights turned red and I realized I had blood in my eye. I remember that someone pulled me out of the warm car into the cold air and I saw a woman lying in the road, and she looked pretty with the light on her hair, and a man was kneeling next to her, holding her hand and screaming.

Then for a long time I felt like I was swimming in deep water, and sometimes I would come to the surface where there was yelling and beeping and pain, and then I would go back under again. Finally one morning I woke up for real, and snow was falling outside, and they said I'd been in a coma. I could see that there was just a stump where my leg should be, but it didn't hit me then, not really. Everything was so easy somehow. I did what they told me—I ate and took my pills and did my exercises—and even though I couldn't walk and sometimes the words I wanted to say got lost somewhere inside my head, it was mostly like being a little kid in school, where if you just follow the rules nothing bad will happen to you.

And then one day it was time to go home. They gave me a walker like I was an old man and I hopped my way out the door. Lauren and Emma made a big banner for me that stretched all across the living room wall, and Lauren cooked spaghetti with homemade meatballs, my favorite, and I ate with a real fork in my own house, and I felt like I was at a party for someone else. That Sunday at church the pastor gave a sermon about miracles, and people kept grabbing my hand, looking into my eyes, hugging me too long and too hard. The ones who had been to see me in the coma talked about how bad I'd looked and how I'd almost died, and finally I got Lauren to tell me that the other driver, the woman with the bright hair, actually had died, even though the doctors had done an experimental operation to relieve the pressure on her brain. Her name was Annie and she was an elementary school teacher and the single mom of a boy, three years old. The police said she'd probably fallen asleep at the wheel. By the time I got out of the hospital, they'd already had her funeral.

THE NEXT TIME I e-mailed Sophie was when the big article in *Conversation* came out. I didn't usually read that magazine but I'd set up a Google Alert on Sophie's name. I knew it was maybe a weird thing to do, but I told myself she was the only person I'd ever known who got famous and it wasn't that weird that I was interested. The article had a picture, bigger than the one on her website. She was wearing a gray shirt, with her hair slicked back, and she was looking up a little bit like there was something above the camera. In the bigger picture I could tell she'd aged since college—her face was thinner and more tired—and I thought about all the ways I'd changed since then too. My hair was getting thinner in front, and I'd put on some weight in my belly and my face. My dad had gotten all jowly in his fifties like an old dog, and I was worried I was going that way too. I wondered if Lauren still thought I was good-looking or if she was just having sex with me out of habit or even pity. The thought scared me, and I told myself I'd start eating healthier, try and lose a few pounds.

The article was called "Into the Woods with Sophie Stark"—the writer had gone to Sophie's house and just talked about her day a lot. It said Sophie and her husband lived in a "light-filled" apartment in Brooklyn and that when the writer came over, Sophie was eating chicken. I wondered what it would be like to be famous enough that someone would come to your house and write down everything about you, down to what you had for lunch. When Sophie and I were together, I don't think I ever saw her eat. We never went to a restaurant or anything like that. I felt bad then that I'd never taken her out.

When the writer quoted Sophie, I could hear her voice almost like we were together again. She sounded more grown-up but also the same. She talked about how she got into making movies in the first place: "I started getting really interested in how people move, and you can't really show that in still photos—or you can, but it's difficult, and you can only get little pieces of it. So I decided I wanted to make movies, and I made *Daniel.*"

It made me shiver to read my own name, even though it was the name of the movie. I hoped she'd thought about me when she told the writer that. Next he asked her about Allison Mieskowski, the actress who played Marianne. He said there was a rumor that they had been lovers and the movie had broken them up. I tried to imagine Sophie with Allison, who I thought was not pretty but sexy—the gap between her front teeth, all that red-brown hair. It had always been hard for me to picture Sophie with girls—I'd asked her once if she was the man or the woman, and she just rolled her eyes. Another time, also early on, I'd asked if she'd ever gone all the way with a girl, and she said of course she had. Later I wasn't sure. It took me three visits to Sophie's room before I got the courage to lean over all the junk on her bed and kiss her on the mouth. When I did, she didn't melt like other girls but pushed back strong and hard, and she tasted smoky like there was a fire inside her. I thought she was different because she'd been with girls or because she was so experienced in general. But the next time I came over, we took her clothes off, and she was rough and strong until the moment I got inside her, and then she squeezed her eyes shut and held on to me like she was scared. She kept saying I wasn't hurting her, but I couldn't finish, and when we stopped, there was blood down the insides of her thighs. I asked her if it was her first time and she said no, just her period, but the next time and the next it still seemed to hurt her, and I always wondered if she'd been lying.

"Jacob wants me to get a publicist so they can tell me what to say to questions like that," Sophie said when the writer brought up

Allison. "But I'd probably still forget and mess up, and then they'd get mad at me. I guess what I want people to know about Allison is sometimes you see someone and it's like, 'There, that's the face, that's what I've been looking for all this time.' And then everything they do becomes interesting. It's not always the face, though—it could be the way they move, or the way they stand, or even just one of their ankles. It's like someone walking over your grave when you meet that person, and after that it's the best feeling, like fitting puzzle pieces together."

The writer asked if she was talking about movies or love.

"It's hard for me to talk about love," she said. "I think movies are the way I do that."

I remembered when I'd told Sophie I loved her. We'd just had sex and we were lying in her bed looking at each other. She looked like a fighter naked—she was so skinny, but her arms and her belly and thighs were hard with muscle. She was using her hands to measure my chest. Her hands were little and red and chapped, and I wanted to hold them in mine and let them heal, but she slid them out and kept measuring.

"Your chest is wider than three of my hands," she said.

"You have three hands?" I asked, but she was serious.

"Does it feel weird?" she asked me.

"Does what?"

"Does it feel weird to be so big?"

I hadn't thought about it, but now that I looked back, I could remember how things changed when I was thirteen, fourteen, when I grew. Not just girls liking me or my dad's friends joking about how I could beat them up now. I remembered feeling different. I used to swing my arms around when I was by myself just to feel how heavy they'd gotten. When I ran I felt the new length in my legs. I felt dangerous. I didn't know how to say any of this so I just said, "I guess it did at first, a little. Now it feels normal."

"Stand up," she said then.

I was confused. I thought maybe there was a bug in the bed.

"Why?"

"I just want to see you."

I reached for my clothes.

"No," she said. "Like this."

And so I stood naked in front of her. It had been years since I'd felt embarrassed taking my clothes off in front of a girl—I was always looking at them, thinking about what we were going to do. But I was embarrassed then—I could feel my face getting red and my chest too. I was worried about how I looked to her, my hairy legs, my balls. Then she said, "Stand up straight. You're beautiful. Stand up straight."

At first I was offended. "Beautiful" made me think of a male model or something, the kind of person my dad wouldn't respect. But then there was nothing about Sophie my dad would like; none of my family or my friends would have anything to say to her. It made me feel special that I had something nobody else knew about. She wanted me in a way nobody else would understand. And even though she never used the word, I thought she loved me. I pulled my shoulders back, and I didn't feel stupid anymore. I felt like I was doing something great, even though I wasn't doing anything at all.

When I got into bed with her again, I was tingling all over. I put my arms around her and felt her back against my stomach, and I whispered that I loved her. She didn't say anything, so I said it again, louder. The room got so quiet I could hear the crows calling in the parking lot and the trucks on the highway. Then she turned around to face me.

"My grandma died when I was eleven," she said. "And my brother, he cried and cried. I didn't cry at all. Afterward my brother asked me, didn't I love her? And I said of course I loved her, I thought about her all the time. And he said, then why wasn't I sad?

"And I didn't have an answer for him. It was like if someone asked you how did you know blue is blue. And ever since then I've been scared, I guess, when people talk about how they feel. I never know if we mean the same thing."

Now I think she was being honest, which is more than I ever did for any of the girls I was with before her. I told CeCe I loved her every day, even while I was sleeping with Sophie. It came easy to me, telling girls I loved them, but I never thought about what it meant. I'm still not sure.

After I finished the article I looked up Annie the schoolteacher on Facebook. She was blond and had kind of crooked teeth and she looked really happy and normal. Her account was public and so I could see all the messages on her wall saying it was too soon and they knew she was watching from heaven. I didn't read them all; I just scrolled through them to the messages she'd gotten when she was alive, like, *"Had so much fun w you and TJ and Sara loves her new Barbie so much!"* Or, *"Was so great to talk, never forget you are the smartest and bestest friend."* Just from looking at the normal silly things her friends and family said to her, I could tell she was a kind person with a nice life. After I read all her Facebook messages and read them again, I wrote Sophie for the third time.

Dear Sophie,

*I don't know if you're getting these e-mails. You might have
someone who reads your e-mail for you and tells you which ones
are important. If you do I'm not sure that person would think this
is a very important e-mail. But if you are reading this, I want to
tell you another thing about my life, which is that I was in a car
accident this year. I am doing a lot better now and will probably go
back to work soon, but the accident has made me think about my
life in some ways. It's hard to explain but I guess what I'm asking
is, remember when we were first talking and you asked me to prove
I was interesting? I guess I'm wondering what you thought and
what kind of person you ended up thinking I was. Would you say
I was a good person? I know it's a weird question, and it's been a
long time, but if you could take a minute to think about it, that
would mean a lot to me.*

Talk soon,
Daniel

Lauren signed me up for an appointment with a therapist. She
said she was worried about me, staying up so late and spending so
much time on the Internet. She showed me a pamphlet the nurse had
given to her when I was discharged, explaining that people who had
been in accidents might get depression or posttraumatic stress. She
had a whole stack of pamphlets I'd never seen before, which made me
feel like a kid, like the adults were talking about me after I went
to bed.

I wasn't stressed. I didn't have a leg anymore, and that made me feel like a freak, but it didn't make me *nervous*. I wasn't sure if I was depressed. I played and replayed the accident over and over again in my head—the headlights, the woman lying in all that brightness, the man screaming. The pamphlet on posttraumatic stress said therapy could stop people from reliving the traumatic event, but I didn't want to stop. I knew it was important. But I agreed to go because Lauren wanted me to—I wanted her to be happy and not worry.

The therapist was a nice man with a beard and a round face. His office had a houseplant and some paintings of beaches and sailboats. He was burning one of those scented candles. I felt big and clumsy like I was going to break something.

First he asked me questions about myself and my family, and then he asked me a lot of questions I answered no to. Did I have nightmares? Did I have intrusive thoughts about the accident? Was I afraid it would happen again? Did I have panic attacks? Did I have thoughts about hurting myself or someone else?

Then he asked me how I felt about the accident. I didn't know how to answer because I was still trying to figure out how I should feel.

"Okay, I guess," I said.

He nodded. I thought he would be a good game-show host, because his face would never give away whether you were on the right track or not. Then he put his notepad down and leaned toward me.

"You know," he said, "I see a lot of men in my practice, and one thing we really have trouble with is expressing our feelings. We tend to feel like we have to be strong and keep everything inside, because that's how we were raised—that's how our dads were. But it's not the only way to be."

I didn't know what he was getting at, but I nodded anyway. I didn't want him to think I was stupid.

"The truth is, there are lots of different ways to be strong. We can be strong in the old way, the never-talking-about-our-feelings way, and that has certain advantages. In the short term, it might be easier. Or we can recognize that another way to be strong is asking for help when we need it and letting people in a little, even if it's scary. More often than not, if we can learn to do that, we feel even better about ourselves and more able to take care of the people who need us than we did when we were trying to be strong and silent. Does that make sense?"

I was thinking about my dad. I wouldn't call him strong and silent—he laughed a lot, and sometimes he yelled, but he certainly didn't talk much about his feelings. I thought if he were sitting on the therapist's couch, he'd probably say he wasn't keeping anything inside. He'd say if he was ever feeling something important, he'd be sure to let somebody know. And really, I didn't think he'd been hiding a lot of complicated stuff all those years we were growing up, when he'd come home whistling from his job at the Grain Board, eat his dinner, have a beer, and go to bed. He always said we were a lot alike, he and I, and mostly I agreed with him.

"I guess," I said.

I knew that wasn't what he wanted to hear, but he smiled anyway. He would've been good at poker too.

"Look," he said. "Let's try a little exercise. If you don't like it, you don't have to do it again."

"Okay," I said.

I was expecting inkblots or word association or something, like on TV, but instead he just told me, "Try to describe, in as much detail as you can, a time when you felt helpless."

I thought he was trying to get me to talk about the accident or the hospital, but "helpless" wasn't the right word for what I'd felt. When I was at the hospital I had so much help—help eating and help falling asleep and help going to the bathroom—so much help all the time that I barely had to feel anything at all. And now I didn't feel helpless when I sat in front of the computer at four a.m., clicking and clicking like the next website would have answers written on it. Maybe it was because I'd been thinking about Sophie so much lately, but when I thought about helpless, I thought about the last time I saw her.

It was December, the end of the first semester of our junior year. I'd been seeing Sophie for a month while I was still dating CeCe, and Sophie never asked about it or acted like she even cared. I cared, though. Before when I cheated on CeCe I could forget about it quickly—if she ever called me on it I would've actually had trouble remembering. But Sophie was under my skin—I could smell her room on me even after I showered, and I could tell CeCe was suspicious. She'd never asked so many questions about where I was or asked me so often if I loved her. She was worried in a way she'd never been before, when I stayed out late or said I had to practice so I could go off and be with another girl. I felt guilty every time I looked at her, and also confused. She and I made sense together—she was fun, she was pretty, my parents liked her. Before the Sophie thing, she'd been jealous enough to show she cared but chill enough to let me do what I wanted. But I couldn't get back to feeling about her the way I did before I met Sophie, the way my heart used to race when I looked at her or touched the back of her neck.

Finally I decided I wanted Sophie to be my real girlfriend. Once I made the decision I knew it was right. I practically ran across town to her apartment so I could tell her. I knew something was wrong as soon as I got there, because she was cleaning. She had a giant trash bag on the floor and she'd cleaned off the desk and half the bed already.

"I've never seen you clean before," I said.

"I'm moving out," she said. "I got a job."

My stomach fell. "What kind of job?"

"It's a fellowship in New York. For young directors. They give you some money and train you to make better movies."

"What about your classes?" I asked. "Are you going to skip next semester?"

It wasn't what I wanted to say but it was the easiest question I could come up with.

"I guess I'll apply for leave or something," she said. She didn't seem to have thought about it.

"For how long?" I asked. "When are you coming back?"

"I'm not sure," she said.

"Well, you have to come back in the fall, right? So you can re-enroll?"

"Yeah," she said. "I guess so. Probably."

That was when I knew I was going to lose her. When she was in New York making movies, why would she come back here where people made fun of her and guys shaved her head? I was sad and pissed off, and I let myself get mean.

"You're going to get eaten alive there, you know," I said. "What's the biggest city you've been to? Des Moines?"

"I've never been to Des Moines," she said.

"See? You've never been anywhere and you think you can just go to New York and everything will be fine?"

She looked confused and—the first time I'd ever seen it—hurt.

"Why are you talking to me like this?" she asked.

I felt bad that I'd hurt her, but I was still mad.

"I just want you to think through this before you rush into it. You can't just move across the country without thinking about how it's going to affect you." I couldn't stop myself from adding, "Or me."

"You have a girlfriend," she said.

I'd always liked her plain way of talking, like everything was simple and obvious. Now it made me feel like an idiot.

"So this is it?" I asked her. "I'm never going to see you again?"

She looked really upset then, and I couldn't tell if she was sad to be going or if I was just bothering her.

"I don't know," she said. "We might see each other. How do I know?"

I couldn't stop. "And you're not going to miss me at all?"

She sat in the clean space on the bed, wrapped her arms around her knees. "Why are you asking me this stuff? I thought you liked how things were."

"Well, maybe I wanted more," I said. "Did you ever think about that?"

She looked up at me then, and now her face was different. She looked like I'd suggested she jump off the roof.

"What did you want?" she asked. "Did you want me to be your girlfriend?"

Her voice wasn't nice, but I wasn't giving up.

"Yes," I said. "I want you to be my girlfriend."

I thought she might change her mind then, that once I'd made the offer she'd decide to stay. Part of me thought she might be leaving because of me, because she was in love with me and I wasn't giving her what she wanted. I knew I was the only one who'd used the word "love," but I also knew she'd stalked me for three months, and I didn't believe she could be done with me so fast. I thought a lot of myself then; nowadays it's hard to remember why.

"And then what?" she asked. "Were you going to take me to the frat formal with my shaved head? Were you going to introduce me to your parents? What were you going to say when they asked what the fuck you were thinking?"

I was offended that this was what she thought of me, that I was too much of a pussy to stand up to my family or my friends.

"I'll tell them I'm in love with you," I said.

She scrunched her eyes tight and shook her head. She opened her mouth and shut it again. For a long time I stood there in front of her waiting for her to say something. Finally she just said, "I want you to go."

"No," I said. "I'm not leaving until we talk about this."

She looked so mad then that I was scared. She looked like I'd tried to force myself on her.

"I want you to go," she said again, louder. And there was nothing I could do then but turn around and leave.

WHEN I TOLD THE THERAPIST this story I took out the part about CeCe. I told myself I wasn't that person anymore and that bringing up cheating on my ex-girlfriend just made things complicated. I told the therapist Sophie and I were casually dating, and I wanted more and she didn't, and even saying that much to another person made me sweaty and uncomfortable. When I was finished the therapist nodded seriously and said he could tell I was a very thoughtful person, and he gave me some sheets to write down how I was feeling, and then our time was up.

On the drive home Lauren asked me how it went, and I said, "Fine," and then I tried to think of something else to tell her. It was true that I hadn't told her how I was feeling since the accident, and I didn't know why—I trusted her opinion more than anyone else's. I decided I needed to try harder.

"It was good," I told her. "He says I need to be more open with my feelings."

She nodded, in that calming way she had, and she said, "You know you can always talk to me."

And so I told her I'd been feeling at loose ends since the accident, and out of sorts, and maybe it had to do with not working. And she said she totally understood, and it was good that I was going back to work soon, but in the meantime maybe we could try to do more things together, like taking Emma to the park or playing board games. We also decided I would volunteer more at church. I felt relaxed and then we ate dinner and had sex, but it was still hours before I could sleep.

A couple of weeks after my first therapy appointment, I found out Sophie was coming to Chicago. Her movie was opening there, and she was going to answer questions afterward. I'd read all about the movie, and I was already planning how I'd explain to Lauren that I wanted to see it, but I'd never thought I'd actually see Sophie. If I could relearn how to drive, I realized, I could drive to Chicago.

I e-mailed her again:

Dear Sophie,

I noticed that you're going to Chicago on tour for your movie. It turns out I will be there for work that day. Do you want to have some coffee after the screening is over and catch up? It's such a funny coincidence I figure we should take advantage of it. Let me know if you're interested.

Also, sorry if my last e-mail came off as weird at all. I was having a hard time but I'm doing much better now. Although if you would like to discuss anything in the e-mail in person I would be happy to do that too.

Talk to you in Chicago, I hope,
Daniel

I started slow, with Lauren in the passenger seat next to me putting her hand on my arm at every stop sign, asking if I was okay. At first I wasn't; my right leg felt unbalanced without the left one, and I kept pushing the gas pedal way too hard so the car lurched forward, scaring Lauren and embarrassing me. But I thought about going to Chicago and I did some breathing exercises my therapist had taught me, and soon I started to feel good, like this was a type of moving I could still do.

The next week I went back to work. My thigh muscles were working better with the prosthesis now, and I'd graduated from a walker to a cane. So hobbling back into my building I just looked like an old man and not an almost dead one. The office staff got me a cake, white with WELCOME BACK written on it in red frosting. My desk was just like I'd left it the day of the accident, down to the bag of Mini Oreos that I'd eaten all but one of so I could tell myself I hadn't finished the whole thing. I realized if I'd died that night the desk would probably have stayed untouched for a few days, like a shrine, and then someone would've taken all my stuff and thrown it away to make room for my replacement. I wondered who my replacement would've been, and what he would've looked like, and I imagined him replacing me in my whole life, not just work—as Lauren's husband, Emma's dad, my parents' son. I wasn't sure they'd miss much about me after a while. If I disappeared for a long time and someone else came to take my place, someone who was nice to Lauren and played with Emma and went to work and came home, they'd probably forget about me pretty quickly.

I didn't get much work done my first day back. A couple of times I realized I'd been staring into space; I hoped nobody noticed. As the week went on I got better at acting normal; I went to therapy and physical therapy; I felt guilty that I had so many people helping me. The therapist asked me if I was scared of driving, but it was the opposite: driving made me calm. I started taking the long way home, the old county road instead of the highway—and then I started turning down roads that didn't even lead home at all but took me out past cornfields, old farmhouses with rusted trucks in their driveways, a blond-haired kid tossing handfuls of dirt into a drainage ditch.

One of the back roads off the county route ran past a quarry. I'd never seen it before, even though in high school we used to drive around looking for places just like it to get drunk on summer nights. Two nights I drove past it slowly, without stopping, but the third night I got out and looked down. It was so deep I couldn't put a number on it. The walls were straight up and down on both sides where they had cut the rock out, and at the bottom there was nothing but dark icy water, far, far down.

I could already feel what it would be like to crash through the ice and swim in the water. It would be so cold, so cold that soon I'd lose the feeling of coldness, and then the feeling in my fingers and toes and leg and arms, and then I'd just lie back; above me I'd see the quarry's black walls rising, and between them the stars.

I was thinking about the accident again, about the question I couldn't answer. I knew the other car had come swerving across the road at me. What I couldn't remember was if I'd cranked the wheel hard and tried to get away, or if I'd kept driving right toward it. I knew I loved my wife and my daughter and I wanted to live, but I also knew that night in the hospital when I was a kid wasn't some crazy fluke. I knew that ever since I'd blown out my knee, ever since my life was just about going to work and coming home and not about flying around the court and feeling all that power in my arms and legs and heart, some part of me had wanted to die. And I knew if anyone could understand that it would be Sophie.

After a long time a truck came down the road with its brights on, and there I was leaning on my cane next to the quarry like a deformed villain in a crappy movie, and I was so embarrassed that I got right in my car and drove home. Lauren was worried about me; I told her I'd been working late to make up for all the time I'd lost. I could tell she didn't quite believe me, but she kissed me anyway and we had beef stew with egg noodles, and I read Emma a book about horses, and when I checked my e-mail that night I had a message from Sophie.

Hi Daniel,

Sorry I didn't respond to your other messages. Sometimes I'm bad with e-mail. Please come to my show and we can get coffee

afterward and talk. I haven't talked to anyone about Iowa in a
long time.

Sincerely,

Sophie

I read the last line over a couple of times. Had she not talked about Iowa because she never thought about it or because what we had together there was private and couldn't be shared with just any-body? I hoped it was the second one. It made me feel better to believe there was something between us that no one else would understand.

That night I didn't sleep at all. I felt light, like if I wasn't wearing my heavy fake leg I might shoot up to the ceiling. At about five in the morning, when the sky was just starting to turn gray, I had a scotch to weigh me down a little. I came up with a plan of what to tell Lauren. I already knew about a company outside Chicago that made herbicide. It wasn't really our area—we dealt mostly in hardware—but maybe it was time to expand. I'd make an appointment with them that morning; I'd tell Lauren right away. It wouldn't be a lie.

Lauren was nervous when I told her. She didn't want me driving all that way so soon. She wanted to see what the therapist thought, but he said it was a good idea. He said it was good for me to stretch myself. He asked me if I was doing the journaling exercises he'd given me—I said yes, which was true, except that I hadn't written anything about Sophie in my journal or about going to the quarry. He said it sounded like I was getting a lot of benefit and I should keep up the good work.

In the two weeks I had to wait, I tried to act normal—I didn't drive around, I went to bed at a reasonable time. I didn't e-mail

Sophie. Lauren and I had sex every other day or so, which had become our pattern, and only once Lauren looked at me afterward and said, "Are you okay?"

My heart raced.

"I'm great," I said. "Why?"

She shrugged then and put her head on my chest. "No reason," she said. "You just seem a little high-strung these days."

"Probably because I'm feeling better," I told her. "I think the therapy is helping."

She looked up at me, and I thought she was going to ask me another question, but instead she kissed me on the cheek and said, "I'm glad."

I'D ONLY BEEN TO CHICAGO a few times before, and I'd forgotten how confusing it was, how so many streets ended all of a sudden or turned into something else. It took me a while to find the theater, and I started to worry that I'd be late, that maybe it would be full and they'd turn me away and I'd have to drive back home the next day without seeing Sophie at all. When I finally got there, my polo shirt—I hadn't known what to wear and I'd changed clothes three times—was soaked with sweat. The short-haired girl in front sold me a ticket, but there were no seats left—I had to stand up against the wall in the back. It was hard to stand on the fake leg and I had to sort of lean over on my cane, but there was no way I was walking down to the disabled seats in the front where everyone could see.

I realized I'd dressed wrong after all—everyone was wearing tight jeans and T-shirts with pictures of states on them, even the old people. I tried to think about the last time I felt out of place—I remembered freshman year in college, when I'd gone to the semester's first meeting of the drama club, just to see what it would be like. I was used to people liking me, trusting me right away, but the president, a skinny guy with hair in his eyes, kept saying things like, "If you're all *sure* you want to be here," and then looking right at me. I didn't go back.

For the first twenty minutes of the movie, I was still nervous. I was scared that my left leg would give out and I kept looking around for things to lean against if that happened. There was nothing; just the backs of people's seats. The beginning of the movie didn't have much talking, just a lot of scenes of a little girl in a hospital, getting operations on her hands. The scenes weren't graphic—no blood, just shiny, cold-looking instruments, gauze being unwrapped, Jell-O on a tray. Everything moved slowly. At one point a clown came to the hospital and gave balloons to the girl and a bunch of other kids, but the scene wasn't happy or funny—it was dreamy and sad. I was worried there was something about the movie I wasn't getting. I was worried everyone understood it except for me.

Then the girl got out of the hospital. She stood at the doorway to her bedroom, big and empty-looking with its made-up bed, its stuffed animals lined up along a shelf. And then she was at a bus stop, in a plaid skirt and knee socks—pretty, I thought, like the girls I'd gone to high school with. And then time jumped again, and she was a grown woman, giving a baby a bath in the sink the way Lauren used to do with Emma. You could see her hands clearly and I had a hard time looking at them, the little fingers curved and pointing inward. Then a man came up behind her and lifted the hair off the back of her neck and kissed her, and she smiled a little bit, but instead of shutting her eyes like you would if you were lost in that moment with your husband and your baby, she kept hers wide open, serious, like she was watching for something. And that was when I knew, even though I didn't really understand what the movie was about yet, that the woman was so, so lonely, even with people who loved her. And then I forgot everything I was feeling and watched her without thinking, without even knowing I was watching something, until the very end when she went out into the woods and it was so beautiful, like a church, full of light.

Then it was over. The lights came on and people started saying things to each other and again I was self-conscious, worried that everybody else was making smart comments when all I had was a feeling I had a hard time finding words for, a kind of relief. My left leg was almost completely out of juice and I had to lean heavily on my cane to rest it. Then a man came onstage to introduce Sophie, but I didn't listen to anything he said because my palms were sweating and my heart was racing and I was craning my neck, trying to see her.

She looked the same. She was dressed differently, in a dark gray dress with long sleeves that looked like something from one of Lauren's fashion magazines, but even the way she walked up onto the stage looked familiar, and I knew her body under the dress would look the same as it did when we were together in her room. I know it sounds stupid but I hadn't really thought about how I would want her again like I used to. It hadn't been like that when I looked at the pictures on her website. And I'd felt guilty on the drive over—I had to turn my phone off so I wouldn't see Lauren's calls and texts—but not because I was going a see a woman I wanted to sleep with. I'd felt guilty because I was doing something important without talking to Lauren about it and because part of why it was important was that

Lauren wouldn't understand. Now I felt guilty for all of it. I thought about Sophie's husband, the musician with the stupid beard, and for the first time I was really jealous of him. I wondered if she really loved him, and I discovered that I hoped she didn't.

When she started taking questions, I could tell something was different about her after all. She sounded more polite, more grown-up, but also tired and nervous. She'd never been like that when I knew her—I'd always liked how she said what she wanted without worrying about how it came off. She was fidgety, too—she kept scratching her arm through her dress. Someone asked what her favorite recent movie was, and she said *Aero-Man*, which I thought was funny because I hadn't pegged her for a superhero fan.

"The way Veronica Dias plays the Parachutist," she explains. "You'd think she'd be really tough, and she is, but she also looks so sad. Like it's lonely to be a superhero."

The audience laughed. I was proud of her then; maybe she knew how to work a crowd after all.

Then a woman asked, "Is it true this movie was based on your husband's mother?"

Sophie looked behind her like maybe someone else was going to step up and answer the question. When no one did, she said, "Most of it, yes."

"Did he work with you on this script?" the same woman asked.

"No," Sophie said. "I wrote it on my own."

"How does he feel about the movie?" a man in a weird, old-timey black hat asked.

Even from where I stood at the very back, I saw her face change—she looked scared and upset like she had when we talked that last time, thirteen years before. I wanted to tell the guy in the hat to shut up, but I also wanted to hear what she said. Sophie was quiet for a minute. She scratched her arm and looked from side to side of the theater. Finally she said, "I guess you can't really know how someone feels about something like that, can you? I mean, you can ask them, but they might not say. Or they might say one thing and then change their mind, but by then it's too late to do anything about it."

Hands were shooting up all over the room.

"Wasn't *Marianne* based on Allison Mieskowski?"

Sophie bowed her head for a second. "That's something I wouldn't want to talk about without Allison here."

"Do you ever feel guilty about using the people in your life as material?"

This one came from a man, too. I lifted up on my good leg to see him—scrawny, an ugly patchy beard. I thought about taking him outside and beating him up. I hadn't hit anyone since eighth grade but I thought about punching him in the face. Sophie looked so weak and small then; she looked like she needed someone to hold her up. She lowered her head again, and I was worried she was going to cry. When she lifted it her face was different, harder.

"I don't understand any of the words in that sentence. 'Guilty'—I know what that means, but I don't understand the point of it. And 'use'—people say that like it's so awful, but it's just when you make something into something else, and people do that every day. And 'material'—that's like saying there's some defined thing you have that you make movies out of, like clay or something, and everything else you leave out. Maybe some people make movies that way, but their movies are shit."

Everyone was talking then, everyone's hands were in the air, some people were just shouting questions out, but I didn't want Sophie to have to answer any of them. I was proud of her, and I thought she should have a rest from these people who didn't know her. I raised my hand. I couldn't tell if she recognized me, but I was tall and in the back and so she pointed at me, and I had that feeling of relief again, like finally I was here.

"I don't usually get very emotional about movies," I said. My voice sounded so loud in the theater. I was afraid of sounding stupid, so I raced through. "But when I watch your movies I do have really deep feelings. I'm just wondering how you do that."

Sophie nodded. She didn't smile, but she gave me that plain, serious look I remembered. I felt my heart race.

"For me, when people see my movies, it's kind of like a translation. I put the images together, and when people see them, sometimes it translates into a feeling. Then they tell me about it, and I know a little bit more about them, and about the movie, too. But I have to start with the shots and scenes and let the emotions come if they can. I don't understand them well enough to plan them."

I wasn't fully satisfied when she stopped talking—I didn't really buy that she didn't understand other people's feelings, even though she'd said that same thing to me when we were twenty. It sounded too much like the kind of thing I would've said to some girl in college when she wanted to know why I hadn't called her. But I knew we could talk more about it—I was sweating under my arms, thinking about how soon I'd be sitting right across from her.

"I think that's all we have time for," said the man who'd introduced her, and then I started shoving my way to the front. A bunch of reporters were already up there, asking Sophie more questions. She was tired again. I started to get anxious, waiting there, and I saw her turn like she was going to walk off backstage, away from me. I panicked.

"Sophie!" I called out.

All the reporters looked at me like I was crazy, and Sophie turned around all startled, like I'd slapped her.

"It's Daniel," I said. My face was hot. "We were supposed to have coffee."

She looked stunned for a minute, then tired again.

"That's right," she said. "Okay."

We walked out together, not touching or talking. We hadn't hugged. I realized I'd never walked with her anywhere. She walked fast, her head down against the wind. She had on one of those expensive coats that don't look very warm. I had to struggle to keep up, but I liked that she didn't say anything about the cane. We found a coffee shop and she went in without saying anything to me. I followed her.

We both got coffee and she poured half of hers out and filled the cup back up with milk and sugar. When we sat down she wrapped both her hands around the cup. They were dry and cracked, her nails all bitten down. She looked at me over the lid.

"When you knew me," she asked, "did you think I would ever get married?"

I was so unprepared for the question that all I said was, "What?"

She kept staring at me. "Did you think I would ever get married?"

I thought about it. When I'd wanted her to be my girlfriend, I'd daydreamed about walking her to class, about taking her on a date downtown where she'd wear a fancy dress. I'd thought, for some reason, about going to a cabin in the woods with her, holding the sides of her waist while she looked out the window. But I'd never thought about marrying her, and it was true that when I thought back to how she was then, how she never called me or wanted more from me, and how easy it was for her to leave, I was surprised she'd been able to share her life with someone else.

"I guess not," I said. "You seemed pretty independent."

She nodded at me, fast and hard, like Emma sometimes did when I guessed the right answer to a riddle.

"I didn't think so either. I never thought I would get married. And now here I am. I've been married for three years."

I wanted her to tell me something was wrong in her marriage—I was excited to think I could be the person she told that secret to, something she had to hide from all the reporters and critics and jerks in stupid hats who wanted to know about her and her life. I leaned forward. I could smell her—it reminded me of her messy bed and the first time we lay there and the last time, when she pinned me down like I was nothing and I let her, or made believe I let her. She was small but the longer we were together, the stronger she got.

"Do you like being married?" I asked her.

"Do you?" she asked.

That question felt like cold water. I moved back, away from her. I'd been trying not to think about Lauren. But the truth was I did like being married. I'd been afraid of it for all the usual reasons—I was worried I'd miss the feeling of being in bed with a new girl, the excitement of having her want me. But instead I liked the feeling of knowing who I'd be lying down with, what she thought of me, how to make her laugh. I used to get this cramping feeling in the back of my neck at the bar in college, looking at all the girls and wondering which of them would want to go home with me, and one morning a few weeks before Emma was born, I realized I hadn't felt it in years. There was no question that marriage—which meant Lauren, her face and her voice and the way she sighed when she was mad but she was letting me know it would be okay—was good for me, and knowing that made me feel sick to be sitting in a coffee shop with a woman I'd loved over ten years before, who I wanted to talk to about things I couldn't tell my wife. But I didn't get up.

"Yes," I said. "I love it."

She nodded. I couldn't tell if she was disappointed. I wanted her to think we had things in common.

"I mean, it's really hard sometimes—" I started, but she interrupted me.

"That makes sense. You would be good at being married. But I'm just not good at it."

I thought about what she'd said to me about love back in college and all the things I'd heard or read her say about feelings since then. I got excited—I could help her. She had a problem, and because I'd known her for so long and followed her so closely, I could solve it.

"I don't think you're bad at it," I said. "I think you're just different from other people. Other people talk about their feelings, but you actually show them, with your movies. And maybe that's even better."

She was shaking her head, but I kept going.

"I've thought about this. Some people, regular people like me, we play by the rules. We act a certain way, we say what we're supposed to say. But if everybody was like that, the world would be a pretty boring place. That's why there are people like you, who shake things up a little bit. And maybe it's not always easy for the people around you, but overall you make the world better for everyone."

She was shaking her head still. Now she was smiling too, but in a sad way.

"I used to think that," she said. "I used to think I was special and that was why I seemed to fuck everything up all the time. But now I know it's just because I'm not a very good person."

When she said that I almost sobbed. For the first time I really said to myself what I'd been thinking for months, that I was counting on her to make me better. And now I knew she was feeling just the way I was feeling, maybe worse.

"That's a terrible thing to say about yourself," I told her.

She shrugged. "I call 'em like I see 'em," she said. The phrase sounded weird, like she'd learned it from TV. She looked miserable, but she wasn't crying. She looked like people look when they've cried all they can and they still don't feel any better.

"I think you're a great person," I said.

She raised her eyebrows. "Yeah?" she asked. Her voice was almost mean. "What possible evidence could you have for that? What have I ever done for you?"

I wanted to tell her that I thought she might know me better than anyone. But I knew that wouldn't be enough. I needed something specific. And then I thought of a day.

It was October, after Sophie started filming me but before we ever got together. I'd hurt my knee the week before—it was just a twinge, but the ACL was starting to tear, and the next season it would tear all the way, and I'd have to quit basketball forever. I didn't know that yet, but I was anxious about the knee anyway—I wasn't used to anything going wrong with my body. CeCe was acting weird, too—she was clinging to me when I tried to get out of bed in the morning, and she kept talking about friends of hers who were getting engaged. We were having an Indian summer—the days were windy and warm, and at night the moon was fat and orange. I felt itchy under my clothes—I felt like something was about to happen, and I wasn't sure if it was bad or good.

One day I felt like I had to get outside. We didn't have practice—I should've gone to the gym to lift weights, but I was too restless to sit down. Instead I went to the park. It was midafternoon on a weekday, and there was nobody around.

When I was a kid I had a way I liked to let off steam. I'd go out in the field behind the house, all the way till it met the trees and no one could see me, and I'd spin around as fast as I could. I'd spin until I couldn't stand up anymore, and then I'd fall to the ground and feel it pitch and roll under me like a ship. And then I'd get up and do it again. Finally I'd go back to the house all red-faced and sweating, and if anyone asked what I'd been up to I'd just say, "Playing." The game was kind of like a pure version of basketball, just moving around for the excitement of it.

The truth was I hadn't completely stopped the game when I started college. I never told anybody, obviously, but sometimes when the park was deserted I still played it. So that day, when I found the park empty and covered in dry leaves, I started to spin. All the red and brown October colors turned to stripes, and when I let myself fall, the ground humped up to meet me like a living thing. It'd been so long since I'd been just happy that I'd forgotten how it felt—even when I was drunk I never felt that loose and excited at the same time. At some point I kind of started yelling—not words, just sounds that welled up inside my body until I couldn't help but let them out.

I'd stopped spinning and was just yelling, and maybe jumping a little, and waving my arms, when I saw some movement in the trees up by the swing set. It was Sophie, with her camera.

I charged her like a dog.

"What the fuck do you think you're doing?" I screamed at her. "Why can't you leave me alone?"

The air was getting cold finally and she was only wearing a light fall jacket. She was shivering a little. She looked so small to me; I hadn't realized how small.

"I'm sorry," she said in that plain voice. "You looked really happy."

And the tension went out of my muscles, and my hands unfisted, and it seemed ridiculous to be angry on that pretty day, the last one we'd have for months, because somebody thought my happiness was important enough to videotape.

SOPHIE SMILED when I finished that story.

"I remember that," she said. "You were so mad, and I didn't understand. I was pretty dense back then."

"No," I said, "I'm grateful."

"Why would you be grateful?"

I knew that now was the time to ask her my question. I'd been planning it for so long, but now everything seemed hard to explain.

"Why did you like me?" I asked instead.

"What do you mean?"

"I might've done something really bad," I said. "In the accident. I might've . . ." I trailed off, tried to start again. "Remember the story I told you, the time I had meningitis?"

She nodded.

"That's how I feel all the time now," I said. "Like it's not worth living. Ever since I had to stop playing. Maybe not that strong, maybe not planning like that, but it's always there."

Sophie nodded again. I was glad she didn't say she was sorry or I should get help, or anything a normal person would say.

"I'm not smart, I'm not interesting. The only thing that was good about me was basketball, and I don't think you really cared about that. So I want to know what else there is, because that's all that's left now."

Sophie put her cup down and looked at me the way she used to, that naked, direct stare, and then she reached out and put the palm of her hand on the side of my face. I could smell her skin strongly then, musty and spicy like I remembered, but I wasn't turned on. I knew what it felt like to be touched sexually by her, and this wasn't it. But it wasn't maternal either. If anything it felt like the old movie about Helen Keller, where the nurse spelled words on her skin. Sophie wasn't spelling anything, but I felt like she was trying to say something comforting to me. And it's true that I was comforted, maybe more than if she'd tried to talk.

After a long time she took her hand away. She checked her watch—it was big and cheap-looking and didn't fit her, unlike the rest of her nice clothes.

"Shit," she said. "I have to go do a radio interview."

"I'm sorry," I said. "Do you want me to go with you?"

"It's okay," she said. "It won't be a big deal. I already know this guy likes the movie."

"That's good," I said. "He should. It's great."

"Thanks. Most people seem to like the movie, actually. It almost makes it harder."

And before I could ask her what she meant by harder she was out of her seat, throwing away her empty cup, buttoning that expensive coat.

I wanted to say something about how much she meant to me and how I hoped we could see each other again, but she took my hand and shook it firmly and said, "I'll e-mail you," and walked out onto the street.

THE NEXT FEW WEEKS were kind of hazy. Both Lauren and my therapist asked if I was feeling worse—my therapist even said I should think about taking medication. But I wasn't worse. It was true that I hadn't gotten to ask Sophie any of the questions I wanted to ask her, and I was disappointed about that. But more than anything I just felt quiet, like when you first go outside on a winter day and let the cold start waking you up. Lauren and I went to Emma's dance recital and even though I'd been bored and fidgety at every other recital I'd ever been to, this time I just watched. I went for another drive out to the quarry, but I didn't stop there. I drove on deep into the country so I could look at all the old houses and the women outside planting bulbs in the thawing ground and the mixed-breed dogs, and when it got too dark to see anymore, I drove home.

A week after I got back from Chicago I got an e-mail from Sophie. The subject line was *"I thought you might like this,"* and there was no text in the body, but there was a video attached. I waited until Lauren was asleep to watch it, and there I was, spinning and spinning. The video was shaky; Sophie must still have been learning then. But she kept zooming in on my face, like that was the important part. I was spinning so fast at first that it was blurry, but as I slowed down, right before I charged at her, she got a good, clear shot, and there I was, red-faced and crazy with joy. I paused the video and looked at my face a long time. I could see how someone might have loved me like that, and I didn't know if I could ever look that way again, but I thought I could try. *"Thank you,"* I wrote back, and then I turned the computer off and got into bed.

CONVERSATION

Into the Woods with Sophie Stark

By Benjamin Martin

There are some directors who care a lot about whether you have seen their movies. I know this because as a young reporter for the *Burnell College Mongoose*, I had the bizarre good fortune to meet indie film god William Cockburn, all of whose films I happened to have seen. On learning this he took me under his wing and spoke only to me the entire evening, causing my already overinflated 21-year-old ego to swell nearly to bursting. (I did not tell him that I found all but one of his movies tired and obvious, and indeed this fact faded from my memory as he praised my intelligence and discernment.) Sophie Stark, whose hotly anticipated second feature, *Woods*, will be released in March, is not one of these directors. When I told her I was pretty sure I'd seen everything she'd ever directed, including the short film *Daniel* and the music video she directed for singer-songwriter Jacob O'Hare, she said only, "Good."

When I asked her to elaborate, she said, "Well, you're writing a thing about me, so it's good you've seen my movies."

We were talking in the small but light-filled living room of the Brooklyn apartment she shares with O'Hare, now her husband. Stark is 28, but she moved with the economy of an old person, or one conserving energy. She wore a light gray dress with loose sleeves like wings, and she perched on the edge of the couch as we talked, carefully picking clean a chicken leg.

She seemed by turns oblivious and hyperaware of my presence—when I asked to use the bathroom, she ignored me, but when I paused on the way back to examine a photograph on the wall behind her, she turned around to stare at me. The shot was of a young boy eating an ice cream sandwich, and it had a certain quality I associate with Stark's films—an attention to framing that seems to convey a subject's emotional state almost by accident. Stark confirmed that she'd taken it.

"It's my brother," she said, "when he was nine."

The boy in the photo looked less serious than Stark, a little nerdy and put upon, but the resemblance was striking. Stark wouldn't talk much about her brother—asked if the two were close, she narrowed her eyes at me as though it was a strange question. She was willing, however, to talk about how photography led her to film.

"I used to feel kind of isolated a lot of the time," she said, "like I was in a box and the rest of the world was outside the box. After I started taking pictures, I felt less like that. But I started getting really interested in how people move, and you can't really show that in still photos—or you can, but it's difficult, and you can only get little pieces of it. So I decided I wanted to make movies, and I made *Daniel*."

Daniel is a fascinating, if flawed, first film, but noncompletists probably became aware of Stark after *Marianne*, the hyper-low-budget feature debut that won Stark the Cleveland Fellowship and the admiration of a number of critics. Even Stark gets animated, in her way, when she talks about it.

"I wasn't sure I could do it," she told me between chicken bites. "*Daniel* was a documentary, kind of, and I wasn't sure I could write a whole movie and film it and have it be anything like life."

Really, *Marianne* is almost more like life than life itself.

Over the course of her career, Stark has been perfecting a particular wide shot, with the camera placed slightly above the actors and giving a nearly 180-degree panorama. It's not a viewpoint any human being could actually achieve—Stark seems less interested in reproducing life than in transcending it, showing us what it would look like if we were able to step back beyond the bounds of what's humanly possible.

When I floated this theory to her, she seemed unimpressed.

"Mostly I just try to make what I see," she said.

Stark's eyes are huge, and she never seems to blink; it's possible that she's able to see a wider angle than most people can.

Marianne was also notable for introducing the unconventional but strikingly talented Allison Mieskowski, who will not be appearing in *Woods*. Rumor has it that the two were lovers and broke up during the production of *Marianne*; Mieskowski did not attend the premiere. Stark would not comment directly on these rumors:

"Jacob wants me to get a publicist so they can tell me what to say to questions like that. But I'd probably still forget and mess up, and then they'd get mad at me. I guess what I want people to know about Allison is sometimes you see someone and it's like, 'There, that's the face, that's what I've been looking for all this time.' And then everything they do becomes interesting. It's not always the face though—it could be the way they move, or the way they stand, or even just one of their ankles. It's like someone walking over your grave when you meet that person, and after that it's the best feeling, like fitting puzzle pieces together."

I asked if she was talking about movies or love.

"It's hard for me to talk about love," she said. "I think movies are the way I do that."

She is, nonetheless, married, and O'Hare seems deeply protective of her. Several times during our conversation, he came into the room to let me know how much of our allotted time was left—forty minutes, ten, five. Her agent had given me a hard ninety-minute time limit and warned me not to overstay my welcome. When I asked about it, Stark said, "They know I get tired really easily."

Asked what happens when she gets tired, she responded, "I say things people don't like."

It's one of the perks of genius that you can be difficult or even impossible and not only escape censure but enjoy praise and the careful ministrations of others. This is a source of especial jealousy for those of us who are merely difficult without the benefit of genius.

My ninety-minute audience did include a screening of a small portion of the unfinished *Woods*. Any resentment I might have felt lifted as I began to watch.

It was a cut without sound—Stark says this lets her look at each shot with no distractions. In a rare moment of openness, she told me it was like when she taught her brother to draw—for the first year, she made him draw everything upside down so he'd really look rather than work from memory. I said she sounded like an unusual kid; she agreed. As a former unusual kid myself, I couldn't help but ask if she'd been bullied.

"Sure," she said. "Once in junior high, a boy took a cup of his own pee and poured it down the back of my dress. It smelled bad, but it didn't bother me that much. At a certain point, I figured out I could learn a lot about people from how they teased me—I could learn what kind of people they wanted to be and how they wanted other people to think of them. And since I've never been that much like other people, I've had to learn about them any way I can."

The scenes we watched featured star Olivia Warner and newcomer Jason Koutsakis as her teenage son. The film is said to be loosely based on O'Hare's childhood, something I asked about when I saw Koutsakis noodling with the guitar. Stark wouldn't comment, but soon it didn't matter. A scene in which Warner and Koutsakis argue until she strikes him was fast-paced and, even without sound, riveting. Then came a scene shot, Stark told me, in the National Aquarium in Baltimore. The scene required delicate negotiations with the aquarium management over its lighting; they were concerned that too much artificial light would harm or disturb the fish. A consensus was apparently reached, because the scene begins with the ambient light and brilliant colors of a good dream; the fish themselves appear to glow as Warner and Koutsakis walk by them. They pause in front of an octopus, whose writhing purple arms and dark central shadow (what's in there, you realize, is its *mouth*) are completely hypnotic. Meanwhile the light is changing—the shadows deepen, the octopus and the two humans are marooned together on an island of light. Is this a good dream or a nightmare? And then the wide shot, the camera pulling back to reveal all the fish, pulsing silently in their tanks, and Warner planting a kiss on Koutsakis's forehead. Amid all this, how could anyone be reassured? The scene feels like a terrifying exposure of the insufficiency of love.

Afterward I couldn't stop myself from saying, "That was amazing."

Stark merely nodded.

With my last five minutes, I asked her the question that had been plaguing me since the beginning of our interview: "Do you care if people like your movies?"

She was quiet for a long time. I could hear the ticking of the wall clock and then O'Hare's footsteps, coming to shoo me away. Stark seemed to be looking at a surface a few feet in front of my face.

"Yes," she said finally, "I do."

And our time was up.

George

THE YEAR I GOT THE SCRIPT FOR *ISABELLA*, I WAS JUST SO TIRED of making bad movies. The company was doing well; the old bad days of not paying our electric bill were behind us. But in those days we'd made movies I was proud of. Now we kept the lights on and I made enough money to rent an apartment by the beach and send something to my daughter, Kat, every now and then, but we did it mostly by making shitty movies for women. The movies were all the same; they had that indie lighting, kind of crappy the way people like now, and a controversial-seeming premise, like a daughter finding out her dad is a cross-dresser. At the end the point of all of them was to make women feel like the world was an okay place and even if you were a little bit fucked up, you would eventually find happiness in it. I got it. I knew life was hard for women. I'd made it harder for plenty of them myself. I understood why they'd want something to calm them down without making them feel too dumb. But I was tired of feeling like a therapist, and every time I saw a movie that was actually good, I got terrified that I'd never make a movie like that again.

I felt that way when I saw *Woods*. I'd liked *Marianne*—loved it, even—but I thought it was a little green. Stark would linger on one of her actors' faces for a beat too long or show some fingernail clippings on top of a dresser for no reason—it was like she hadn't quite learned how to communicate with an audience. But in *Woods* she knew exactly what she wanted to say. The nurses crowding Beth at the beginning, one entering as soon as the other left, the kids in the schoolyard, the guests at her wedding, her family swarming to pick up a fork she'd dropped—nearly every scene stuffed with the sad fumbling of human love, the way well-meaning people hurt as often as they help. Those few scenes where Beth was alone and her whole body relaxed, like she was free. And the final scene, when Beth made it to a clearing in the woods full of green-gold light, a place clearly more beautiful and comforting than anything her family had been able to offer her, a place that would welcome her away from life. I stood up and clapped at the end, even though I think standing ovations are stupid—it just felt so good to see a movie that didn't try to make me feel good.

After that I watched *Marianne* again, and then I tracked down Stark's other work—a couple of music videos, a weird, beautiful short called *Daniel*. It wasn't all as flawless as *Woods*, but it all had that quality—as if an alien had come down and filmed humans and shown us what we were like so much more honestly than any other human could. I talked about her to everybody I knew, which was easy, because *Woods* was blowing up—people were talking about Oscars. After a little while, I stopped talking about her, because I was worried somebody else was going snap her up, give her a big budget to make their movie, and I wanted to get her first. I felt like

I'd discovered her, which was how I'd felt my whole life about anything I loved, even though it was rarely true.

Isabella wasn't an obvious fit for Stark. She'd never done anything period, and the script was sort of schlocky and commercial in a way none of her own screenplays were. But it was the most serious property we had—it was the only one I could imagine being an Oscar contender. And it had a woman at the center who was strong but in some ways isolated, which I convinced myself was a connection to her previous films. Still, I didn't think she'd call back. I figured people were probably beating down her door. And her agent was someone I didn't know, a young guy with a confident-sounding voice even on voice mail. There were more and more people like that in the industry—ten years ago when I walked into a party, it would be full of my friends, but now I was in my fifties, and half the time I was the old, weird guy by the vegetable platter, pretending to text people. When I got ready to go out at night, I knew I didn't look bad, just nondescript—gray hair, a little bit of a gut but not a lot, something gone out of my face in the last ten years or so. People I met now tended not to remember me. I was worried her agent would tell her not to call; I definitely wasn't expecting her to show up at my apartment.

It was a Saturday afternoon in October. I was rereading the script for *Stuffed* (a bereaved woman finds love with a taxidermist) and watching *Babylon 5*. At first I thought the girl outside my window wearing a backpack and a flannel shirt was one of the beach drifters who sometimes went door-to-door looking for food or money. Then I recognized her face from *Conversation*. I hadn't had a visitor, expected or unexpected, in months, and I had no idea what to say. I went with, "It's so great to meet you."

"Yeah," she said, and I wasn't sure if she was saying that it was great to meet me, too, or agreeing that yes, she was great. Her voice wasn't rude, just flat, without feeling.

"This is an unexpected surprise," I said, and I felt gross—my Hollywood politeness sounded so fake in front of her.

"Well, I needed to get out of town for a while," she said, "and you called, so."

From her films, and from the few pictures I'd seen in *Conversation* and newspapers, I'd expected someone cool and tall, elegant and forbidding. But Sophie was short, and her voice was casual and familiar. I knew she was around thirty, but she sounded like a smart twelve-year-old. I thought of Kat at twelve, bringing her books into my office to talk to me about molybdenum or stag beetles. It would be two years before she learned to hate me.

"Can I get you anything?" I asked. "If I'd known you were coming, I would've . . ."

I gestured awkwardly around my little living room. My apartment wasn't messy, but it was embarrassingly empty—I'd moved there two months ago, after Taylor kicked me out of the place in Silver Lake I thought was ours. I'd gotten rid of most of my stuff when I moved in with her, not that I'd really had much since divorcing Nadia thirteen years before that, and since I'd been on my own again, I hadn't really bothered to accumulate anything. A coffee table, an IKEA couch, a bed, a few photos of Kat, and some driftwood I'd picked up on the beach were pretty much all I had.

"Can I use the bathroom?" Sophie asked.

I showed her the tiny room—its window onto the beach was my favorite thing about the apartment, because I could watch the waves while I showered. She left her backpack in the living room—I almost wanted to go through it, just to see what I was dealing with. Her showing up at my place had thrown me. I had a pitch planned, but it was for the phone, and all my comparisons between *Isabella* and Sophie's previous movies sounded dumb and pretentious when I imagined making them to her face. I guessed it was a good sign that she was here, but I didn't know her—maybe she always showed up at people's houses to catch them off guard.

"Who's the girl?" she asked, coming back from the bathroom.

I had a photo of Kat, eight years old, in a picture frame painted with fish that she'd made in her third-grade class. At the time she'd said that fish things were for the bathroom, in that funny-serious way she had, like she was a judge delivering a verdict, and I'd kept it there in every house I'd lived in since the divorce so she'd feel at home when she visited. For the last ten years, though, since she'd become an adult and could make her own decisions, I'd mostly seen her for lunches in nice restaurants, and the only fatherly satisfaction I got out of those meetings was that I always knew what she'd order (Niçoise salad) and what she'd leave on her plate (we could never get her to eat capers, no matter what we did). I was surprised that Sophie asked, but I liked talking about my daughter. I missed the days when she was little and people would ask me about her all the time.

"It's my daughter, Kat," I said. "A long time ago."

Sophie sat down, not on the couch but cross-legged on the floor.

"It's a good name," she said.

I thought so, too. I always planned to call her that when she was born, and I couldn't help using it still, even though I was pretty sure it annoyed her.

"She goes by Ekaterina now," I said. "It's Russian. Her mom picked it out."

"You're not together anymore?" Sophie asked. Her tone was non-judgmental, the way you might ask if I liked seafood, but I didn't like talking about Nadia the way I liked talking about Kat. I was aware again that I had a stranger in my house, and I wasn't sure what she wanted.

"Let's talk about *Isabella*," I said. "You must have questions."

"Oh, yeah," she said, scratching her leg. "When do we start shooting?"

I was surprised, and a little disappointed. I realized that I'd been looking forward to being able to convince her.

"So you're interested?" I asked. "That's great news. I know you must get a lot of offers."

She shrugged. "Yeah, but I need to do something different now."

"Different how?" I asked.

She shrugged again. "I like *Isabella* because somebody else wrote it, so I can't fuck with it too much. When I have too much freedom, I make mistakes."

"But *Woods* is wonderful," I said. "Your original work is some of the best I've seen."

"Yeah," she said, not humble but not flattered either. She stared out my window at the clouds rolling in over the ocean. I was annoyed with her then—I'd been hoping for a smart discussion with someone I respected, not a surly girl sitting on my floor. I wondered if I'd made a mistake.

"Maybe you'd like to talk a little bit about your vision for the movie," I said. "Do you have any specific inspirations? Other films, visual art—"

"Actually," she said, "I haven't eaten. Could we get food?"

I didn't have dinner plans—I was just going to eat Pop-Tarts and have my own sci-fi marathon like I did pretty much every night. But it made me even more frustrated that there was nothing I could say she was interrupting. I still tried to cultivate an air of importance, even though it was clear I'd never be the big studio honcho I'd dreamed of becoming. I screened my calls; I tried not to let people schedule meetings with me any less than a week out. I didn't like that she thought she could come in and take over my day.

"Listen," I said. "It's been great to meet you, but I'm pretty busy tonight. Why don't we set up a time while you're in town, and you can come into the office, and we can really talk seriously about the movie."

Then she put her face in her hands. I thought she was crying, and I was terrified. I've never known what to do when someone cries. But when she lifted her face she was just breathing hard, her nostrils flaring.

"I'm sorry," she said. "I just don't have anywhere else to go."

I TOOK HER to the taco stand near the boardwalk. We got chicken soft tacos—she wanted hers plain, no salsa or even onions—and sat on the beach. The sun was going down behind the clouds, and the light was all muffled—it could just as easily have been early morning. The beach was mostly empty; it was just us, a few joggers, and a guy walking a brown dog he'd let off the leash. The dog ran up to us and stuck its nose in Sophie's face. She didn't flinch, just petted it calmly between its eyes until its owner whistled and it ran to meet him.

"My ex-wife used to say if you could read a dog's thoughts, they'd be smells," I said, to break the silence.

Sophie didn't answer. She bit into her taco.

"I know I shouldn't have barged in on you," she said after a minute, still chewing. "Things just got really bad really fast, and I'm not that good at having friends."

"What got bad?" I asked.

I was still annoyed with her, but I didn't want to turn her away now. It had been so long since anybody had asked me for help.

"Did you know *Woods* was sort of based on my husband's mom?"

I nodded. I'd seen something about that in a write-up of a screening in Chicago, but I hadn't paid much attention. I've never thought the backstory of a movie was very important—I don't watch making-of documentaries either. It was strange to think of Sophie as someone's wife—only now did I notice the ring on her finger, below a bitten-down nail.

"Well, at first he was really into it," she went on. "He said it would be a relief to have his mom's story out in the world, not just in his head anymore. Then he saw the movie."

"Once it was real, it didn't seem like such a good idea anymore?" I asked.

I'd seen this before with biopics—the family's so flattered that someone wants to tell their famous grandpa's story, and then they realize the screenwriter put in the coke and the cheating and they freak out. Like they didn't get what made the story interesting in the first place.

Sophie shook her head. "No, I fucked up. I knew that Jacob wanted it to be a happy story, like about his mom finding peace. And I let him think I'd make that. I thought I could make it. But then I got into it, and I realized there was a much better way to make it that would be really beautiful and interesting. And I knew I could either make it happy or I could make it good."

I remembered the second-to-last scene in the movie now. Beth leaves the house, weak and fragile, and looks across the lake to the beach where her family is playing, and just for a second her face flashes total contempt. You had to be really ballsy to show an audience that, to let us see someone who, on her last day on earth, hates the people who took care of her. And if those people were your husband and his family, you had to be a little cruel.

"I'm glad you made it good," I said.

Sophie shrugged. "I knew I shouldn't do it. But once I see the best way to do something, it's hard to do it any other way."

I admired her then; I was almost jealous. I'd hurt plenty of people in my life, but never because of my artistic integrity. I'd been all too willing to compromise that just to get a steady paycheck, a decent office. When I was really young, I thought Hollywood was going to be full of geniuses—ambitious, crazy people like you see in movies about movies. But mostly it was full of people like me, people who thought they had big ideas but really just wanted to make money and be famous and ultimately couldn't even quite manage that.

"He can't blame you for that," I said. "He gave you permission."

She shook her head. She used her empty taco container as a shovel to scoop a hill of sand.

"He didn't know what he was getting into," she said. "Neither did I. I keep thinking it's going to be different, but it never is."

She used her fork to draw a road up the hill, then stuck the fork in the top, a flag.

"Different how?" I asked.

She looked up at me then, and I recognized her face. It looked like mine in the mirror after I got the last of my stuff from Taylor's house, or after I finished eating brunch by myself in between two happy families, or after I came home from a night out at what used to be my favorite bar, now filled with people who would never be my friends.

"I thought making movies would make me more like other people," said Sophie. "But sometimes I think it just makes me even more like me."

Again I thought about Kat when she was twelve. I thought of the stories she'd shown me—the science teacher who discovers aliens in his backyard, the unpopular boy who turns into a tiger. I knew a good story when I saw one—I knew it wasn't just because she was my daughter that I thought her writing was funny and surprising. I gave her pointers here and there, and I imagined doing this for years—mentoring her, helping her become the great writer I knew she could be—and then when her first book was published and dedicated to me, I could know I'd done something good with my life. But Kat had stopped showing me stories and, as far as I knew, stopped writing them. Now she was an anthropology grad student, the kind who studies old bones, and whenever I asked her about her work she just said, "It's really technical," as if I wouldn't understand.

"Why would you want to be more like other people? You know how many other people can make movies as good as yours? I can think of maybe five who are working right now."

She looked right at me as I talked. It didn't embarrass her to be complimented.

"You have a responsibility," I went on, "to make the best movies you can. It might cause problems along the way, but the value of what you make will outweigh all that. That's what you'll be remembered for."

She smiled, and when she stood up, she looked taller than before, her back straighter. I felt bigger, too, like I used to when I would lift Kat to pluck walnuts from the tree in our backyard. The sea and sky were blue-gray now, and everybody else had gone home; we could've been giants on that beach.

WE MET WITH STEVEN, the head of development at Blackhorse Pictures, two days later. Sophie hadn't booked a hotel, of course. I thought about booking one for her, but when she kicked off her shoes and curled up on my couch, I didn't have the heart to make her leave. I was realizing that she needed more than a place to lie low; she needed taking care of. At night I could hear her from my bedroom, whimpering in her dreams.

She turned out to have brought decent clothes with her—dark jeans, a black blazer—which was a relief, because I had no idea where to take a young woman shopping. The morning of our meeting, she changed and slicked her hair back and put on red lipstick. She looked like a different person, cool and confident, like the first photos I'd ever seen of her, from the premiere of *Marianne*. In Steven's waiting room, though, she seemed nervous, crossing and uncrossing her legs. I wasn't worried. I knew that Steven was getting jealous of execs at other studios who were churning out Oscar contenders. I knew he'd been hurt when the *L.A. Times* called Blackhorse "a clearinghouse for faux-indie fare." I figured that to him Sophie would mean credibility.

"I'm so excited to meet you," Steven said to Sophie when the receptionist finally let us in. "I have a million questions."

Then he wrapped me in a hug, which I'd come to expect but hadn't entirely gotten used to. Steven and I had partied together when we were younger, and he'd been a much bigger piece of shit than even I was. Once he brought an aspiring starlet, maybe twenty years old, to a big party in Runyon Canyon—he'd met her when she waited on him and his wife at a restaurant. He said that like it was something to be proud of; his wife was home that night, pregnant with their son. But then Steven turned forty and met his second wife, and suddenly he got wholesome. He quit cheating, quit doing coke, had two more kids, and now his office was full of their Little League trophies and pictures of the whole family vacationing in Bali. The charm that had gotten him laid when we were young had softened into this constant cheerleadery enthusiasm—his e-mails always included the word "psyched." It made me feel tired, but clearly it worked—Steven was where I thought I'd be at fifty-five, and I was not.

"You have the coolest style," he said to Sophie when we were seated facing the giant window in his office. Against the backdrop of the Hollywood Hills, he looked like he was on a nature show, an effect I'd always found unnerving. From old Steven the compliment would've been a come-on; new Steven just sounded like an eager fanboy.

"Thanks," Sophie said, with no feeling. I liked that she didn't bullshit him back; clearly she hadn't learned the language of meetings, of sucking up. I was glad I could do that for her.

"Sophie's so jazzed about *Isabella*," I said. "Jazzed" was another word Steven liked. "She can't wait to get started."

"Neither can I," he said. "I think this is such an amazing fit. Sophie, your sensibility is so raw and honest, and I'm so psyched to have you bring that to *Isabella*."

Sophie just nodded. I wondered how she'd gotten this far without learning even basic politeness. I assumed she'd been terrible in school. I, on the other hand, had always known how to kiss ass.

"Great," I said. "I knew you were the right person to come to with this. Not everyone would understand what we have with this project, but I think you know it has the potential to be a really big deal, not just critically but commercially. And I think we can do it for thirty million."

Steven's smile got a little tighter.

"Remind me who you have attached for Isabella?"

This was the question I'd hoped he wouldn't ask. I knew he'd want a big name to play her, and I'd sent the script out to five young actresses who were hot right then and who I thought would be interested in something period and highbrow. But nobody had committed yet, and I didn't think anyone would until I could promise them real money. I'd been hoping to lock Steven down and then get the cast in place; now I was going to have to bluff him.

"Marisa Teal basically said yes," I told him.

She hadn't, but of the five she seemed the most likely. She'd done a couple of romantic comedies lately, and I knew she was looking for something that would make people take her seriously. Plus, I'd produced her breakout film; she'd played a young woman who moves to West Texas to escape an abusive husband and ends up managing a rodeo.

"'Basically'?" asked Steven.

I felt stupid for assuming this would be easy. I'd just figured Steven would be as excited about Sophie as I was, but he'd gotten where he was by making lots of money for the studio. And it was true that Sophie had never worked with a significant budget, never had to make real money for anyone. I looked over at her; I could tell she was anxious. Even though she was acting like she didn't give a shit, I knew she wanted this. I tried again.

"She's this close to committing," I said. "I'm sure once we can tell her we've got funding, she'll sign on right away."

Steven nodded, but not encouragingly. He looked like he was humoring a little kid. I remembered one bad night in our twenties, getting kicked out of a club when Steven vomited on the wall. He was drunk and high and crying, and he kept saying, "I'm a shit. I'm a terrible person. I need to change my life." And I'd held him up until we found a cab, held him while he shook and cried and talked about hating himself. Now he looked so smug, like he'd always been better than me, like he'd never been humbled.

"You just get Marisa on board," he said, "and we're good to go."

Meaning that without Marisa we were nowhere.

"WHAT DO WE DO NOW?" Sophie asked.

We were driving down the 10, L.A.'s ugliest freeway, the city lying low and gray on both sides, but Sophie still had her face glued to the window like we were on safari.

"We get lunch with Marisa," I said. "She's my friend. We should be able to convince her."

Again I was exaggerating—Marisa and I had a good professional relationship, but we weren't friends. I hoped she felt like she owed me.

"I don't want Marisa Teal," Sophie said.

I'd been afraid of this—that she'd insist on Mieskowski or some other hyper-indie actress and cause a lot of trouble. I sighed.

"In order to get the funding we need to make the best movie—" I started.

But she interrupted me. "I want to talk to Veronica Dias."

Veronica Dias wasn't the name I'd been expecting. She was just coming off *Aero-Man*, and she'd been *Dude* magazine's hottest woman of the year. She was definitely bankable; I just didn't know if she could act.

"Are you sure that's a good idea?" I asked.

"No," Sophie said. "That's why I want to talk to her. Do you know her?"

I knew Veronica a little—I'd met her at a couple of parties, and her agent was sort of a friend of mine. I found her anxious and fragile and full of herself.

"A little bit," I said, "but—"

"Can we meet her?"

"I just don't know if she's right," I said. "She's never done a project like this before. And I don't think she's very easy to work with."

"I need to see her to decide if she's right."

She was so certain all of a sudden, like she was snapping back into focus. It both reassured and bothered me; I wondered who was in charge.

"We can try to have lunch with her," I said, "if you really want to."

Sophie nodded like she was satisfied. I waited for her to say something, but she didn't. She looked out the window for a long time. We came up on the 405 and the traffic slowed way down. I wanted her to talk to me—every time she got quiet and distant, I felt like I was missing my chance to get to know her.

"Where'd your name come from?" I asked finally.

She didn't answer right away, and I was worried I'd overstepped; I'd heard she wasn't born Sophie Stark, but she'd never explained it in interviews. Maybe it was something she didn't explain.

Then she yawned and pulled her knees up to her chest, her feet on the seat.

"When I was a kid, I used to go all over," she said. "I'd sneak out of the house and go someplace, anyplace."

"Me too," I said, even though the only place I went was my friend Eddie's, because he had comic books and sometimes, if we begged, his mom would take us to the movie theater and leave us there all day long.

"One time I took the bus to Chicago and went to the art museum. They had an exhibit of photos, and I'd never seen good photos before, like ones that weren't just of someone's birthday."

I imagined her as a kid wandering through a big museum, except in my mind the kid Sophie looked just like Sophie now.

"There was one of this woman. It's hard to describe. She was wearing a man's suit and a hat, and she was looking right at the camera with this kind of half smile like she knew exactly how the photo was going to turn out and it was going to be great. I remember I just looked at the photo and I thought, *Yes, this is how I'm going to be.* And the card next to it said '*Self-Portrait,* by Sophie Stark.'"

"That's amazing," I said. "So there's a single photograph out there that completely inspired you? Have you met the artist? You two should do a project together."

I was already imagining a joint show, a retrospective of Sophie's films with the other Sophie's photos in the lobby.

"I tried to find her last year," Sophie said. "I just wanted to see what her life was like. But I couldn't even find the photo again. When I search for the name, I just get me."

I was disappointed. I wanted to know where Sophie came from.

Still, I told her, "Maybe you don't need her anymore. What you do, it's a lot harder than taking a great photo. I know you've had a rough time recently, but to me it looks like you're doing great."

She turned to look at me, and for a second I saw a new expression on her face, just for a second, open and hopeful, like a kid excited to be praised. I could've thrown my arms around her, I was so happy to be getting through. Then she turned away. When I looked at her again, she seemed to be concentrating, like she was doing math.

"Why do you live by yourself?" Sophie asked.

I could've been offended, but she'd asked the question in her flat voice, with no judgment and no pity. It was strange to hear my life questioned so coolly. And I wanted to keep her talking; I wanted to see her face open up again.

"What do you mean?" I asked, stalling.

"I mean, you're friendly and everything. You were nice to that guy back there, even though he was kind of a dick. How come you don't have a wife or whatever?"

For someone who didn't understand people, she was good at getting right to what would hurt me. At the same time, I wanted to answer her. After Taylor kicked me out, I'd had no one to ask me what had happened, how I was. I called Kat, and she listened silently for a few minutes before saying, "Pardon me if I don't have much sympathy for you."

"I was living with my girlfriend," I said to Sophie. "She was a little younger—well, twenty years younger. We'd been together three years, and I always assumed we'd get married someday, but I hadn't done anything about it. Then one day she told me she'd decided she didn't want to be with me anymore, so she kicked me out."

Sophie didn't say anything, but when I took my eyes off the road to see if she was listening, she was looking at me with total concentration.

"I told her I loved her, we should get married. I said I'd get her a ring and we'd go to France for the honeymoon. And she looked at me kind of sadly, and she said, 'I don't want to marry you.'"

"Why not?" Sophie asked.

This was something I'd thought about a lot, obviously, as I moved into my one-bedroom apartment, watched young couples with toddlers building sand castles on the beach.

"I mean, my first marriage didn't go so well," I said.

This wasn't completely true. Nadia and I had been good together a long time. I never wanted to be like Steven and the other guys we hung out with. There were always girls around when we were younger, new, pretty girls with long legs in little jean shorts or white summer skirts, smelling like sunscreen, but my dad had come home to my mom every night, even though he spent all day spreading hot tar on people's roofs and God knows he could have used a little fun, and if I couldn't stay faithful with a nice house and a cool job and a pretty, healthy wife, then how could I ever respect myself? So I flirted, but nothing more, for years, and then I fell in love. It's not important who she was—she had black hair, she was younger than me, but not a lot, she was a lot like Nadia except she was new and she was never mad at me. Nadia and I were going through a hard time then—now I think it was nothing we couldn't have handled, but at the time I convinced myself that we'd grown apart, that our marriage was over. And I did what I thought was the right thing, and I moved out and got a divorce so I could be with the other woman, who I thought would make me happy.

"I left her for someone else," was all I told Sophie. "And then that didn't work out either. So I don't know, maybe my girlfriend didn't think I was a very good bet."

We turned right and I could see the ocean laid out in a shining plate. When I moved, the broker had told me there was something good for the brain about living near the sea, something about ions. But I often felt like the water was insulting me, like, "I'm beautiful and endless—what are you doing with your life?"

"Do you think you're a bad bet?" she asked. She was looking at me with that math face, but I thought I could see some worry in it, like whatever I said next would be very important.

The day I moved out of Taylor's, packed my turntable and a few clothes in my car and drove off all by myself, I thought she was probably smart to get rid of me. And for the next few weeks, as I sat in my almost empty apartment and thought about what would happen if I were to die, I still thought that. But over time I came back to the thing that kept me going in my life, the belief that I had screwed up—badly, even—but that I was capable of loving people well and doing right by them, and if I was given a real chance, I would show it.

"I think I can be," I said.

She didn't say anything, and her face didn't quite get that hopeful look it had before, but she seemed satisfied. And she nodded, and her nod seemed to take me in and accept me, like I was okay, like we were both okay. I thought of Kat, the skeptical way she always looked when I told her I loved her or that I wanted to help her however I could. "There's no way you can help me," she'd said once, after a breakup of her own. At the time I'd been so hurt I could barely say good-bye, but now I thought maybe that was how the world worked;

your parents weren't always the ones who could help you, your child wasn't always the one you could help.

We were home. The clouds were rolling back in, and the evening sun was coming down in streaks. A boy and a girl, probably brother and sister, were flying a bright blue box kite on the beach. The sister held the spindle while the brother watched.

"You should move to L.A.," I said. "I can introduce you to a lot of people. It would be great for your career."

She was looking back at the beach, but she turned and gave me a half smile.

"Actually," I said, "there's a locations guy you should meet right away. He'll be a big help on *Isabella*. He took me to this church out in Alhambra one time that would be great for the wedding scene. And for the Columbus scene, we'll have lots of options, obviously—this guy knows a lot of great beaches."

Sophie nodded. "This is a nice beach."

She sounded like a kid again.

"It's nice," I said, "but probably not so great for shooting. We'll want someplace a little less built up. But we'll find it, don't worry."

She nodded again. She was looking at the ocean.

"It's lucky you came to me," I said. "I think there's a lot I can show you. We're going to work really well together."

Sophie was quiet for a minute then. A gust took the box kite high up above the waves, and the brother and sister cheered.

"You should direct your own movies," Sophie said finally.

No one had said that to me in a very long time, and I'd stopped even thinking about it.

"Why do you say that?" I asked her.

"You'd be good at it," she said, and then she walked into my house.

We met Veronica at one of the fancy bad restaurants where I always met actors. Lots of actresses aren't beautiful in person—they have big, weird features that show up better on screen—but Veronica had a smoky, lush-mouthed sexiness that made everybody look at her, even in a place full of Hollywood types. I could already see her sitting on Isabella's throne, drawing the whole court's eyes to her. We kissed on the cheek. Up close her face looked a little puffy, like she'd been crying; she probably had. There were a lot of rumors about Veronica—that she'd had an abusive childhood, that she was bipolar. I was still worried she'd be difficult, but I'd talked to Marisa that morning, and she'd turned me down sweetly but definitively. Veronica was starting to look like our best shot.

I turned to introduce Sophie, but she was already sticking out her hand.

"I'm Sophie Stark," she said.

"Great to meet you," said Veronica. Her voice was more gravelly than I remembered, but I liked it; it made her sounds serious. "I love your movies."

"Thanks," Sophie said.

I had to keep myself from shaking my head. I'd have to teach her to say, "I love yours, too" whenever someone said that, even if she hadn't seen them.

We sat. Sophie stared at the menu. I started to get nervous; I should've prepped her better. I should've told her you had to make flattering small talk with actors, build them up, make them feel important.

"You were really amazing in *Aero-Man*," I said. "You took a two-dimensional part and really made it three-D." This was my stock line for people who had been in shitty movies; it usually worked pretty well.

But Veronica was looking out the window—she looked a little woozy and unfocused. She smiled vaguely and took a sip of water.

"If you want to be Isabella," Sophie said, "you have to move differently."

My stomach fell. I gave Sophie a *Shut up* look and tried to think of a graceful way to pretend she'd never said that.

"Excuse me?" said Veronica. Now she looked focused.

"Sophie just got here from New York, and she's really jet-lagged," I began, hoping the excuse would start to make more sense as I said it. That didn't happen. Instead the waiter showed up just as I was running out of words. Veronica ordered a salad; I got a burger. Sophie asked for a plain chicken sandwich. None of this distracted Veronica.

"I want to hear what that's supposed to mean," she said. "Move differently?"

Sophie looked totally calm. "You keep your shoulders hunched and your elbows too close to your body. All your muscles are too tight. You move like you don't know you're beautiful."

I hoped the compliment would calm Veronica down a little, but I knew it was too equivocal to do much good. Starlets are used to being told they're beautiful; you have to really drown them in praise for it to have any effect.

"Veronica's been working nonstop lately," I said to Sophie, my eyes yelling, *Shut up, shut up, shut up*. "She can't have perfect yoga posture every minute."

Veronica ignored me. She was staring at Sophie.

"How should I move?" she asked.

Her voice was too loud—people were looking at us. Whatever was up with her, Sophie was making it worse.

Sophie drew herself up straight. She threw her shoulders back, picked up Veronica's water glass, and then, with an easy flick of her wrist, poured its contents on the floor. Then, just as easily, she opened her fingers and let the glass go; it hit the hardwood floor and shattered musically into a million shining pieces.

An older woman sitting next to us yelped. Everybody stared. A busboy rushed over to clean up the mess, and I tried to apologize: "It just slipped right out of her hand."

Veronica pushed back her chair.

"I have to use the restroom," she said, and walked unsteadily away.

"What are you thinking?" I hissed at Sophie. "You can't treat people like that."

Sophie shrugged.

"We need her more than she needs us," I said. "Without an actress we don't have a movie."

Sophie's face had changed. It was stubborn and unreadable. I thought of an animal—a cat, a wolf.

"I'm going to have a movie," she said.

The waiter brought our food. Sophie bit into her chicken sandwich. I sat staring at the glittering orange slices in Veronica's salad. I tried to think of a lunch that had gone as badly as this one. I remembered one fifteen years ago, when I was still making arty, risky movies. I was trying to get funding for a project starring a cult singer-songwriter named Charlie Buck, who I thought was a genius. It was his first movie; he showed up filthy and obviously stoned, and he told a story about having a threesome with a sixty-year-old woman and a sixteen-year-old girl. The older, very square producer we were hoping to get money from just sat there bug-eyed. Finally I leveled with him.

"Look," I said, "it's obvious that Charlie's offensive, unpredictable, and hard to work with. You should only do it if you're brave."

He signed on within the week. So I decided to try the same tactic again. When Veronica sat back down, I got started.

"Listen," I said, "Sophie has very high standards. I know she'd agree she's not the easiest person to work with."

I turned to Sophie, hoping for some sort of recognition. But she was looking at Veronica, not me. Veronica was moving differently now; her joints looser, her shoulders more relaxed. Her eyes smoldered; she looked, I had to admit, queenly.

"Is this what you want?" she asked, her voice dark.

"Better," said Sophie.

Veronica nodded. She speared a single orange slice, brought it to her mouth, chewed. Then she gripped her plate between her thumb and forefinger and, in a single graceful motion, flung it across the room. The busboys looked at each other disgustedly; the manager shot out of the kitchen. Before any of them could reach our table, Veronica stood up and walked out of the restaurant.

I put my head in my hands. I couldn't look at Sophie.

"What the fuck was that?" I asked her from between my fingers.

"That was good," Sophie said. "She'll be good, I think."

I lifted my face. Sophie was eating her sandwich. The manager was hovering a few steps behind her, looking like he was trying to hold in a scream.

"I'm sorry," I mouthed. "We'll pay for it."

I turned back to Sophie.

"She's going to think you're crazy," I said, "and she's not going to want to work with you."

"Then she shouldn't work with me," Sophie said.

I admired her a little then, how sure she was that she was right, how little she was willing to compromise. I took a deep breath.

"I know you have your vision for this movie, and I respect that. You just need to learn how to deal with people. You need to learn to stroke their egos a little."

Sophie was silent for a moment, like she was considering what I'd said. Her eyes were pointed at mine without actually meeting them, like my face was an object she was examining. Finally she said, "I don't think I do need to learn that."

THAT NIGHT I COULDN'T SLEEP. Even if Veronica said yes, I was worried she wasn't going to be able to work with Sophie. Sophie was worse than I'd thought, further away from normal. The coldness I'd seen in her movies wasn't something she just called up every now and then to help her with a scene; it was the way she was. I'd had such a clear picture in my head of us working together—her watching each take with her keen eye and saying perceptive things to me about the actors and the lighting and the camera angles, and me moving easily about the set, my arm around the DP, my voice in the actress's ear, translating what was in Sophie's head into reality. Now I couldn't imagine it anymore.

I got up to go to the bathroom; from the hallway I looked in at the couch. Sophie was sitting awake at the end of it, her arms wrapped around her knees. I thought of going in and sitting down with her and asking what was wrong, but right then I felt so unable to help or understand her that I decided to let it go. I told myself she'd probably rather be alone.

IN THE MORNING Sophie was gone. I looked in the kitchen and the bathroom and the bedroom where I'd just come from, as though she might be hiding under my bed. I called for her on the hazy beach; a jogger with neck tattoos looked at me like I was crazy. A girl came up to me, seven or eight years old, dragging a long string of kelp behind her like a tail.

"Did you lose your dog?" she asked me.

I didn't have Sophie's phone number, so I called her agent, but the line went to voice mail. I went to her website and sent her an e-mail. My apartment had no trace of her, except for a dent in the pillow where she'd laid her head and a smell—maybe it was my imagination—like fallen leaves.

In the afternoon Steven called. I'd been sitting on my couch staring at my TV, watching *Battlestar Galactica* without paying attention.

"I just wanted to touch base," Steven said, "and tell you how excited I am."

"Excited about what?" I asked. I sounded like Sophie, no feeling in my voice.

"About *Isabella*," he said. "I talked to Veronica this morning. I've never heard her so psyched about a project."

"That's great," I said. I didn't want to let on that I hadn't heard from her. I started to feel more hopeful—if Veronica had said yes, maybe Sophie was out meeting with her. Maybe she'd be back, and we could start brainstorming locations. I'd been thinking about beaches, and I remembered a private one where we could film the Columbus scene. It had a little cove we could use as the Spanish harbor, cormorants on the rocks and whales in the winter. I'd already checked to make sure there were cormorants in Spain.

"And I wanted to thank you," Steven went on, "for setting the whole thing up. I'm just really jazzed about it on a personal level. I'm actually heading out to New York in a couple of weeks to look at locations with Sophie."

I thought he was confused; I was glad to have something over him.

"Actually," I said, "we'll be filming here."

"Oh," said Steven, and his voice got tight the way it always did when he was saying something he knew was going to make someone else uncomfortable. "Maybe there's been a miscommunication. It's just—I talked to Sophie, and it sounds like she's been planning to shoot in New York with her crew."

"You talked to her about this?" I asked.

"Well, yes."

My stomach went cold. "You talked to her today?"

"We've touched base a couple of times since we met. I'm sorry, I assumed you were in the loop."

I tried to remember if Sophie and I had ever actually agreed to shoot in L.A. or if I'd just assumed we had.

"Right," I said. "Okay. Well I'll be coming out to New York too then."

"Of course," said Steven. "This is your baby. Like I said, it sounds like she's got everything pretty well figured out, but obviously we totally welcome your input."

I realized then I wouldn't be going to New York. I'd assumed

Sophie wanted to work with me. Now it looked like she'd only needed me to introduce her to the people she wanted to meet and give her a place to stay while she made the deal. I could take the script back, insist on a director who'd give me more control. But I didn't want to work with another director on *Isabella*. I wanted to work with Sophie.

"Thanks for calling," I told Steven.

"See you in New York!" he said.

I hung up the phone.

FOR THE NEXT FEW DAYS, I didn't do much. I just watched and rewatched old movies—*Vertigo* and *Edward Scissorhands* and *I Shot Andy Warhol*, the kind of movies I'd always loved but never made. Two days after Sophie left, I watched *Daniel*. I'd forgotten how amateurish it was—the muddy sound, all the misframed shots. I'd also forgotten how good it was. When I finished it, I watched it again from the beginning. At the end, when Sophie stood in the bathroom with her shaved head, I watched her face—her crooked mouth, those giant eyes. I remembered how she'd looked on my couch the night before she left. I thought there might be a human thing inside her, trying to get out.

The next day I found the note. It was underneath my box of Pop-Tarts, now empty. It said, *"Thanks and sorry. Talk soon, Sophie."*

I was surprised by the last part, coming from her, and I half took it seriously. For months I expected her to show up at my door again, hoping to be fed. I didn't know if I would let her in.

Allison

THE MONTHS RIGHT BEFORE SOPHIE CAME BACK TO ME WERE
some of the happiest of my life. After *Marianne* some other young
directors called me, but I didn't want to be in movies anymore. I
didn't like the feeling of someone else being in charge of me. At least
onstage what I did was what they saw—no cuts, no tricks, no sur-
prises. That summer I had a part in an off-Broadway play about a
family whose dad was a donkey. I thought the play itself was kind of
silly, but I liked my role as the mean, moneygrubbing youngest sister, and I liked that the director and the rest of the cast respected me
and treated me like a real actor. We were friends and we went out
together after the show. During the day I worked at a coffee shop in
Chelsea that was clean and not too crowded, and my boss paid me
on time and never tried to grab my ass. I lived in Prospect Heights
with my boyfriend, Abe, who was kind and funny and who I loved,
but not enough to keep me awake at night or make my chest hurt
with wanting. On the night Sophie showed up, he and I were re-

watching *Close Encounters of the Third Kind*, and he was rubbing my feet. It was fall and raining hard, and she stood at my door soaking wet, no umbrella, in this little ugly dress that looked like it cost a lot of money. I could've punched her.

"I'm sorry I came here," she said.

"Why are you sorry?" I said. It still knocked the wind out of me, seeing her, even though it had been over three years. "I never said I didn't want to see you."

Actually, I'd tried to get in touch lots of times—I'd called and e-mailed. I couldn't bring myself to congratulate her on *Marianne*, but I'd sent her a long e-mail when *Woods* came out. She never responded to any of it. I assumed she was mad at me, and I got mad at her for being mad.

"I know," she said. "I'm sorry I didn't talk to you all those times, and now I'm talking to you because I need to."

"Okay," I said. "Jesus, come in."

I was surprised she'd made it anywhere in such heavy rain—she'd always hated water. At first she made it sound all mysterious and existential, but later she told me the older kids had held her head underwater at the pool one time and she almost drowned. It was easy to forget sometimes that Sophie wasn't always Sophie, that she used to be just a weirdo kid the other kids made fun of.

Now she was dripping on the living room carpet. Abe stared at her, and as I introduced them, I had this terrible feeling of dread. She did that thing she used to do when she met people she didn't care about, where she just looked right through them like they didn't exist in her universe. I thought about how I'd apologize for her later. I told myself Abe and I would be in bed together and we'd laugh about how crazy she was. I walked her to the bathroom, where she immediately took her dress off. She wasn't wearing underwear.

"Jesus," I said again. I shut her in the bathroom and stood outside trying to act like I wasn't remembering every time we'd ever fucked, every time she'd thrown me down or held my wrists back or pinned me to the bed so hard I thought her little body must be made of iron—and that I wasn't also having this protective feeling I'd never had before, like I wanted to wrap myself around her and dry her off with my skin.

"What?" Sophie said from the bathroom. I didn't even answer. After some time she must've figured it out, because she said, "Okay, I'm dressed now."

I was worried Abe might've heard, so I rolled my eyes at him like. *Who knows what the fuck is going on with this girl?* But he just looked confused. I went back in the bathroom.

Sophie was sitting on the edge of the tub. She was swimming in my sweatpants and Abe's old Virginia T-shirt. She was looking down at her feet.

"You know how people say you can tell your health by your toe-nails?" she said. "I think my toenails mean I'm unhealthy."

"I've never heard anyone say that," I told her. "Are you okay? Are you on drugs?"

I hated myself. I sounded like some suburban mom I'd only seen on TV. Sophie smiled at me. I'd forgotten how tiny and perfect her teeth were, how sharp the canines.

"I'm not on drugs," she said. "I just need help."

I put down the toilet lid and sat on it. "Help with what?"

"I'm supposed to do this movie, and I can't do it."

"What movie?"

She dropped her face into her hands, stuck her fingers up in her wet hair. "God, it's so bad. I don't even want to tell you."

I just waited. Finally she lifted her head.

"Okay," she said, "the first thing is, I didn't write it. The second thing is, it's a period piece. The third thing is, it's set in Spain."

I laughed. I imagined Sophie trying to direct a bunch of matadors and ladies in flamenco outfits.

"What is it?" I asked. "What's the story?"

She rolled her eyes. "It's about Queen Isabella. Like as in Columbus. This woman who wears big necklaces and smiles too much wrote a book about her, and now they want me to make a movie."

She sounded like an angry teenager, and in my baggy clothes she looked like one too. I didn't have a lot of sympathy for her. Most people would be excited to have people begging them to make movies.

"Why are you doing it?" I asked her.

Her face changed then, and I remembered she wasn't actually a teenager anymore. She looked older than when I'd seen her last; lines were starting around her eyes. I had a flash of what she'd look like as a really old lady, with bright white hair and knobby fingers.

"I figured the stuff I write just gets me in trouble," she said. "Then I got this script. It wasn't good, but I liked Isabella. I could see how I wanted her to be. I thought that would be enough and the rest of it would come to me. I thought it would be like a project, doing something I wasn't as close to."

"And it's not enough?" I asked.

"Nothing else is coming to me. I mean, I've got a cast, I've got locations, but I'm not excited about any of it, and I can tell it's not going to be good."

I just waited. If she wanted help, I was going to make her ask.

"I want you to be in the movie. I think if you were in it, I might care."

"You want me to be Isabella?"

"I did," she said, "but I'm working with a studio this time. Not a big one, but still, they won't pay unless there's a star. So Veronica Dias is going to be Isabella. But I want you to be her handmaid, Beatriz."

I thought of the movies I'd seen where the queen has a handmaid. Usually this is what she does: giggle, whisper, say people's names, put shoes on the queen's feet.

"Why would I want to do that?" I asked her.

"We can pay you twenty thousand dollars," she said. "And also, I need you."

Sophie understood a lot more about people and how to play them than she ever let on. I think she knew that I still loved her and that I'd be flattered that she needed me. I think the minute I opened the door, she knew she had me around her finger. I thought all this even then. And I'd talked a lot over the years about how Sophie was bad for me. Just the week before, I'd told my castmates after a couple of beers that I thought she was too self-centered to ever really love anyone. But now when I think about that night, I think about something my stepdad once said when my mom yelled at him for quitting AA. He just told her in this sad, quiet voice, "Sometimes the sick part of me just seems like the truest part."

And if it was a sick part of me that wanted to do whatever Sophie asked for, then I thought maybe it was the truest part too. Also, I couldn't stop looking at her wrists, those little delicate bones.

"Okay," I said. "I'll do it."

"Thank you," she said, and it was sweeter than any thanks I'd ever gotten.

Then she added, "Also, I need a place to stay."

BEATRIZ WASN'T A BAD ROLE. In one scene she serves rotten meat to the cruel and ugly Afonso V to make him sick and sabotage the plan to marry Isabella off to him. In another scene she explains sex to Isabella before her secret meeting with Ferdinand—it turns out Beatriz has been sleeping with a nobleman. Plus, it was exciting to work on such a big movie. We'd made *Marianne* for almost no money, and now there was a PA who'd bring you a sandwich if you asked and five guys just to work the lights. For the palace where Isabella lives as a teenager, we had this old Eastern Orthodox church in Bay Ridge— I'd never cared about old buildings before, but I liked to walk up and down the pews when it wasn't my scene, touching the dark wood and thinking about ghosts. I knew that really all the people who'd prayed and been married and baptized and buried there were normal Brooklyn people with jobs in stores and offices, but I kept thinking of royalty sitting there in heavy jewels, daggers hidden in their clothes. I started to feel like I was part of a dark, exciting story.

I think Sophie felt it too. Nobody would've known she was nervous about the movie—the very first day, she walked onto the set with a swagger I'd never seen. She wore boys' pants and boots and red lipstick and everybody watched her in a way that would've made me jealous if she hadn't pulled me aside at least once a day to tell me, "I couldn't do this without you." How could I not be flattered? On *Marianne* she'd been smart, but also weird and distant and twitchy, like a robot that didn't work very well. But she'd grown up since then; now she could be graceful. She took Ferdinand aside and taught him how to hold his head like a king; she joked with the lighting guys; she yelled, "Perfect!" and we all felt like we were.

"Move your hair off your shoulders," she told me as I approached the throne. "I want to see your neck."

I knew everyone in the church could feel the tension between us, and I was embarrassed and also proud. But Veronica was always the center of attention. She was the one Sophie talked to most often, telling her how to stand and walk and how Isabella's face would look when she was sitting on the throne for the first time. I knew Veronica wasn't Sophie's type—too thin and nervous, more beautiful than sexy—but I still noticed how much of Sophie's focus she took up, how often Sophie touched her on the arm to show her how to move. When I watched the two of them, it was hard to believe Sophie really couldn't make the movie without me.

At home Abe treated Sophie like a pet. When she didn't eat the chicken and asparagus he cooked for us her first night, he started making the things she liked—canned peaches, oatmeal with cinnamon and sugar. He served them to her in a little bowl with flowers on it, and she scarfed them like a hungry cat. I asked him how he knew what to feed her, and he said he'd asked, of course. I wondered when they'd talked without me hearing. I realized I really wanted them to hate each other. Once I even caught him patting her on the head after she did some tiny chore, and I wanted to grab him by the arm and tell him to be afraid of her. I didn't say anything. In bed at night he told me how glad he was that we could help her, and that she could stay as long as she wanted.

When I could get her alone—in the kitchen, doing dishes, when Abe went out for a cigarette—I asked her about her husband.

"It didn't work out," she said. It was one of those normal-people phrases I figured she'd memorized from TV.

"Are you getting divorced?" I asked.

She was bad at doing dishes. She started to put one away with tomato sauce still sticking to it, and I took it from her hand.

"I don't think he wants to," she said.

"Do you want to?" I asked her.

She shrugged. "I don't care. I don't want to live with him anymore, though."

"Why'd you marry him anyway?" I asked.

I guess I was hoping she'd tell me she did it for money or because she thought it was time to get married, even though neither of those reasons seemed like Sophie at all. Instead she started going at a nonstick pan with a wad of steel wool. I took it from her so she wouldn't ruin it.

"You didn't really need anything," she said finally. "I thought it would be good for me to be with someone who needed something from me."

I needed you, I wanted to scream, but then I thought, *Let her think I was strong. Let her think I didn't take every pill I could buy or steal in the year after I left, hoping one of them would delete the person that was me. Let her think I didn't have to fuck thirty different terrible men just to forget the way she smelled.*

"He needed someone to listen to him really well," she went on, "and I thought I could do that."

"And you couldn't?" I asked.

"Well, I didn't."

She picked up a jar lid I was going to throw away and washed it very carefully, like it was expensive china.

"Or, I did and then I didn't," she said. "Maybe that's worse. I did a lot of things wrong."

I bet you did, I thought, but I felt sorry for her too. I knew she didn't ask to be the way she was. I thought of my stepdad, how every time he came back to us he wanted to get it right, stay out of trouble and be a good dad. But he just didn't know how to think about the future or how to keep his mouth shut, and those things were always going to get him in shit whether he wanted to be good or not. And I thought of my mom, too, who let him keep coming back, even though she knew as well as anyone that he was never going to be any different.

"I'm sure it wasn't all your fault," I said.

"No, it was." She paused with her hands in the sudsy water, like she was taking a bath. "You know, right before I left, he asked me to quit making movies."

"That's awful," I said. "Who was he to ask you that?"

"Well, he was my husband. He still is my husband. And he might've been right. I might be better if I didn't make movies."

I thought of Peter forcing his face at me, and I thought she might be right. But I'd survived that. If I could suffer to let Sophie do what she loved, then everyone else in her life should have to do that too.

"Making movies is your life's work," I told her. I'd read that phrase somewhere and I thought it was cheesy, but it was what I had. "Anyone who loves you should understand that."

She shrugged. "It doesn't matter that much," she said. "At this point if I stopped making them, I'd probably die."

And then Abe came back in with the cold air, smelling like smoke, and she went back to being his little cat again.

ON SET THE PROBLEM was Veronica. I'd been sort of scared to meet her, because she'd been on the covers of all the big magazines, but when I saw her the first day I just thought, *Oh*. It'd been a long time since I'd lived with one, but I could still spot an alcoholic right away. It was okay in the first few scenes we shot, where she just had to look queenly and pissed off; she had that drunk-lady way of lifting her chin and narrowing her eyes like what were any of us staring at? But when we tried to shoot the scene in her bedroom—the prop guys had hung expensive-looking tapestries in a back room of the church and wheeled in a gigantic bed—she totally fell apart. Our lines were pretty modern-sounding—the screenwriter didn't want anything flowery—but she still couldn't deal. She got through the very beginning of the scene okay—Isabella tells Beatriz about her money-grubbing half brother Henry's latest plan for her marriage, a rich nobleman who will top up Spain's treasury. Beatriz at first isn't too sympathetic—the guy's rich, after all, and he'll take care of Isabella. But Isabella explains that she's not going to let herself get shipped out to the countryside to be somebody's wife, that she's going to sit on the throne like the queen she is. I liked the speech because it wasn't about freedom and love like some Disney princess; it was about power. I knew I would've nailed it; I practiced it sometimes when no one was around, just to see how it sounded. But Veronica couldn't handle it.

"I'm not made to be a rich man's wife," she said, and then she just paused and stared at me, like I had the lines printed on my face. We cut. The script guy showed her the line and she nodded and looked annoyed, like she knew it all along. But the next time she got to the same spot and crashed again. The third time she got as far as, "I'm not going to move to Osuna and supervise servants," before she stopped and looked up at Sophie hopefully, like maybe that was it. The fourth time she said, "I'm not made to be a man's rich wife," and instead of laughing she looked like she was going to sob.

"I'm sorry," she said, "I need a minute." And then she ran to her trailer in her big heavy Isabella dress.

Sophie was scratching her arms. She started to follow Veronica, but she looked exhausted.

"Let me talk to her," I said.

Sophie looked relieved, but a little dark thought was growing in my brain.

Veronica said, "Come in," in a thick voice, and when I opened the door, she shoved something behind her mini-fridge. The trailer was full of little-girl stuff—a pink teddy bear and a unicorn poster and a jewelry box with rainbow stickers on it. Veronica lit a scented candle and then lit a cigarette from it.

"Are you okay?" I asked her.

"Sure," she said. "It's a tough scene, you know."

"It's a tough role," I said.

She looked at me like she was grateful. She'd rubbed away some of the makeup under her eyes, and the skin there was greenish and shiny.

"I used to have an easier time," she said.

I remembered just a few years before, when she'd been in her first big movie. They called her "the thinking man's starlet." She'd gone to Columbia and spoke three languages and her dad was some kind of diplomat and she looked so pretty and classy and smart and she always said the right thing in interviews, like she'd gotten the best of everything her whole life but she knew how to be humble about it. Of course I was jealous of her.

"This must be really hard for you," I said. "All the pressure, the attention."

She pulled her knees up to her chest. Her big skirt was getting wrinkled, but I didn't say anything.

"I used to feel like I was in control," she said. "I'd step out of my house in the morning and think, *Anything I want today, I can have.* Now I don't even feel like I control my own brain."

She reached behind the fridge, pulled out a bottle of green tea, drank deeply, and winced.

"You want some?" she asked.

I didn't, but I said yes. I needed to be on her side. The bottle was about half tea and half vodka. It was disgusting, like lukewarm bitter gasoline. That had always been one of the saddest things about drunks to me—the shit they were willing to put in their mouths. One summer my stepdad quit beer and switched to cough syrup, and that sweet smell in the sticky heat made me heave every time I walked into the house. Even my youngest sister wouldn't go near him.

"You are in control," I said, "but not for long."

She looked pissed off, set the bottle down. "What's that supposed to mean?" she asked.

"I'm not the only one who knows you have a problem," I said.

This was a cross between the truth and a lie. I hadn't actually talked to Sophie or anyone else about Veronica's drinking. But I was pretty sure they'd pick up on it soon, if they hadn't already. Veronica looked worried but not convinced. I went on.

"I'm not going to tell anybody," I said, "but there's thirty other people working on this movie, and a lot of them are pissed off at you right now. It's only a matter of time before somebody talks to the press."

"I'm sorry," she said, "are you threatening me?"

She was trying to sound cold and unimpressed, but I could hear the fear in her voice. She'd never be able to play Isabella, I told myself; she couldn't even act powerful with me.

"I'm trying to help you," I said. "Look, I know you're going to get it together. You just need a couple of months to clear your head, and you'll be fine."

This was what my stepdad always said—he just needed two months of total calm and no distractions, and he'd get sober. Once he even put it on the calendar, a big X on the first of October. But then October came, and my youngest sister got bronchitis and shook the house with a cough that sounded like a wild dog barking, and then she had to get chest X-rays, which meant my stepdad had to take another house-painting gig so we'd have the money, and his Calm Months got postponed. He wasn't mad about it, just shrugged and said he'd do it in December, in January, in June.

"I know that," Veronica said. "After this I'm going to go on this meditation retreat in Vermont. I've done it before. It totally cleans out your whole system—it's like being a new person."

"That's great," I said. "You should do it now."

"I have to finish the movie," she said. She didn't sound excited or even indignant; she sounded like she was talking about homework.

"If you drop out now," I said, "it'll be news for a day. A few people will wonder about it, and you'll have to figure out something to tell them."

"More than a few people," she said. "I have a contract."

I didn't actually know much of anything about being a famous actress or how their contracts worked, but I didn't think it mattered.

"If you stay, somebody's going to tell *Us Weekly* that you're a drunk who can't say her lines. And that will be news for a lot longer, and it could permanently fuck up your career."

She didn't say anything, but I knew I'd gotten to her. Her whole body stiffened.

"I don't need this from you right now," she said finally. "You don't know anything. You've been in what, one movie?"

"Suit yourself," I said, and left her there.

VERONICA DIDN'T LEAVE RIGHT AWAY. She limped along for a few more days, mangling her lines and making the crew roll their eyes every time she opened her mouth. Then, when someone snuck an empty vodka bottle into the shot for her big monologue about Ferdinand (it wasn't my idea, but I did help the grip find the bottle), she looked at all of us with this kind of ruined pride, more regal than anything she'd shown us before, and stalked off to her trailer. The next day her agent told Sophie she was pulling out.

What I wasn't prepared for was how Sophie took it. She folded up in my armchair like a sick bird and said in this dull, hollowed-out voice, "It's over. The movie's over."

"It's not over," I said. "We'll find another Isabella."

"You don't understand," she said. "The financing was contingent on Veronica. Now the studio will pull out, and we'll have no money."

I hadn't thought about that. When we made *Marianne*, we just did whatever Sophie wanted, and I'd figured this would be the same.

Now I remembered the trailers and the mini-sandwiches on the craft-services table and the five lighting guys, and I realized how dumb I'd been.

"We'll find someone even better. Veronica was no good, you know that. She could barely read her lines. We'll find someone who will really impress them."

Sophie lifted her head. Her face was awful. It was the first time I'd seen her like that, all the lights out behind her eyes.

"Like who?" she asked.

I sent Abe out for some ice cream. He was happy to go; he felt bad for Sophie. He didn't know it was my fault.

"Like me," I said when he was gone. "Like you wanted in the first place."

She looked confused, just for a second, but long enough for me to realize she'd lied to me. She'd never wanted me for Isabella. She'd always thought of me as Beatriz, the maid.

"I'd love that," she said, her voice so clearly fake it was insulting, "but they're going to want a big name."

Some people just turn away when someone disrespects them. They don't give that person a second chance. But I've always been the kind who stands and tries to show the other person where they went wrong. This has gotten me in a lot of trouble.

I got right up in her face. She blinked. I hoped she was afraid of me.

"Who do you think made *Marianne* great?" I said. "Do you think it was you? It wasn't even your story to begin with."

"I know," she said. Her voice was so small. Later I'd look back and realize I'd never heard her so weak before. But I kept right on going.

"You need me," I said. "And not to be your maid. Not to hold your fucking hand. You need me to star in this movie, because it's the only way it's going to be any good."

I didn't know until right then that I believed that, but it was true.

Sophie looked at me, and her face was exhausted, like after you cry and you just want to lie down by yourself for a while, but her eyes were completely dry.

"You're right," she said, and soon Abe came back with the ice cream, and we ate it and watched *The Blair Witch Project*, and I wasn't sure I'd won at all.

THE NEXT DAY on the subway platform, in the morning, while we waited for the train that would take us to Sophie's meeting with the producer, Sophie got a look in her eye like an animal hunting. I was looking down the tunnel for the train's first light, and she pushed me up against the dirty wall with everyone watching, put her mouth on my mouth, her hand up my shirt. I should've punched her; she knew what it meant to come at me like that, without warning. But she didn't pin my arms—I could've pushed her away. Instead I put a hand in her hair and pulled her closer into me. What can I say, except her smell, the taste of her breath. The memory of every single thing we'd done when we were together, and all the years I told myself we'd never do any of it again. The way we knew how to move against each other even after all that time.

EVERYONE WAS PANICKING. The screenwriter and a guy named George, who Sophie said was an executive producer in L.A., were calling her every day to yell at her. The studio gave Sophie a list of names, people she could replace Veronica with. My name wasn't on it. We made a tape of my marriage speech, and I said those lines like I was made to say them, but they weren't interested. So we started sending the tape around to other independent studios and to rich people Sophie knew who had liked *Marianne* and *Woods*. We waited.

I saw my friend Irina, the girl who'd booked me in the storytelling show years back. I told her Sophie and I were working together again, and she raised an eyebrow and asked if we were *together* together too. I said of course not, I was with Abe. She said that was good, he was a kind person, and Sophie wasn't kind. I nodded, pretended that I agreed with her. I didn't tell her I was realizing I wasn't very kind either. Or that Sophie and I had already fucked secretly in a cab (coming back from a failed meeting with a rich movie buff) and in the alley behind a Crown Heights bar (after drinking whiskey to cover up the failure). Just that morning I'd snuck into the bathroom while she was showering, pretending to bring her a towel, really licking the water off her skin. It felt right to do it in bathrooms and alleys, without telling anyone. I was ashamed of cheating on Abe and manipulating Veronica; sneaking around and looking over my shoulder and never getting to lie in bed with Sophie on a lazy morning felt like the appropriate price to pay for the things I wanted. And when sex was a secret, the movie almost felt like a secret too, something the two of us could enjoy together without anyone else messing it up.

After a couple of weeks we did get an offer, about a quarter of what the studio had promised. We'd have to lose a lot of the crew and the nonspeaking cast—the footmen and scullery maids, Columbus's sailors. We'd have to cut all the scenes with ships and horses. And we'd lose the big old church that had made me want to play Isabella in the first place. Sophie took a week to think about it. I was afraid she'd give up. We went to old buildings we could use cheaply, warehouses and restaurants where Sophie knew people, but none of them looked right. Then we found the old bottle factory. The floor was covered in broken glass, and the walls were full of holes where the equipment had been ripped out. I figured we should move on to the next place on our list, which was a high school gym, but Sophie got a look in her eyes like when a dog smells something on the wind, and then she went crunching around in the glass in her little expensive shoes, muttering to herself. Finally she turned to me.

"Let's just get rid of Spain," she said.

"What do you mean?"

"I mean it's not going to look right no matter what. Let's just put it in New York and use whatever locations we want."

I knew she was right—none of the buildings we'd been to looked anywhere near as good as the church. But I wasn't sure anybody would feel what I felt there—"haunted" I guess would be the word— if they watched us saying our lines in a banged-up warehouse.

"I don't know," I said.

But Sophie was looking all around at the scabby walls and the high barred windows and the place in the corner where a big snarl of copper wiring came right up out of the floor. I could tell she was excited—I knew her face when she was all lit up with a new idea. What I didn't know then was how to tell her deep true solid joy from the kind of excitement that came from panic.

"I promise," she said, "it's going to look really beautiful."

"Okay," I said, "I trust you."

It took a week to convince everyone else. Both the screenwriter and George threatened to take the movie away from us. But Sophie told them the same thing she'd told me: the movie was going to be even better this way. She said things I'd never heard her say before, like "boundary breaking." She had this ability to sound completely confident, like it would be insane to ever doubt her. Finally she got her way.

So we started to shoot again. The bottle factory became the dank old farmhouse where Isabella's brother puts her after their father dies. Isabella's carriage to her brother's castle was a yellow cab—the driver asked me if I was going to a Renaissance fair. The castle itself was a fancy old building on Eighty-sixth Street, and the throne room was an apartment in a Williamsburg high-rise with a view of the city. The owner was a friend of the producer—she was excited that we were making a movie in her house, and she kept giving us unhelpful tips about the light until we put her in a dress and gave her a nonspeaking role. The banquet hall was an actual Italian banquet hall in Bensonhurst. We hired the real staff to serve us dinner for the party where Isabella meets Ferdinand for the first time; in that scene we're eating spaghetti bolognese and eggplant parm. Then they helped us put the tables and chairs away and we danced the way the choreographer had taught us before we had to stop paying her.

I thought it all looked good enough—the banquet hall even seemed kind of royal to me, with its fake marble floors and fat velvet curtains we kept bumping into as we danced. But Sergei, who played Ferdinand, kept getting more and more upset. He was short and black-haired and pretty, and he'd been great in his scenes with Veronica—he had pale blue eyes and on cue he could make them flare up with desire. But at the banquet hall he acted like a teenager who has to babysit little kids at a party. He was supposed to kiss my hand and look up at me like he already loved me—instead he looked over my left shoulder at the door to the street.

As good as Sophie was sometimes at getting down to the soft core of you, she could be really shitty at giving notes.

"That doesn't look right," she said to Sergei. "You need to look like you like her."

He rolled his pretty eyes. "You've made that a little difficult, haven't you?" he asked.

Sophie looked at him with a blank, empty face, which made him madder.

"Come on," he said, "this is a surprise to you? You throw me in a smelly party room with a girl twice my size and you expect me to act like nothing's different?"

I tried not to show that this bothered me, but it did. I wasn't twice his size—he was short and slim, but he had broad shoulders and big gym-rat arms. He probably outweighed me. But I was a lot bigger than Veronica—her Isabella dress wouldn't zip up my back, and I had to wear the Beatriz costume with extra gold brocade we got at the craft store. And I was bigger than I'd been in *Marianne*. I knew how this worked—if the movie did well enough, there would be before-and-after pictures of me on the Internet, strangers calling me a cow. I didn't really care so much—when I was by myself, with no cameras around, I liked the way I looked just fine. But I wanted Sophie to tell Sergei how stupid he was being, how beautiful I was, and how if he couldn't do the scene it was his problem.

Instead she said, "Think about someone else if you have to. Just make sure you look at her face when you do it."

In the next take he did make eye contact, but his mouth had a mean twist when he looked at me. I didn't know who he was thinking about—his Russian wife with her big breasts over a tiny waist, her pretty calves in stiletto boots; Veronica, so delicate her arms looked boneless; or some other small, elegant woman. Whoever it was, I knew in his mind that person was much more beautiful than me.

When we were finally done for the day and Sophie and I were curled on the saggy couch of a bar called Stan's, I asked her, "Do you think I'm not pretty enough to play Isabella?"

I'd never been the kind of person who asked that—I'd always hated girls who fished for compliments, who forced their boyfriends to tell them how pretty they were until the word lost all its meaning. And I knew Sophie wanted me; already in the bar's graffiti-covered bathroom she'd made me come with her hands. But I didn't like the way she wilted in front of Sergei. And I knew he was right in one way— for the movie to work, the audience had to want Isabella. I wanted Sophie to tell me that they would. Instead she said, "I don't know."

My thigh was touching hers and I jerked it away. "What do you mean, you don't know?"

"I mean I like how you look. In the dailies you're beautiful, with all your hair down. But you and Sergei don't look good together."

"He's just not trying," I said. "He's pissed that I don't make him look like a big man."

"That's probably true," Sophie said. "But it still looks bad."

"You're the director," I said. I was almost yelling, and a guy by the pool table looked over and gave me a smirk. "You're supposed to direct the actors. That's your job."

She let her neck go slack, rolled her head away from me so she was talking at the wall.

"I just don't feel it with this one," she said.

Then she turned to look at me.

"Sometimes I feel like I'm fading," she said, "Like I'm getting more transparent. Do you ever feel that way?"

"What do you mean?" I asked.

"Never mind," she said, and put her head on my shoulder, something she did all the time now that she never used to do. We sat like that for a minute while I worried about her, and was mad at her for making me worry, and then mad at myself for being mad. Just when I started to relax again into the smell and feel of her, she said, "Abe knows."

I'd been cheating on him for three weeks at that point, and I hadn't been careful at all—sneaking out to the living room to see her while Abe was asleep, going down on her in our bed before he got home from work. But I'd still been having sex with Abe, I still loved him, and I thought those things would keep him from suspecting. He wasn't dumb, but he was easy to please, and I thought that if I just kept him warm at night and told him sweet things sometimes, he wouldn't suspect I was fucking my ex-girlfriend in our house.

"How do you know?" I asked.

"We were eating cereal—" she started.

"What? When?"

I was annoyed that they still talked to each other without me, even now. A few nights before, Abe had told me he was worried about her—I'd just rolled over and pretended to be asleep.

"While you were in the shower," she said. "We were joking about how long you take. And then he got all serious and said to me, 'It's okay, you know. I understand.'"

This was worse than him knowing, that he might know and not even be mad. It made me feel like he must not love me as hard as I wanted him to.

"How did you know what he was talking about?" I asked. "Maybe he meant something else."

"I asked him," she said. "And he said he knew you and I had a history and he didn't want to get in the way of that. He said he just wanted you to be happy."

I tried to imagine that—the man I'd lived with for over a year and Sophie, who'd been back just a few months, talking about my happiness. Like I was a kid or a crazy person who couldn't make decisions for myself.

"What's that supposed to mean?" I asked.

"I asked him that too. He said he knew you loved him and he didn't believe in being jealous. He said you had enough love for both of us."

It takes a lot to make me miss my family, but that did it. I remembered when my sixteen-year-old sister's boyfriend cheated on her with his ex, who had a kid with another guy and dirt-colored greasy hair like a stray dog. My sister sobbed on the phone so hard she choked, and when he came over with a fat pink teddy bear to win her back, we all came screaming down at him, my mom and all my sisters, whirling like a hurricane until he ran back to his car, terrified of us. Then we all got into my mom's bed and petted my sister's hair while she cried and told her she didn't need him, she didn't need anybody too weak to give her his whole heart.

And now here was Abe, saying lines out of some hippie relationship book. I was disgusted with him.

"What did you say?" I asked Sophie.

"I said okay."

"That's it? Okay?"

I didn't know what I expected her to do, but I didn't want her to just agree with him.

"Listen," she said, "maybe it's good. He makes you happy, and I'm not that good at doing that. Maybe you can have both."

"You make me happy," I said, but I knew she was right. Sophie would never know that on those nights when I felt like I didn't belong in the city or maybe the world, like I'd given up my only home and I was never going to find another, what I really wanted was for someone to make me get dressed and take me dancing. She wouldn't remember what my favorite ice cream was and buy it just rarely enough to surprise me every time, and she would never learn that the thing to do when I froze up during sex was to look me right in the eye and remind me, again and again, that I was safe. But Abe had known all these things without my telling him. He was good at loving me; it came easy to him. It was true I didn't want to give that up.

"I said we'd talk about it later," Sophie said, "but what if we don't? What if we just keep doing what we're doing and let it be?"

She looked tired—she was looking that way more and more lately—and now I was tired too.

I remembered something else from back home, when my stepdad was in the hospital after he missed one of our front steps drunk in the dark and fell down and broke his nose. It was so stupid I couldn't look at him, and while he was in with the doctor, I asked my mom if she loved him.

"He's pretty good to me," she said. "He keeps me company. He helps out with the kids."

"That's not what I asked," I said.

She looked me in the eye then, which she almost never did, and said, "I know, honey. But I don't ask myself questions like that."

And maybe it was good she didn't. Maybe that was how you had to live, eventually—just let things be and never ask yourself if they were what you really wanted. The waitress came by—she was pretty and sad-eyed, and, up close, older than I'd thought—and I ordered us each another whiskey. I drank mine fast and the night got fuzzy around the edges. Sophie and I kissed on the train home, but when we got there I got into bed with Abe and we fucked quickly without talking. I fell asleep against him thinking, *Maybe, maybe, maybe.*

THE NEXT DAY was the big scene between Isabella and Ferdinand—they think she's about to marry someone else, so they agree to have sex at the house of a sympathetic noblewoman. We used a Holiday Inn on Third Avenue in Gowanus, warehouses out all the windows and the chemical smell of the canal whenever the wind turned. The address was written in permanent marker on the bedsheets. While the grip set up the lights, I sat on the bed in Abe's bathrobe. Sergei was fully clothed.

"Look," he said, "maybe we don't do this scene at all. Maybe we just cut to, you know, flowers blooming or something."

"Don't be a dick," I said.

"I'm trying to help. If we try to make this movie sexy, it's going to look ridiculous. Maybe we take the high road, go for the Merchant-Ivory types, the grandmas."

I looked at Sophie, but she was ignoring us, staring over the DP's shoulder at the viewfinder and scowling.

"Okay," she said, "let's do this."

I shrugged off my robe. I was wearing a nude thong Sophie and I had bought together; at the time I'd looked forward to wearing it and having her watch me. Now I just felt ashamed, like someone had pulled my pants down on the playground.

The first take was terrible. We were supposed to start lying on the bed, with Sergei straddling me, and then he'd pull me up so our faces were touching and say his line: "Never belong to anyone else." But he never pulled. He just let me lie there waiting, looking confused, and then when I was sure he'd forgotten the line he said it, blandly, like it was a suggestion.

"You guys need to do that way better," Sophie said, and I was mad that she was talking to both of us when Sergei was the only one not trying.

On the second take he did pull, but roughly, like I was dead weight, and my breasts slammed against his chest and he pulled back like I was disgusting, and we had to cut before he even said his line.

On the third take he scooted back as he pulled me, so we were a good two feet apart, and then he held my hand while he said the line with no heat in it at all.

"That time you looked like first-graders," Sophie said.

I pushed myself out of bed. I didn't bother to put on the robe. Sergei and the pimply grip and the angry DP and Sophie herself were just going to have to put up with my tits and belly and ass as I walked to the bathroom.

I locked the door and stared at myself in the mirror. I thought of how many people had seen me naked in my life—my mom, my dad, my sisters when we went swimming in the quarry where the water snakes came up from their secret nests to scare and excite us, the boy from tenth grade whose name I'd forgotten and who rubbed me between my legs until he came in his own pants, Bean, Barber, all the men in New York I saw for a night or a week or a month and wanted nothing from except their skin on mine, Abe, Sophie, Sophie, Sophie. But probably almost nobody saw Isabella naked. Her nurse, maybe, the maid who bathed her. (I remembered hosing off my little sisters in the backyard after they got into an old can of house paint, their bodies wriggling like puppies.) Before she met Ferdinand, she herself was probably the only person who looked at her body and saw sex. And her brother was about to marry her off as a bargaining chip, not a body but a name. Ferdinand was a teenage boy—maybe if he was lucky he'd seen a naked woman once in his life, a hooker working her way through the court. It would be up to me to show him I was something to fight for.

BACK IN THE ROOM, we were getting gold late-afternoon light through the cheap window blinds. I could feel it in my hair and on my skin as I walked back to the bed. Everybody got quiet.

"Let's go," I said.

This time instead of waiting for him to pull me I reared up on my own. Instead of waiting for him to come close I wrapped my arms around his waist and pressed my belly against his. I thought of when I'd first met Abe, at a dance club in Harlem, how he lifted me over his head like it was nothing and on the way down I put my hands over his hands, pressing his fingers into my flesh. I thought of when I'd first met Sophie, how I'd been the one to move toward her on the street outside my house. I thought of how I'd chosen them both, about how badly I'd wanted them, how badly I wanted them still. I looked hard into Sergei's blue eyes and said, "Never belong to anyone else."

For a minute it was silent and I could hear the trucks on Third Avenue, the blood in my ears. Then Sophie said, in a soft voice, "Okay, that's good, I think we got it."

The rest of the day was smooth—the light was beautiful, Sergei behaved, I felt calm and good in Isabella's head. We finished ahead of schedule. And then, while everyone was packing up and I was getting dressed, Sophie came to me and grabbed my wrist so hard it hurt. Her eyes were huge. She said, "I want you to leave him."

THEN WE HAD THE FIGHT I'd been wanting. We told Abe together, standing in the living room, holding hands. He looked at Sophie with a cold rage I'd never seen before and said, "Get out of here so I can talk to Allison."

"No," she said. I could tell she was scared, but I wasn't sure of what.

"Fine," he said. "Allison, let's talk in the bedroom."

I followed him like a child. I expected him to scream at me for betraying him, and if he'd done that, maybe I would've stayed. Instead he said, "You know you're making a huge mistake, don't you?"

I just looked at him.

"How long is it going to last? A week? A month?"

"I don't know," I said.

I wasn't an idiot. I knew that Abe and I had a good shot at being old together and Sophie and I did not. But all I wanted then was to be with Sophie; I couldn't hold anything else in my head.

"When it's over," he said, "don't think you can just come back. I won't be here."

"I know," I said, even though I hadn't till right then. He'd been a safe place for me to go for such a long time; I guess I thought maybe he'd always be one.

"This is your last chance," he said. "You can change your mind now, and we can go back to how we were. Better, maybe, because we've been through this."

I saw how much it was going to hurt to lose him. I saw it far away, like a thing on the horizon, like a mad dog we watched walk down our street one ugly Sunday back home, its mouth full of disease. But I couldn't feel the hurt yet. I was filled with a dull calm.

"I'm sorry," I said. I went to get my suitcase from the closet.

I heard him walk to the door, stop, turn back.

"I hope you know what you're getting into," he said.

It made me angry that he would condescend to me like that.

"I'm a grown-up," I said, rolling my dancing dress up into a ball. "I'll be fine."

"I'm not talking about you," he said. "I know you'll be fine. You always are. But Sophie's heading for something bad, and if you're the one that's with her, that's going to be on you."

"You don't know anything about Sophie," I said, but when I left the house with everything that was really mine in a suitcase and a garbage bag, I was scared.

WE WERE AT THE SUBWAY STATION—her holding my hand, me shaking—when we realized we had no idea where to go. All we had between us was a little money Sophie had saved from a few lectures and classes she'd done after *Woods* and the now-tiny amount I was getting paid for *Isabella*. We ended up going back to the Holiday Inn where we'd just been shooting. The room we'd used was taken, but they put us in one exactly like it, except the mirror had some kind of dark stain that looked like a ghost when we turned out the lights. At first it was kind of a joke for us, staying there, but then it started to feel safe, like we could drop out of the real world and live in our movie. We finished the shoot—the last scenes we had were Isabella's meeting with the rebel leader (shot at a coffee shop on the Upper West Side, where they wouldn't let the actors carry their fake swords) and Isabella's marriage to Ferdinand (in Prospect Park, between rainstorms, a dog running back and forth across the shot). Then Sophie started editing, and it was just like *Marianne*—the two of us lying awake together, talking about how great we'd be. Except now Sophie knew what success looked like, so her daydreams were more specific. She wanted to premiere at Sundance. She wanted a big nationwide release in lots of theaters. She wanted a review in *The New York Star*.

I wanted all that too, mostly because Sophie wanted it. But unlike with *Marianne*, I also had dreams for myself. I wanted a big magazine profile like Sophie had gotten, where they'd praise my acting with words like "luminous" and talk about my favorite breakfast cereal like it was something important. I wanted the Coen brothers to call me and offer me a role in their next movie—I'd turn it down because I was already shooting another movie with Sophie, but then they'd work around my schedule because there was just no way they could make the film without me.

It wasn't that I wanted to be famous, exactly. For one thing, I didn't want my family to see the movie—I didn't want any connection between them and my life now. And I didn't think about people stopping me in the street, or women's magazines putting me on the cover, or fancy restaurants saving a table for me. I just knew that for the first time in my life I'd done really, really well at something, and I wanted important people to talk about it.

I didn't tell Sophie about any of this. She was nervous—she came home every night from editing with her shoulders all hunched together. I did things to make her days easier, like getting single-serving packets of oatmeal and making sure she left with a few every morning, and at night, after she curled away from me, I lay awake with my excitement.

We didn't get into Sundance—Sophie said she wasn't upset, but then she got into the bathtub and stayed there for hours, until I had to fish her out of the cold water, dry her off, and put her to bed. We did get into the Hudson Film Festival, though, and that seemed to calm Sophie enough that she could eat real meals and look me in the face when she talked. She started working on something new—she wouldn't talk about it, but she said I could see it as soon as it was done—and we had two months of good time. She wasn't paying much attention to how she looked then; she'd stopped slicking her hair back and it fell soft around her face, and sometimes while she slept I could imagine the child she'd been before she met me. I knew she'd been Emily when she was little, not Sophie, and sometimes I called her that in my mind, a secret name nobody who saw our movies would ever know.

I got my job at the coffee shop back, and I picked up shifts at a midtown bar too. Living at the motel was stupidly expensive, but every time I talked about leaving, Sophie got all closed off, and I learned not to mention it. I was good at being good to her then. Sometimes she came to the bar at the end of my shift and we would tease the drunk businessmen together. She liked to tell them we were sisters, and I'd play along—"Twins, in fact," I'd say. "We're very close." And if the men reacted right, I'd lean across the bar and kiss her deeply, they'd cheer and buy her shots and over-tip. Once, right before the festival, a middle-aged guy with a corned-beef face was hitting on me—nothing intense, just asking if I was single and what kind of guys I liked. I laughed, but Sophie interrupted—"You know that's my wife you're talking about." I knew she was kidding around, but that word made me excited and scared. The beef-face guy apologized.

"I didn't mean anything," he said.

"No, it's okay," she told him. "This happens all the time. And it's only going to get worse."

"Why?" he asked. I didn't know the answer either.

"Because she's about to become a movie star. Her movie comes out in a couple of weeks, and then everyone in New York is going to want her."

He was impressed and tried to ask us more questions, but I was busy trying and failing to read Sophie's face. On the way home I wanted to ask her what she meant by "wife," but she was quiet on the subway, gripping my hand and staring straight ahead, so I didn't bring it up.

. . .

ON THE NIGHT OF THE PREMIERE, I wore a dark blue dress Sophie had bought me, cut low and tight in the bust and flowy around my hips and thighs. People who knew Sophie kept telling me how beautiful I looked and then asking her where she'd been and if she was going to whatever other event or party or screening they wanted to show off their invites to. I knew she could work a crowd if she tried, but today she just mumbled some excuses about being really busy and sat down in the back with me, clutching my hand.

I hadn't been in the editing room, so the way the movie looked was a shock to me. In *Marianne* Sophie always made us wait for the most beautiful light, even for the saddest scenes, so the whole movie looked golden. The few reviews we got all mentioned that. But *Isabella* opened at the Brooklyn Navy Yard, on a cloudy day with a yellow-gray sky. I didn't remember shooting the scene—Sophie must have gone without me. The opening credits rolled over the gray water and the empty boats; once a seagull flew across the frame. I thought maybe the shot was supposed to be sad in a poetic way, but instead it looked flat, like Sophie's face when you couldn't tell what she was thinking. I started to worry that I was already missing the point of the movie. Then the scene changed and there I was, in the bottle factory in my Isabella dress.

At first I was vain and nervous and I stared at myself on the screen to see if I looked fat. But then I forgot to look at my chin, my waist, the neckline of the dress where the flesh of my breasts came up, and instead it was like when I was little and I would wake up early in the morning to hear my mom crying. She could never sleep then, after my dad went away for the last time and before she met my stepdad, and she'd be up sobbing at four a.m. and banging mugs and bowls around in the kitchen, I think hoping I or my sister would wake up and go make her feel better. I tried it once, but it didn't work—she just cried harder and talked about being a bad mom—and so after that when I couldn't go back to sleep I'd just lie in bed and pretend to be someone else.

Sometimes it was Charlotte, a tall, pretty girl in my grade whose parents already had a college fund for her. Sometimes it was Tom Winston, Mom's second cousin who moved to Richmond and bought a car dealership and came back every year for the Fourth of July with a fat watch and pictures of his wife and daughters, all blond and perfect-looking, like they'd never in their lives stayed up all night crying. But it wasn't just people who had it good that I thought about. Sometimes I'd pretend to be the old man with no teeth who sold peanuts at the bus stop in town, while all the high school boys kicked dust on him and made fun of his baby gums. Or I'd be Melissa Osburn, who lost her leg all the way up to the hip when drunk Brandon Phelps ran her over, and now her mom wouldn't even let her go to school anymore because something else might happen. The point was just to leave myself and run away into somebody else's life, and I got really good at it—so good that I carried the other person with me long after it was time to get up, through breakfast and waiting for the bus and the first sludgy hours of school, and when I passed by a mirror I'd be surprised to see my own face looking back.

That was how I felt all during the movie, and when the lights came up I was still sitting straight and queenly, holding my hands in my lap like they were covered with heavy rings. So I was surprised when people started coming up to me, trying to shake my hand. A woman in thick makeup said, "I want you to know I cried when you told Henry he couldn't push you around anymore. I thought of all the times I wanted to do that and couldn't, and I just bawled."

I looked more closely at her—her eyeliner was all smeared and feathered, her eyes red.

A man asked, "Why haven't we seen you onstage?" And before I could tell him he could have, he shoved a business card into my hand and closed my fingers over it.

Another man, tall and thin and old, told me, "You shone out of that movie, just shone out of it."

I thought that was a strange thing to say, and then I saw that Sophie was already heading for the exit, all by herself, and nobody was trying to talk to her.

In the lobby people kept stopping me, and I knew I should just push past them to get to Sophie, but it was hard when they kept saying everything I'd hoped someone would say. I started to feel like I'd won a big race, a marathon. I wanted to put my hands in the air. When I reached the glass doors of the theater I could see Sophie—she was sitting on a bench, far away from everyone, with her blank face on. I was going to run and join her when a woman tapped me on the shoulder. She was less dressed up than everyone else, jeans and a blazer, and she looked calm and a little bored and immediately I wanted to please her.

"I'm Lucy," she said. "I write for *Conversation*. I'd love to talk to you more sometime."

I felt like kissing her. Instead I said, "How about tomorrow?"

She smiled like she was surprised, and I realized I should've tried to act busy.

"How about Wednesday lunch?" she asked.

I thought of pretending I had something to do then, to seem important, but I couldn't make myself do it.

"Great," I said, and she gave me her business card, which I put in the special tiny pocket of my purse so I'd never lose it.

By the time I got outside, Sophie was gone.

I called her phone, and when she didn't answer I ran all around the theater and side streets, calling her name.

Some older ladies in nice clothes were chatting by the side entrance; I charged at them breathless and panicked, and asked if they'd seen her.

"Well, yes," said the tallest one, with a big ugly opal necklace in her cleavage. "We saw her in the theater."

"No," I said, "I mean after that. Just now."

They edged away from me. They looked the way strangers sometimes do when you're really freaking them out, like you might infect them with something.

"We haven't seen her," said the woman with the necklace.

As I ran off she called, "You were very good."

Finally I had to give up. On the train I felt guilty because I'd just been lapping up compliments instead of taking care of Sophie, but also I was angry, because couldn't she just let me feel important for a little while? By the time I got back to the motel, I had at least ten apologies and as many accusations all written out in my head.

Sophie was sitting on our unmade bed, with her computer open.

"What are you doing?" I asked. "Where have you been?"

She showed me the screen. It was full of listings for apartments.

"I think we should find a real place to live together," she said.

I was still mad at her for scaring me.

"Now you want to?" I asked. "I've been trying and trying to get you to move out of this shithole for months."

She looked at me with the same face she'd worn when she decided to make the movie modern—big-eyed and hopeful—but too much somehow, I could see now. Kind of desperate.

"I want to move in together as soon as possible," she said. "I want to start a real life together."

I sat down on the bed with her. I was worried now.

"What's up with you?" I asked. "Why did you run off?"

Her face shut down then. She looked at the computer instead of at me.

"The movie isn't good," she said.

"Of course it is," I told her. "It's great. Everybody was saying nice things about it."

"No," she said. "You're good. The movie is bad."

I hadn't seen her like this before—after *Marianne* wrapped, she'd been excited, full of plans. I tried to think back to the movie, take myself out of it and look at it like a stranger would. I thought about the opening shot of the harbor, how it looked bleak and gray and flat, like Sophie's face with all the feeling sucked out of it. Other parts of the movie were like that, too, I remembered now—the glass-and-metal front of the building that was Henry's palace, the conference room where Isabella makes her deal with the rebels, even the stretch of Sixth Avenue where Ferdinand and Isabella have their wedding procession. Now that I thought about it, it was true that the movie had started to lose me whenever Isabella wasn't talking. But that had to be normal—I'd never seen myself on the big screen before. I'd waited years to watch *Marianne*. Of course, like all the egomaniac actors I knew, I'd be most interested in watching myself.

"That's ridiculous," I said. "The movie's beautiful. You're just nervous because it's the premiere, that's all."

Sophie didn't nod or look up.

"What if we moved to Maine?" she said. "I've been looking there too."

"What's in Maine?" I asked. I was getting exhausted trying to follow her train of thought.

"We could get a little house on the beach and catch fish. We could build a boat. We could really get away from everything."

I was a little mad at her again—why would I want to run away now, when for the first time in my whole life I was in a place where people thought I was great? But also I was pretty sure Sophie had never been in a boat, let alone built one, so I decided not to take her seriously.

"Okay," I said, "but if we do that I want lobster pots. I want to eat lobster every day."

"We'll do that too," she said. "Maybe we can get jobs on a lobster boat, and they'll pay us in lobster."

Her face and voice were dreamy, like a little kid's. I took off my clothes and got under the covers with her, and we held each other and talked about lobster until she fell asleep.

THE FIRST REVIEW WASN'T TERRIBLE. It was a short blurb in the *Daily Bridge* calling the movie "flawed" but "well acted" and "occasionally moving." Sophie seemed nervous but not too upset; she made a list of apartments to visit, and we saw two on Monday. The first one was nice enough inside but sat between two chicken plants, so the air all around it smelled like shit and old blood. The second was pretty, on a street with trees and an elementary school, but the landlady squinted at us and said, "If you live here, you can't be coming and going all the time. To work, okay, but we can't have people coming in and out at night. This is a family building."

We couldn't figure out if she was bigoted or insane. Tuesday we took the day off from looking, and I went to meet the manager of a new bar where I was applying to be shift manager. He liked me and hired me right away, but I explained I couldn't start till Thursday.

"Tomorrow," I said, "I have an interview with a magazine."

I met Lucy at a fancy vegetarian restaurant in Chelsea. She was just like I remembered, calm and pretty in jeans and a blazer and leather moccasins, and looking at her made me think maybe a person could fit in everywhere if they just had the right clothes. She told me the Korean-style rice bowl was delicious, and I ordered it to be polite and because nothing else on the menu looked very good anyway. The waitress brought us tea and then pumpkin soup in little bowls, which was lukewarm and sweet and reminded me of my sister's baby food, and while I tried to find a way to like it, Lucy asked me where I was from. I sometimes lied about this to people, especially people I'd never been close to, not because I was embarrassed but because I didn't think I should have to think about home just to satisfy some stranger's curiosity. But I was scared to lie to a reporter, and also I wanted her to know what I was really like, where I came from—I wanted people who read the magazine to know that and like me anyway.

"West Virginia," I said, and when she said, "Oh, it's beautiful down there," I said, "Not where I'm from."

Immediately I was worried that was rude and she'd be mad at me, but she just went right on to the next question. I told her about my dad and my mom and my stepdad and my sisters, and I only stopped telling the truth when we got to Bean. No good had ever come from exposing that weak part of myself. When she asked me why I left home I just said I was getting away from a bad boyfriend, and she nodded, and the main course came. I'd been expecting something that looked like fried rice, and I burned myself right away on the heavy iron pot that was still cooking my food. I was ashamed, and I stared stupidly at the red blister rising on my finger, until Lucy noticed and said, "I do that all the time," and told me to hold my finger against my cold water glass until the pain went down.

"So when you took the Isabella role," she said, her own iron pot steaming untouched in front of her, "you were replacing someone much higher-profile. And correct me if I'm wrong, but it seems like you don't have any formal training. Were you nervous?"

"No," I said. "I wasn't nervous at all."

She cocked an eyebrow at me, like we were friends and it was okay to tell her what I *really* thought, and it occurred to me that if I knew her better, I might not necessarily like her.

"Really?" she asked. "Not even for a minute?"

I looked right at her, wishing I hadn't burned my thumb or shown up in a flowered dress that was both too fancy and not fancy enough, and I said, "I knew I'd be great. And if anybody doubted that, I was going to show them."

Lucy nodded, neatly scooped up a piece of tofu from her pot, and blew on it. "Did Sophie doubt you?"

"What?"

I knew what she'd said, but I needed her to say it again so I'd have time to calm down. The suggestion—and the way she smiled when she said it—made me want to smack her.

"You weren't her first choice. Was she worried you couldn't handle it?"

Of course I'd been afraid of that. And maybe part of the reason Sophie was acting so weird about the movie was that she never expected me to be so good. I was even madder at Lucy because I thought she might be right.

"Sophie's always believed in me," I said.

Lucy nodded. She picked up a mushroom with her chopsticks, popped it in her mouth.

"Is it ever hard to work with your girlfriend?" she asked.

I tried to eat some of my rice bowl. It was still steaming hot; a bite of rice and some spinachy vegetable burned my tongue and made me pant. I tried to think of an answer that would make her feel dumb for asking and also would make me feel better about me and Sophie and our future.

"No," I said finally. "She motivates me. Being with her makes me want to be better."

"And this movie hasn't strained your relationship at all?"

I was starting to sweat. I thought of Sophie at our grungy motel, looking at pictures of Maine on her computer.

"What do you mean?" I asked.

"Well, you've gotten so much praise, and she's gotten a lot of criticism."

"No she hasn't," I snapped back. "What criticism?"

"Well, the *Bridge* review and the one in the *L.A. Times* and then the blogs. And Martin's got a review coming out today or tomorrow."

I'd avoided learning that much about movie criticism; I didn't even know what blogs she meant. But I did know that Ben Martin was the movie critic for the *Star* and that his review would be more important than any other.

"A bad one?" I asked.

But she just waved her hand vaguely, took another bite of tofu.

"Look, I'm not trying to say anything bad about the movie. I loved it. I'm just curious about how you're handling the response as a couple."

I wondered if they'd taught her this in her journalism classes, what to say if a subject got upset. I wondered if she'd thought that I'd be easy to interview, that I'd give up all kinds of dirt because I didn't know any better. I promised myself I'd disappoint her.

"We don't care what other people say about us," I said. "Especially Sophie. The only important thing is making good movies and making each other happy."

"So she's supportive of your career, even if it doesn't involve her?"

The idea that I would do movies without Sophie really hadn't occurred to me until right then. I had no idea how she'd feel about that. But I was on a good track now, and I was going to stay on it.

"Of course," I said. "We're behind each other a hundred percent. We don't have any choice. We're each other's everything."

On the train ride home, I was proud of myself for what I'd said. I'd tell Sophie, and she'd be proud too. We'd both do a lot more interviews, I thought, and we'd keep saying the same things, and eventually we'd have no choice but to live by them.

At the motel Sophie had her suitcase out on the bed. She was carefully folding her clothes into it.

"Where are you going?" I asked, smiling even though I was already scared. "Maine?"

"No," she said.

She folded up a boy's button-down shirt that I recognized from our old days together.

"Sophie," I asked, "what's going on?"

"The *Star* review came out," she said. She pointed to her laptop.

I'd been so worried about what to say to Lucy that I'd almost forgotten the review. But once I started reading it, I couldn't look away. Ben Martin started by talking about Sophie's career, calling her movies "deeply unsentimental." Then he said, "There's a fine line between unsentimental and outright unfeeling, and *Isabella* has crossed it." I had the thought that I should stop, go comfort Sophie, tell her that what that asshole said didn't matter. But I kept reading. He talked about Sophie's "fundamental flaw." He compared her to a robot. He said the only good thing about the movie was me.

I still think that after I read the review, there was a chance for us. If I'd told myself it was bullshit, if I'd slammed the laptop shut, and looked at Sophie with all the love and respect I'd felt when we were first together, and gone to her and told her she was so much better than he said, and believed it, I think we would've come through. But instead I believed him. Not completely—I didn't think Sophie was a no-talent loser who would never make a good film again. But looking back, I did think the movie was drab and ugly. And I did think I was the best thing about it. It felt good to let myself believe that—after letting Sophie convince me that she was the only one who could make a movie good, that sometimes she had hurt me to do it and that had to be okay, I wanted to feel like actually I was the one her movies couldn't live without.

So I did go to her and rub her shoulder and kiss her cheek, but all I said to her was, "What do you care what that guy thinks?"

"I care if it's true," she said. Her voice was flat and dull.

"Of course it isn't true," I said, but I didn't sell the line, and when she turned to me, she saw I didn't really believe it.

"I'm going to go stay with my brother for a while," she said.

Sophie didn't talk about Robbie much, but still I'd always been jealous of him. She'd once said he was the only person she could talk to without feeling bad about herself—when I asked her if I made her feel bad about herself she said no, but it sounded forced.

"How long are you going for?" I asked.

She shrugged. She was doing something that always scared me, moving like she had almost no strength in her body, like she was about to fall right down on the floor.

"A month," she said, "maybe longer."

"A month?" I almost yelled. "I thought we were going to look for a place together."

"I thought so too," she said. "I thought that would help. But I don't think so now."

I hated when she talked like that, like she was so mysterious. I thought she was being petty, so I was petty right back.

"You're so mad that I got a good review and you didn't that you don't want to live with me anymore? Maybe you need to grow the fuck up."

She didn't flinch, just sat down on the bed and looked up at me.

"You know," she said, "when I met Veronica, I knew she was fragile in all the right places. I knew I could break her down. But I couldn't do that to you again. Once you came on, I just had to let it be your movie."

"That's the only way you know how to make a movie?" I asked. "By making other people miserable?"

She just gave me a sad laugh and one of those huge shrugs I used to find so charming. But I'd given up my life for her and I didn't have any sympathy.

"Fine," I said. "Go rest somewhere else. Get the fuck out of here."

"I'm sorry," she said, standing. I turned to face away from her, like a little kid.

"Jump off a fucking bridge," I told her.

I didn't feel guilty when I said it or when I heard her close the door on her way out. I was sure I would see her again.

NEW YORK STAR

A Queen Dethroned

By Benjamin Martin

The story of Queen Isabella of Castile—the persecution by power-hungry elders, the secret marriage to her first love, the transformation into ruthless monarch and early architect of imperialism—is long overdue for the biopic treatment. Sophie Stark, whose films have long focused on strong, unusual women, would seem like the ideal director to steer this story away from period schlock and toward the truly revelatory. She has accomplished the former, but not the latter.

Stark has always been a deeply unsentimental filmmaker. But there's a fine line between unsentimental and outright unfeeling, and *Isabella* has crossed it.

The film looks like it was made by a robot. Stark has always had an acute visual sense, so there must be a reason she chooses to set *Isabella* in modern-day New York City and to show us the flat, ugly interiors of motel rooms and apartments and industrial Brooklyn at its most dull and gray. It's impossible to determine, however, what that reason might be. *Isabella* was reportedly conceived as a much larger-budget film than it eventually became, and the more expensive version might have been more entertaining—maybe Stark's sensibility would have subverted the tired conventions of corsets and throne rooms. Here it's just removed them, replacing them with nothing.

Much of the acting is similarly empty. Stark doesn't appear to understand the emotional thrust of Ana Valdivia's script, or maybe she just doesn't care. Whatever the case, the actors seem to have received almost no guidance and are acting in about eight different movies. Gabriel Zielinski plays Isabella's greedy half brother, Henry, as a mustache-twirling Disney villain; Sergei Gavrikov's Ferdinand is like a feckless lad in his first year at Cambridge. The only exception, somewhat oddly, is Allison Mieskowski, who overcomes Stark's lack of directorial vision to give us an Isabella who is regal, cruel, loving, and riveting. She singlehandedly saves her love scene with Ferdinand, tearing into him like a lioness (or, with her corona of red-gold hair, maybe a lion).

As for Stark, *Isabella* may be evidence of a fundamental flaw. Her films to date have been stories of strange and lonely people trying to carve out lives for themselves, and only for themselves. But Isabella has to triangulate between her lover, her brother, and the country she will one day rule—it's a film of relationships, and Stark has never been good at relationships.

Stark is famously private, at times verging on the reclusive. In interviews she is not so much evasive as simply absent, as though the human interaction of answering questions is uninteresting to her. But true loners don't make the best directors. *Isabella* reveals a basic inability to communicate with actors (and possibly with crew—who thought it was a good idea to light Ferdinand and Isabella's wedding like a middle school dance?). It also reveals a misunderstanding—or, worse, a disregard—for what an audience might think and feel. Stark's brain must be a fascinating place, but she seems incapable of seeing outside it.

Robbie

WHEN JACOB MARRIED MY SISTER, I WAS SORRY FOR HIM. NOT at first, not when they met me at the airport and I saw how carefully she listened to him talk, how interested she was in him. Not at the altar, where she wore high-heeled shoes and looked beautiful and serious and said "I do" like she meant it. I felt sorry for him later, when the party had gone on well into the night, his friends laughing and playing music on the little spit of beach next to the house and quietly, without telling anyone, Sophie had slipped out of her dress and stepped into the lake. I didn't see her go in. I turned with my glass of wedding wine and saw the dress lying on the dock and, far away, her bony shoulders in the lake, and when I turned back to the party, I saw that Jacob was watching, too.

"When did she learn to swim?" I asked him.

It made me sad that I had to ask, but long ago I'd had to accept that I would see and know Sophie on her terms and not mine. When she called to tell me she was getting married, I hadn't talked to her in a year.

"I taught her," he said.

He sounded proud, but then we both watched her swim out into the middle of the lake, putting her own wedding farther and farther behind her.

"She's a quick study," he said, and I wanted to tell him then to get used to it, that all my strongest memories of Sophie were of her leaving.

So when she said she wanted to stay with me for a while, I kept my expectations low. A weekend, maybe a week, and then she'd fly back to New York one day while I was teaching and, if I was lucky, leave a note. My wife, Reese, was worried.

"She always makes you feel bad," she said.

It was true and it wasn't. Our mom was dead, and I was the only family Sophie had, and I was pretty sure I understood her better than anybody else. Sometimes that felt good, like when she was giving an interview and she talked about *The Tick* or *Batman: The Animated Series* and I felt like she was winking at me. And sometimes it made me angry, because she didn't let me help her. I knew she never should've gotten back together with Allison, for instance, but she wouldn't listen to me. In fact, I thought she should never have gone to New York in the first place. She should've stayed in Iowa and built her career more slowly, and I could've helped her, and she wouldn't have made so many crazy decisions or had so much pain in her life. I'd learned my lesson with CeCe; I was ready to protect her. But every time I told her to come home and figure things out from here, she said no. And now she was coming without my asking. I was glad, but I felt a little robbed too, like she always had to make things her idea.

On a rainy Wednesday she showed up at our door. It was always easy to forget how small my sister was, because she was square-shouldered (all the way up through high school my shirts fit her snugly) and stood so straight and had those big serious eyes. But that day on my doorstep she looked tiny, her shoulders all hunched in. Her hair was greasy and her face had aged since I'd seen her last—she had lines on her forehead, dark stains under her eyes. She was thirty-four.

"Do you have any oatmeal?" she asked me.

For the first couple of days she barely talked. I tried to ask her about her next projects and give her what I thought was good advice, but she just answered me in monosyllables or not at all. She ate tiny amounts of oatmeal and canned fruit cocktail; she lay on the couch, wrapped in a blanket in the sticky heat of the Iowa summer, while Reese went to her office and I went to teach film theory to a bunch of twenty-year-olds. I was in the third year of my Ph.D., and my house was full of movies—movies we'd loved as teenagers (*Alien, The Silence of the Lambs*), movies Sophie had taught me to love in college (*Rebecca, Paranormal Activity*), movies I'd gotten into since then and wanted to show her (*Inside, Sunshine, Rampo Noir*). But all she wanted to watch, over and over, were the animated *Lord of the Rings* videos we'd watched as kids. She was especially obsessed with *The Return of the King*. One sweaty afternoon I caught her at the end of it; she looped right back to the beginning without even getting up to go to the bathroom.

"What is it with this movie?" I asked her. It wasn't even our favorite from growing up—if she wanted to be nostalgic, she could've watched *E.T.*

"I like the elves leaving Middle-earth," she said.

"Why?" I asked her. I didn't like how her voice had been since she'd arrived, even flatter than usual, like she was reading aloud from a technical manual.

"I like how when they didn't belong in the world anymore, they could leave and go somewhere safe."

On screen, the elves were sailing their white ships into gray mist, disappearing.

Reese was the one who said we should take her to the doctor. Reese was loose-limbed and easygoing; she loved silly jokes and cheap beer and dancing. But she was also a tax accountant, and she had a wide seam of practicality running through her, and the older I got, the more grateful I was for it.

"She's batshit," Reese said calmly. "She needs help."

I didn't like the idea of taking Sophie to a stranger, but I thought maybe a doctor could get her to open up a little bit, and then she and I could go from there. I didn't know much about therapists, and Sophie didn't have insurance, so the first shrink I took her to was a weird old Freudian who only wanted to talk about Sophie's dreams.

"I never remember my dreams," she said in the car afterward. "Why didn't he believe me?"

I knew it was true. As a kid I'd been jealous of how quickly she could fall asleep, while I lay awake terrified of the red-toothed old woman who crawled out from under my bed as soon as I shut my eyes.

"We'll find you another one," I said.

The second shrink was a sweet lady whose waiting room smelled like incense and who told Sophie the solution to her problems was to cut out gluten and get a Reiki massage.

"This is stupid," Sophie told me. "I don't need a doctor. I'm not sick."

It was evening, June, hot and humid. In the old house where Reese and I lived, all the doors were swollen open.

"I don't know how to help you," I said. I was getting scared of the way her face looked.

"You are helping," she said, and at dinnertime she made ravioli for us, which we ate even though she'd overcooked it. Then she let me make her watch *Sunshine* and listened patiently while I pointed out all the best parts, although her favorite scene was the very end, with the Sydney Opera House surrounded by snow.

I thought it would be a good idea for her to come visit my class. She liked talking about movies, and when she had a chance to explain things to people, she got very confident and authoritative. I wanted to see that side of her again. I asked her to talk a little about what it was like to be a director, and I showed the kids *Marianne* before-hand—I knew she was feeling sensitive about *Isabella*.

It got off to a decent start. She stood up straight, and her hair was clean. When she introduced herself, she put air quotes around "director," but she seemed good-humored about it, and the kids laughed. The first person to ask a question was Mandy, who was always the first person to ask a question. She matched her sweaters to her socks and her pens to her notebooks, and I suspected the other kids didn't like her.

"How did you know you wanted to be a director?" she asked.

I didn't know the answer to that question. All I knew was that she'd shown up one day and demanded to use my camera. Sophie nodded and answered right away.

"There were things I wanted to talk about in the world," she said, "but I had a hard time expressing them in words. So I learned to draw, and I did that for a little bit, and it was closer. And then I learned to take photos, and that was even closer, but it still wasn't right. Finally when I was in college I learned how to make movies, and that was the closest, even though there's always a gap between what I want and what's on the screen. I think that's just how life is, but it still makes me sad."

I'd been hoping she'd mention me, and even though I knew it was stupid, I was hurt when she didn't. The students, though, were intrigued.

"Is it hard to get the actors to do what you want?" asked Tim, whose essays always compared movies to things that had happened in his frat.

"Sometimes," she said. "But sometimes they know what to do better than you do."

She sounded so sad when she said it that Tim looked shocked, like she'd flashed him. I'd read the reviews; I knew what people were saying about Allison. I'd read her interview in *Conversation*, and I thought she sounded stuck-up—she never acknowledged that she'd be nowhere without Sophie. But I had to admit she was talented; her face held your eye, and she knew how to tell a story with her hands, her shoulders.

Amy raised her hand. She was my youngest student, a seventeen-year-old trying to get a head start on her freshman year. She still had braces on her teeth, and she stuttered when Sophie called on her.

"What's it like being famous?" she finally got out.

I thought it was sweet, but Sophie was stone-faced.

"I'm not famous," she said, "so I wouldn't know."

Amy tried again. "But, I mean, what's it like having people talk about you and stuff?"

Sophie looked right at her with that raptor gaze. Amy blinked back, innocent.

"It's like having everybody mispronounce your name, every day. And at first you try to correct them, but they keep fucking it up, and then you start to wonder if maybe you're the one who's wrong and that really is how to pronounce your name. And after a while you start to wonder if you even have a name. Are you even a person? Do you even exist? Who fucking knows!"

Amy was confused. My other students stared down at their notebooks or turned to one another looking freaked out and maybe pitying. I shot Sophie an expression that said, *Stop it*, but she wouldn't look at me.

"Well," I said with fake lightness, "if there are no more questions for Sophie, I guess we can move on to discussing *Frankenstein*."

Then Helen raised her hand. Helen was a senior, black-haired, dark-eyed, still growing out of a bad case of acne. She wore the same thing to almost every class, a loose black dress that was nothing like what the other girls wore, and I'd never seen her laugh or gossip or check her phone. She didn't talk much, but I felt more connected to her than I did to the other students, and now that she was in the same room as my sister, it was easy to see why.

For a minute I ignored her, though, hoping she'd give up and the Q&A would be over without Sophie saying anything sadder or more embarrassing. But Helen kept her hand up.

"I have a question," she said in an uncharacteristically loud voice. Sophie looked her up and down, then nodded.

"I read your interview in *Conversation*, where you talked about not fitting in when you were younger. I was wondering if you had any advice for people who feel like that now."

A couple of the other kids smirked at each other—one of them wrote something in her notebook and showed it to the boy next to her. I wanted Sophie to give Helen something, some piece of wisdom that would salvage what had clearly been a bad idea.

When Sophie spoke, her voice was a little kinder than before.

"If I did," she said, "I wouldn't be here. I'd probably be off having a nice life somewhere."

The rest of the class was getting bored and uncomfortable, but Helen didn't give up.

"I don't want to be clichéd," she said, "but what about art? Haven't you used movies as a way to kind of get through to people?"

Sophie shook her head. "Nothing has driven me further away from people than making movies," she said.

"So why do you do it, then?" Helen asked. "What's the point?"

Sophie was quiet. She was quiet for so long that the kids started putting their books away and zipping up their backpacks. She was quiet for so long I started to worry something was wrong with her, but she didn't look sick or upset. She looked like she was figuring something out.

"I don't know," she said. "But maybe that's fine. Maybe it's for other people to figure out what the point was."

Helen nodded like she understood, but I didn't understand.

"What did you mean by that?" I asked Sophie when we were safely in the car. "You say you're okay but you really don't sound okay."

Sophie rolled down the window. A storm was gathering; I could smell the ozone.

"When did I say I was okay?" she asked.

"You said you didn't need a therapist."

A flock of crows flew over the road, squawking about the storm.

"I don't need a therapist," she said.

"Then you have to talk to me. I don't even get what you're so upset about. A couple of bad reviews? What do you care? You don't even give a shit about people."

I immediately felt guilty, but she didn't look mad. She had that unreadable face that used to drive me nuts when we were kids. We reached the house. Out the back window of the car, the sky was black and low.

"Did you know I didn't talk until I was three?"

"I didn't know that," I said.

"I learned to talk when you were born," she said. "I never wanted to before."

I didn't know what to say. A rabbit paused on the lawn, looking at the sky.

"But you were just a baby," she said. "You didn't understand anything."

"Is this seriously a guilt trip for not getting you when I was an infant?" I asked.

Sophie didn't react. She just kept talking.

"That was okay. I figured you'd understand when you got older. But then you did, and there were still so many things I wanted to tell you that I couldn't say."

I rolled my eyes. Reese was home; she came to the kitchen window of our apartment and looked down at the car. I gave her an *In a minute* wave. My patience was low.

"Like what?" I asked Sophie. "What are these super-important thoughts that you can't possibly express to mere mortals?"

Sophie shut her eyes and ran her hands through her hair. She looked tired, but she still didn't look mad.

"Somebody told me once that if you could read a dog's thoughts, a lot of them would probably be smells. For a long time, I thought maybe if you could see my thoughts, they'd be like my movies, but I don't think that anymore."

"So what do you think, Sophie? What is your problem? I've known you my entire life, and I still don't understand what it is."

I heard the tears in my voice before I realized my eyes were wet. Just that year I'd started to feel like I'd built a good life. Reese and I had started talking about having kids, and even though I was scared, I thought being a father was something I could do. And then Sophie came back to remind me that I'd failed at being close to the person in my life I was supposed to be closest to, the one I'd loved first and most.

She opened her eyes and looked at me. "I didn't come here to fight with you," she said. "I came to tell you I love you and I trust you. That's all."

"I love you, too," I said. "But what do you mean, you trust me?"

"I trust you to do right by me."

"Of course I'll do right by you," I said. "Just tell me what you need."

"I will," she said. "Right now can we make dinner?"

Soon after we got inside, the rain started. It lashed the windows and fell in an unbroken sheet from the awning above the door. Reese set up a pot under the leak in the closet, and Sophie and I started dinner. I remember thinking she seemed better—warmer and more alert. She agreed to eat spicy beans and rice for dinner instead of asking for oatmeal. She looked out the window and said, "It's so beautiful," and it was—the soaked bright grass, the dark pin oak, the streaming sky.

When it got dark, Reese and I watched TV while Sophie wrote in her journal. When I asked what she was working on, she said it was a new thing she was trying out.

"A documentary, kind of," was all she would say.

"It's good that you're working on something new," I told her, and instead of shrugging she nodded.

"I think it's going to be good," she said.

Reese and I got ready for bed. As she left the bathroom, she kissed me and squeezed both my arms, something she did that always made me feel at home and safe. Sophie saw; for a second we'd forgotten she was there. Reese went into our bedroom, but Sophie kept looking at me.

"What?" I said.

"You're happy," she said.

I couldn't tell if it was a question. "I am," I said.

She smiled, the first time I'd seen her smile since she came to see me.

"I'm glad I couldn't screw you up," she said.

I smiled too. She lowered her head, and I put my hands around it and squeezed like I used to do. I imagined her mind as a thick forest where animals darted, hunted, hid. She put her hands on my hands for a second, pressed, took them away.

"Good night," she said.

"Good night," I told her, and I went to bed feeling calm.

Our bedroom ceiling was flush with the roof, and the rain rang loud as cymbals above our heads all night. In the morning the sky was clear and Sophie was gone. I'm embarrassed now at where I looked for her. In the park, under the dripping trees, water gushing up around my shoes with every step. In the parking lot of the old church. In the cemetery, where one evening recently I'd seen a falcon take apart a mourning dove, its feathers falling like snow. In all these places I called out for her, and I double-checked all the vantage points with the most scenic views, as if she'd gone sightseeing. And when I went home to regroup, I still thought she might be there with canned peaches, or pudding cups, something she'd wanted in the early morning and just run out to get. I was less worried than mad she hadn't told me where she was going, and when the officer came to the door, at first I didn't understand what he was saying.

"That can't be," I said. "She's staying with us."

And the poor policeman, who must've drawn the short straw to have to tell me in the first place, had to explain again.

That morning around three o'clock—later I'd thank a God I no longer believed in that she'd done it then, and not while I'd been looking for her in the park like an idiot—my sister had checked in to the La Quinta Inn across the river. She'd written a note to the housekeeping staff, which she posted on the bathroom door. It read, *"Danger. Do not enter. Please call 911 immediately."* Then she'd run a bath and slit her wrists all the way up to the elbows.

For the first two days I was consumed with rage. All I could think about was how careful she'd been with the feelings of people she didn't even know, how she'd tried to make sure the women who cleaned the room wouldn't see her body. And still she hadn't worried about how the people who loved her would feel when we found out we weren't enough to keep her in the world. She hadn't thought that someone would have to identify her, and that person would be me, and I would look down at her body like a carved bone, thin and small as when we were kids together, and I'd have to think about all the things I could've done over the course of my whole life to keep my sister from wanting to destroy herself. For those two days I couldn't cry or talk to Reese when she tried to comfort me. I could only bite my nails down to blood and drink coffee and whiskey and whiskey and coffee until I vomited in the sink.

On the third day, abruptly, I was sad. That day was beautiful, Iowa in the midst of its green summer, the sun in the oak leaves and the cicadas singing and everything full and lush and living. I thought of how if we'd had a day like this instead of the storm, Sophie might not have killed herself. If the rain hadn't made such a racket in the house, I might've heard her getting up from the couch where she lay pretending to sleep and sneaking out the door into the night. And I could've caught her by the shoulder and asked her where she was going, and after a couple of unconvincing lies—she was never a very good liar—I would've gotten it out of her. And then I could have taken her to the hospital and found her a real doctor and the right drugs, and maybe she would've gotten better not just from what was hurting her the last few weeks but from whatever was wrong her whole strange life. She might've finally been healed.

On the fourth day, I started arguing with her out loud.

"You had a fine life," I yelled at her ghost in our house. "Nothing was wrong."

The ghost was silent, frustrating as when she was alive.

Then I started going through her things. I wanted something that would answer for her. I unpacked her clothes from the little suit-case where she'd been storing them and laid them out all over the house. Her boys' button-down shirts, her one nice cashmere sweater, a few of those floral dresses, threadbare now, still ugly. Which of these was drag? They all smelled like her—dark and musky, like something that slips through the woods, unseen. She'd brought so little else with her—a toothbrush, a blunt-handled hairbrush I'd never seen her use. A tube of bright red lipstick that made me so sad I had to throw it out. A key card from a Holiday Inn.

And then, in the top drawer of my desk, I found something I'd forgotten: her journal. I opened it—at the top of the first page were the words "The Life and Death of Sophie Stark." And then a list of names, a cast and crew. I saw Allison's name, Jacob's, my own. I started reading, and then I got out my phone to call Allison. I didn't want to talk to her, but I needed to tell her that Sophie was gone and that she'd left something for us to do.

The Life and Death of Sophie Stark

I had no desire to appear in *The Life and Death of Sophie Stark*. When I heard of her death, I felt—even more strongly, I'm ashamed to say, than sorrow—a sense of mingled guilt and embarrassment. I felt guilty for giving the last film she ever directed a bad review and for contributing, in any way, to whatever she was feeling at the end of her life. At the same time, I felt embarrassed for thinking that anything I did could have mattered to her. I didn't want to talk to anyone about Sophie Stark; I wanted to be left alone.

For almost a year prior to that, I'd been concerned that I was wasting my life. I'd always been liberated by the feeling that no one was really paying attention to my writing; it didn't matter if my opinions were stupid, because they didn't matter anyway. Then, finally, I was in a position where they did matter, and I felt like a terrible fraud. Writing about movies had always been fun to me, a way to play with ideas, an escape from whatever was lonely and unsatisfying about my life. I knew that I could see the same movie on two different days and have two totally different opinions, and that what I thought said less about the movie than about me and how tired or sad or angry or nostalgic I was when I walked into the theater. Then, suddenly, I was the film critic for the *Star*. I kept writing up my unreliable, could've-been-different-if-I'd-had-a-better-breakfast-that-day opinions, but now people quoted them on movie posters or cited them as evidence that someone's career was going south. Both made me feel horrible. My review of *Isabella* bothered me especially—I'd tried to psychoanalyze Stark, and it was clear after her death that I'd known nothing whatsoever about her. But all my reviews, toward the end, disgusted me. I asked to be transferred to the foreign desk, and my editors generously agreed.

I was in Mexico City when I got Robbie's e-mail. I was shocked that Sophie would want me to be in a movie about her life, and then I was disturbed—if she'd been thinking of me at the end, it couldn't have been good. I wondered if it was some sort of trick, a way to humiliate me somehow. I wondered if I was crazy to think this. Ultimately I just said no—I was abroad, I told him, and I wouldn't be able to get back for filming. I also told him I'd quit criticism, hoping that would stand in for an apology.

Over the next few months, though, it ate at me. I felt guilty—here was a way to do something for her, the only thing I could possibly do, and I was pushing it away. Also, I'll admit that I was curious—Sophie Stark had made me want to watch movies for a living in the first place, but I knew I hadn't fully understood her as a director or as a human being. I thought if I agreed to be in the movie, if I met and talked to all the people who loved her, then I might get a better idea of what was going on inside her head.

Still, I might have put it off forever if I hadn't gone to a party for a reporter who was moving back to the States. There were a lot of Americans there, and one woman recognized my name and wanted to talk about Sophie Stark.

"It's sad, of course," she said, "but it was bound to happen."

Usually I excused myself when Stark came up, as she did from time to time, her death having significantly increased her fame. But I had had a couple of beers and some good ceviche, and I was feeling generous.

"What do you mean?" I asked.

"Well, she just saw people so clearly, you know? You can tell from the work. She saw people for what they really are, and I think if you're that perceptive, you just can't live in the world for very long."

I thought maybe if I didn't say anything, she would stop. I took another sip of beer.

"Think about it," she went on. "To see the truth of life the way she did—it would become unbearable."

I called Robbie as soon as I got home. If I could keep people from reducing Sophie Stark to some kind of magical prophet—a tendency fed, to some degree, by my earlier work—I was willing to do whatever it took.

I'm not sure that I succeeded. Those who have seen the film know it's essentially a documentary. Stark left behind detailed instructions for lighting (those for lighting and styling Allison Mieskowski run several pages), location, and editing and outlined some events she wanted us—myself, Robbie, Allison, Jacob O'Hare, Daniel Vollker, and the producer-turned-director George Campos—to address. I, in what may have been a cruel joke, was tasked with reading my reviews of Stark's films aloud on camera. I tried to make this a little easier on myself by offering commentary on Stark and on my relationship to the films, much of which George (or Robbie, who assumed a lot of directing duties, even though his sister hadn't asked him to) chose to cut. I find my portions of the film unbearable to watch; others I return to often.

As a whole the film did not dispel the notion of Stark as prophet—it remains all too common, especially among her younger fans. Nor, I think, does the film enable the viewer to understand Stark. I appeared in it and spent months talking to the people Stark loved most, and I still don't understand her— that is, I don't feel I know what she was thinking at any point in her life. This continues to worry me; when I watch her films now, I'm always looking for clues.

I've tried to find the photographer from whom, at least according to Campos, Stark took her name. I haven't had any luck. I suppose it's possible that she made the whole thing up. Stark wasn't above feeding her own myth when it suited her, and she may have created a fake origin story just for the sake of misdirection. Or maybe cooking up a false namesake made her feel better about the way her life had gone. Whether she meant to or not, Emily Buckley created a character that was Sophie Stark, and while that character made brilliant movies, she also caused a great deal of pain. Maybe she wanted to offload the responsibility for the name at least onto somebody else. Ultimately, though, I believe the story about the photograph, even though I can't find any evidence for it. I believe that Stark told Campos the truth; especially as she got older, I believe she wanted to be known.

And despite its limitations, I feel *The Life and Death of Sophie Stark* served a purpose. Forcing your loved ones to tell your life story after you commit suicide seems, on the face of it, like an act of unforgivable hubris, and in a way it was. But I think it was an act of generosity, too. Sophie was so often accused—rightly, in many cases—of stealing other people's stories, and now she was letting us tell hers. In a way she left herself to us.

In retrospect most of Robbie's cuts to my commentary were good decisions. But there's one story I wish he'd left in—the story of the last time I saw Sophie. It was 2016, after my *Conversation* profile came out but before *Isabella*. She was at Sundance, by herself, drinking whiskey and dressed all in white. I was standing directly behind her, trying to think of something polite to say, when she wheeled around and said my name.

"How did you know I was here?" I stammered.

She smiled then, the only time I ever saw her do so in person. She tapped the corner of her eye.

"I have superhuman vision, remember?"

At first I didn't know what she meant—then I realized she'd read my profile and was making fun of my idea that maybe she could see more than everybody else. I was embarrassed then, even resentful. Now it's one of my favorite memories. I believe it pained Sophie how poorly other people understood her, how little she could make herself understood, how easy it was to turn her into an angel or a monster. I'm glad to know she also found it funny.

Allison

FOR A LONG TIME I DIDN'T KNOW WHAT TO DO WITH SOPHIE'S ashes. I didn't want to have them and I didn't want anyone else to have them. I didn't want them to exist, of course, because I wanted her alive, but I also didn't want her anywhere near me. I was angry at her for dying. I was angry at her for dying while I was still so angry, before I could bring myself to say I was sorry.

Robbie got a third of the ashes and he scattered them over the train tracks in their old hometown. Jacob got a third and he poured them in the lake. But I held on to my third of the ashes all through the filming of *Life and Death*. I held on to them when it came out and I had to answer questions from reporters about Sophie and our life together and our breakup and her death and what she was like in bed, and I thought I would scratch their eyes out, but then I remembered I had a career and did not. I held on to them when the movie had been out awhile and the requests mostly stopped, and all I got was an e-mail every now and then from a blogger or a film student, like a punch to the back of the head. I held on to them but I kept them out of sight, in a box in another box under a suitcase in my closet.

They were still there when Jacob came for dinner. Robbie and I still can't be in the same room together—it's not that we hate each other, it's just that we actually, physically can't be in the same room. One of us always forces the other out with his or her sadness and guilt and blame. But Jacob and I are friends. We look a little bit alike, and we think it's funny. We ease each other's sorrow; we don't make it worse.

Jacob came on a night my boyfriend, Christian, was away—he and Christian are friends too, and when we're all together we talk about music and tell Bigfoot and windigo and giant alligator stories. But that night Christian was traveling for work, testing the water at a construction site in New Hampshire, and when Jacob and I ran out of windigo stories, we started talking about Sophie.

"Somebody asked me why she did it," he said. "Haven't gotten that in a while."

"Yeah?" I asked. "Who?"

"Some guy in the opening band the other night. Like he was just curious. What do you say when people ask you that?"

I sipped my tea. Usually Jacob and I drink bourbon, but I'm pregnant now, so I'm learning to like chamomile. Christian and I decided it was the right time; he's not my husband and he's not going to be, but we'll be together as long as we're good for each other, and he'll be my child's father forever, and those are the only kind of promises I want right now.

"I tell them to go fuck themselves," I said. "Unless it's someone I have to be nice to. Then I tell them she was depressed."

"Is that what you think?"

I shrugged. I don't always want to talk things through as much as Jacob does. I hadn't wanted to talk about Veronica in the movie. Sophie didn't know I had anything to do with her leaving. It wasn't in the instructions. I could've left it out and by now maybe I would've forgotten it even happened. But I'd already told Jacob, and he said we had to tell the whole story; he said it was our job to make her life make sense. I thought that was too much to ask of anyone, but then I thought maybe if I explained everything in the movie I'd feel less guilty somehow, like I'd discover none of it was my fault. That didn't happen. I felt the same after the movie as before: I wasn't sure Veronica would've stuck around if I hadn't messed with her, I wasn't sure the movie would've succeeded if she'd stuck around, and I wasn't sure that if the movie had succeeded, Sophie would still be alive. But each of those things seemed like enough of a possibility that whenever I thought about Sophie I ended up doing something bad, like drinking a whole bottle of gross gin or breaking all our drinking glasses so the kitchen was covered in shards and the dog cut his foot and I had to tweeze the glass out of his paw pads while he writhed and whined and I thought about cutting my own foot as penance, but I knew that wouldn't make anything up to anybody.

I did get hate mail after the movie came out—that felt like punishment in a way. I thought I'd lose some roles too. I thought I *should* lose some; if there was justice in the world, my career would be over. But even if the movie did cost me some jobs, it probably got me more. It made all of us more famous; to some people it made me exciting. One director told me he wanted to work with me because he needed someone dark, a little bit evil.

"I know she wasn't happy toward the end," I said to Jacob. "Even before the movie went bad. When I first met her she had this strength about her, like nothing could hurt her. By the time we started making *Isabella*, it was gone. Maybe depression is one thing to call that, I don't know. But it's an easy thing to say and it stops people from asking more questions."

Jacob didn't look satisfied.

"Well," I asked, "why do you think she did it?"

"Maybe she just gave up. She was so terrible at being a normal person and doing normal-person things, and maybe she just wanted to quit trying. That's what I think most of the time."

"And the rest?"

"Maybe she thought the movie would only work if she was dead, and she decided it was worth it. That's what really keeps me up at night—that it was just another, like, artistic choice for her."

I'd had this thought too, but it didn't make me crazy like the other ones did—if she killed herself to make the movie happen, at least it wasn't a judgment on me.

"Maybe it was about the movie," I said. "I don't know if that'd be the worst thing."

"That wouldn't bother you?" he asked. "If she was willing to leave everybody who loved her, just to get a movie right?"

"There are things that bother me more," I said.

I got up to make more tea. I wasn't used to this, not drinking with my friends. I was only four months, but I could already feel my body changing, my hip bones moving apart. I missed bourbon, but I liked the feeling of something new leaving its mark on me.

When I got back, Jacob was staring at the liquor in his glass.

"This is bad . . ." he said.

"Can't be worse than me."

"Do you ever wish you'd never met her? Sometimes I think if

she'd never shown up, I would've just gotten past the stuff with my mom. Gotten therapy, I don't know. I'd be this calm person. Instead I've got all this shit rattling around in my head. It's good for the music, but sometimes I just wish I could sleep at night."

I hadn't thought about it, what my life would be like without Sophie. She felt inescapable, like something you're born with. But of course I'd lived twenty years without knowing her. If she hadn't come to hear my story, I probably would've tried to tell a few more— the time my sisters and I found my stepdad passed out so hard at the kitchen table that we put a plastic princess crown on him and he didn't move, so we put a pink scarf with sequins around his shoulders, and a rhinestone necklace around his neck, and a daisy from the yard behind each of his ears, and then my mom came home from work and we thought she'd yell at us, but instead she laughed silently with her hand over her mouth, and then she took a lipstick out of her bag and started putting it on his face, but then finally he woke up and felt the crown and the necklace and the scarf and looked beaten down and ashamed, but Mom and me and all my sisters laughed so hard we had to hold on to each other to keep from falling on the floor. And the time I got scarlet fever and I was so sick I saw trolls stepping from cloud to cloud on the ceiling above my bed, and one night my mom thought I would die, so she told me I had always been her favorite, and I held on to that for years, and it made me want to stay with my family and take care of them, and then one day I asked my mom if she had really meant it, and she said yes, I was her favorite because I was like her, and that made me want to leave and never come back. But then eventually I would've run out of stories— everybody wants to hear about West Virginia, but everybody already knows what it's like to be broke in Brooklyn and twenty, twenty-five, twenty-eight. I know I would've gotten by—if nothing else I know how to get what I need—but I never would've thought I could be an actress. If Sophie hadn't wanted me to be in a movie, I'd never have thought anybody would. I'd have some kind of job and some kind of life, but I know I wouldn't love it as much as the one I have now.

If Sophie had never met me, though, she would've met someone else. There's a lot I still don't know about her, but I know she had a kind of greatness in her that was going to come out no matter what. She needed other people to help it come out, that's true, but she didn't need me. If she hadn't been there that night, she'd still have been a famous director—the only difference is, she might still be alive.

"Sometimes," I told Jacob. "Sometimes I wish we'd never met."

But it wasn't true. I knew I wouldn't trade Sophie's life for mine. I like my life too much. I often think it's good things aren't up to me.

We talked for another hour or so, and then Jacob went home and I sat drinking tea and thinking for a long time.

In the morning I knew what I wanted to do with Sophie's ashes. I got them out of the closet, and I set them on the mantel next to the picture of Christian's parents. When my daughter's old enough, I want her to see them and ask about them. I want her to know where I came from.

Acknowledgments

This book wouldn't exist without my agent, Julie Barer, whose advice has been essential every step of the way. Huge thanks also to Vanessa Kehren for her wise editing, and to Aileen Boyle, Eliza Rosenberry, and everyone at Blue Rider for making the book a reality. Thanks to Margot Livesey and everyone at the Sewanee Writers' Conference for their help early on. For reading drafts and making them better, thanks to Amy Bonnafons, Sam Forman, Colin Shepherd, and Vauhini Vara. For helping me see the big picture, thanks to to Esmé Weijun Wang. Special thanks to Anna Kerrigan for all her help with the details of film and filmmaking, and to Leah Meyerhoff for offering her thoughts when the project was in its infancy. Thanks to my teachers and classmates at Stanford and the Iowa Writers' Workshop, who shaped and continue to shape me as a writer. Thanks to my colleagues at Jezebel, BuzzFeed, Salon, and *The New York Times* for their support of my writing. Thanks always to my parents and my brother for their love and encouragement. Thanks to Toby for reading this so many times, and for everything else.

The Life and Death of Sophie Stark

READING GROUP QUESTIONS

1. Does Sophie Stark give more to the world than she takes away?

• • •

2. Sophie Stark's films are said to be 'more like life than life itself'. Could you see the films in your mind's eye? Or did they remain a mystery to you?

• • •

3. Who would you like to play Sophie Stark in a film of the book?

• • •

4. Is storytelling possible without stealing from others?

• • •

5. What would have become of Emily Buckley?

• • •

6. Did you feel as though you knew Sophie Stark by the end of the novel?

7. Is personal sacrifice necessary to create good art?

• • •

8. What do we lose and what do we gain by never hearing
Sophie Stark's voice?

• • •

9. Which character is ultimately the most betrayed?

• • •

10. Allison's father says when he quits AA: "Sometimes the
sickest part of me just seems like the truest part." Is that
also true of Stark? Is it true in general?

• • •

11. Did Sophie Stark's life have to end the way it did?

• • •

12. "Whether she meant to or not, Emily Buckley created a
character that was Sophie Stark." To what extent do you
agree with Ben Martin?

• • •

13. Sophie Stark says "It's hard for me to talk about love. I
think movies are the way I do that." Are Sophie Stark's
films a way for her to talk about love?

• • •

14. How much of a person's life can really be captured by the voices of those around them?

• • •

15. If you had entered the orbit of Sophie Stark, do you think you would have stayed there? Or would you have run away?

W&N

THE BOOKSELLER
INDUSTRY AWARDS

IMPRINT OF THE YEAR 2015

For literary discussion, author insight,
book news, exclusive content,
recipes and giveaways, visit the
Weidenfeld & Nicolson blog and
sign up for the newsletter at:

www.wnblog.co.uk

For breaking news, reviews and exclusive competitions
Follow us 🐦 @wnbooks

JOSEPH FARRELL ⟨is professor of⟩ Italian at the University of Strathclyde. He is the translator of novels by Leonardo Sciascia and plays by the Nobel Laureate Dario Fo.

"Varesi is something new: while the corruption at the dark heart of *River of Shadows* springs from the bitter clash of the partisans and the fascists, the author allows echoes of the iniquities of history to resonate in the present . . . The real coups of *River of Shadows* are twofold: the author's trenchant analysis of his country's ignoble past, married to the narrative acumen of a master storyteller" BOYD TONKIN, *Independent*

"Opens with a gripping, Dickensian description of relentless rainfall as the river bursts its banks . . . A good line in wry humour" LAURA WILSON, *Guardian*

"A heavily atmospheric narrative . . . an astute analysis of Italy's modern challenges and conflicts" THEA LENARDUZZI, *Times Literary Supplement*

"The slow-burn of the storytelling is refreshing, and matches the pervasive sense of smouldering hatreds Italy harbours. This may not be a carefree country, but the sinister secrets it nurses are fodder for good fiction" ROSEMARY GORING, *Scottish Sunday Herald*

"A dark, interesting mystery" *Literary Review*

"Successful evocation of the impact of the Second World War on the present day . . . Varesi exposes a dark history that still has the power to unsettle" JOAN SMITH, *Sunday Times*